Without warning, he covered her mouth with a gentle teasing kiss.

Laurel's eyes flew open, and she saw Russ watching her with arrogant, knowing eyes, a smile turning up the corners of his mouth.

"Can I do that again?" he asked, looking sure of her response.

She nodded, and before the motion was completed, he had pulled her head forward so their mouths collided. This kiss wasn't light, sweet, questing. This one was hot, with urgent passion and desperate groping hands; his tongue sliding along her bottom lip, seeking entrance.

Laurel moaned. Everything inside her ached and burned, and she slid her hands to his neck, kneading the thick, knotted muscles there. Her chest was pressed to his, her breasts heavy, nipples taut and yearning, and she lost all sense of balance and proportion. She wanted everything he could give her, right then and there, and when his hot tongue touched hers, Laurel dropped her hands to the loops of his jeans and brought their bodies together, hard.

Novels by Erin McCarthy

YOU DON'T KNOW JACK

HOUSTON, WE HAVE A PROBLEM

SMART MOUTH

Erin's stories have appeared in the
following anthologies

BAD BOYS OF SUMMER

WHEN GOOD THINGS HAPPEN
TO BAD BOYS

MERRY CHRISTMAS, BABY

BAD BOYS ONLINE

PERFECT FOR THE BEACH

MOUTH TO MOUTH

Erin McCarthy

BRAVA

KENSINGTON PUBLISHING CORP.

http://www.kensingtonbooks.com

BRAVA BOOKS are published by

Kensington Publishing Corp.
850 Third Avenue
New York, NY 10022

All Kensington titles, imprints and distributed lines are
available at special quantity discounts for bulk pur-
chases for sales promotion, premiums, fund-raising, ed-
ucational or institutional use.

Special book excerpts or customized printings can also
be created to fit specific needs. For details, write or phone
the office of the Kensington Special Sales Manager: Kensington Publishing Corp., 850 Third Avenue, New York,
NY 10022. Attn. Special Sales Department. Phone: 1-800-
221-2647.

Brava and the B logo Reg. U.S. Pat. & TM Off.

ISBN-13: 978-0-7582-0844-6
ISBN-10: 0-7582-0844-8

First Trade Paperback Printing: January 2005
First Mass Market Paperback Printing: November 2007
10 9 8 7 6 5 4 3 2 1

Printed in the United States of America

Chapter 1

"He's not going to show."

Russ Evans didn't even spare fellow detective Jerry Anders a glance, eyes trained on the coffee shop and the woman inside sitting alone. "Ten more minutes."

Jerry didn't protest, but Russ felt him shift in agitation, the heels of his shoes crunching in the hard-packed snow. Russ knew Jerry was cold, because he was, too. Hell, cold was an understatement. His nuts were completely numb. January winds were creeping in under his nylon jacket, and his fingers were stiff wrapped around the binoculars he was using to watch the door of the coffee shop.

But discomfort was part of the job, and he wasn't going to be hanging his badge up anytime soon. In fact, he loved being in Special Operations, got a kick from the watching and the waiting and the thinking—cold nuts or not—because in the end there was nothing like slapping the cuffs on slimeballs.

"He's standing her up."

Thoughtful, Russ scanned the nearly deserted parking lot. Nothing. Their target, petty con artist and first-class bastard, Trevor Dean, was nowhere to be found and it didn't add up. There was no reason to think Dean had figured out the cops were waiting for him, but it wasn't like Dean to pass up a chance to meet a woman.

Women were Dean's source of income, and he liked to live well beyond his means.

"Not his usual type, is she?" Russ took another hard stare at the petite woman sitting in the shop with a cup of coffee in her hand, a thick pink scarf wrapped around her neck. The view of her face was obscured by the glass, the coffee steam, and the rich blond hair that fell over her cheek, but Russ could see enough to feel the prickles of intuition tripping up his spine. Something was off here.

"You mean she's not butt-ugly?" Jerry cupped his hands and blew into them.

Russ laughed. "No. Look for yourself." He handed over the binoculars. "And Dean's women aren't ugly, they're just . . . plain."

"Just plain ugly, maybe." Jerry studied the blonde. "But this one's not bad. Good hair, tight sweater— I'm liking it. Hey, she just licked her lips, did a little nervous tongue thing. Do that again, honey."

"Glad you're enjoying yourself." Russ stamped up and down a little to get the blood flowing in his legs.

"Well, my pants are warmer anyway."

"But don't you think it's strange that this woman looks so different? I don't like it when a con changes a pattern without reason. He's been going after plain women, earning their trust. Letting them think he's in love with them, then stealing everything they've got—and it's been working. That we know of, he's hauled off a hundred thousand bucks so far. And there's probably been more. So why do anything different?"

Binoculars still stuck to his eyes, Jerry murmured, "Maybe this one isn't for business. Maybe this one is just for pleasure."

Russ hauled himself off the brick wall of the bookstore across the street and pitched the cigarette he'd been holding down into a snowdrift, where it sizzled. He'd been hanging onto the thing just in case they were spotted. It would look less suspicious, like he'd just stepped outside the store for a smoke. He dug a cinnamon disk out of his pocket, unwrapped it, and popped it into his mouth.

Crunching on his candy, Russ said, "Like a girlfriend, huh? A real one?" He bent over and picked the butt back up once it stopped burning and dropped it in the pocket of his jacket. "You could be onto something, Anders."

"What can I say? I'm a deep thinker."

"Bullshit." Russ grabbed the binoculars off of Jerry's face. "Pick your tongue back up off the ground before it freezes to the concrete."

"So if Dean's got a girlfriend, why's he standing her up?"

"Because you can stand up your girlfriend. 'Sorry babe, I got held up' and all that shit. You can't do that with a woman you're trying to con." You don't piss off the meal ticket.

Jerry snorted. "Maybe you can stand up your girlfriend and get away with it, but Pam would rip me a new one if I did that. Of course, you don't got a girlfriend, because nobody will put up with your ugly mug."

"I don't have a girlfriend because I don't want one. I'll stick to casual sex. You can keep all that other crap that goes with a relationship." Russ didn't have time for it. Between his job and raising his little brother, Sean, he barely had time to go to the john.

And he'd never met a woman yet who didn't make things more complicated than they needed to be.

"You're a cold man, Evans. But someday you're going to get knocked on your ass by some woman and I'm going to be there taking pictures."

Russ only half-heard Jerry razzing him as he puzzled over the blonde waiting for Dean. If this woman was Dean's girlfriend, was she in on the con? What did she know? And could she be coerced into talking?

Stuffing the binoculars in his pocket alongside the cigarette butt, he started across the street.

"Where the hell are you going?"

"Stay here a minute, Anders. I'm going in the shop, get a better look at this chick. I've got a feeling about her . . ."

"Yeah, I just bet you've got a feeling," Jerry grumbled. "Fine, leave me out here freezing my ass off while you check out the blonde. I'm waiting in the goddamn car."

Russ grinned over his shoulder. "Don't be such a whiner, Jesus. If you're quiet, maybe I'll even bring you a coffee."

"Do that, Evans. So I can spill it on your lap."

The warm air from the shop hit Russ as he opened the door, enveloping him in the scent of coffee beans and chocolate. The bell announced his entrance and the spike-haired guy working the counter glanced over, gave him a head nod. "Hey, how's it going?"

"Good." Russ waited for the blonde to look up, but she didn't. She was reading a magazine, a strand of her hair wrapped around a finger and pulled across her lips.

She didn't look capable of theft. She looked sweet

and innocent, her fleece scarf making her look like an overzealous Old Navy employee on her coffee break. But Russ knew looks were deceiving. He'd seen the most evil hearts lurking behind pretty faces.

His fingers were still frozen, so he went to order himself a coffee. Then he would feel the blonde out, see where she fit in this puzzle so he could track down Dean. The chalkboard menu was riddled with flavors and blends, iced and hot, mochas and javas and lattes, and he gave up trying to read it. "I just want a cup of coffee. Black."

The guy wiped his hands on his green apron. "What kind of bean? You can pick from these." He pointed to the case of seventeen different bean flavors.

"Oh, Jesus Christ." Scanning the variety of French this, vanilla that, winter roast—whatever the hell that was—and hazelnut, he said, "Just give me something with no flavor. Something that just tastes like coffee."

The clerk smirked a little. "You know, there's a Perkins down the street. They have that bottomless coffeepot deal going on."

Wiseass. Russ was debating flashing his badge to scare the little punk when he heard someone call, "Russ!"

Startled, he turned to see the blonde rising from her table, a welcoming smile dancing over her face. "I'm so glad you made it, Russ! I've been really looking forward to meeting you."

What the . . .

Knock him over with a fucking feather, the woman knew his name.

She reached him, took both of his hands and squeezed. She knew his name, looked pleased to see him. He was holding hands with Dean's girlfriend and didn't have a clue what was going on. "Hi," he said.

Wow, that was really thinking on his feet.

"Maybe she can pick a bean for you," the coffee clerk said.

Russ turned and shot a glare at the guy, who just shrugged.

"Oh, go ahead and get your coffee, Russ. I'm sitting right over there when you're done." She pointed to her table, gave him another squeeze and smile, then let go.

How the hell did she know his name, he wondered as he watched her walk. And how had she poured herself into those black pants? That was one beautiful backside. Which was probably the point. Maybe her job was to lure him, confuse him, distract him with sex.

It wasn't going to work. Or at least not completely. He was only slightly distracted.

"Give me any damn coffee you want," he told the clerk.

If the woman was Dean's girlfriend and knew he was a cop, why would she acknowledge him? To throw him off balance?

The coffee boy handed him a cup with a gripper wrapped around it and punched buttons on the register. "Three twenty-six."

"For a cup of coffee?" That pulled him out of his jumbled thoughts. "That is a total rip-off."

"Perkins, man, I tried to tell you."

Russ paid reluctantly, figuring that worked out to about a quarter a sip. Anders wasn't going to be getting any coffee at three twenty-six a cup. The blonde was folding up her magazine, tucking it into an enormous oatmeal-colored bag. To buy time, since he didn't exactly know what to say to her, he walked slowly then set his cup down on her table.

She tucked her hair behind her ear. "Did I mess up the time? I can't keep track of anything it seems, but I thought we said seven."

So she *was* Laurel. They had known nothing about this woman, just that Dean's latest victim had found a note among the scattered junk he had abandoned before skipping out with a cool ten grand that didn't belong to him. The department investigating Dean had lucked out when the victim had come forward. Most were too embarrassed, but this one had been willing to divulge all she knew, including the note Dean had written.

Laurel
Wednesday
7 @ Starbucks, 117ᵗʰ

They'd been waiting outside based on that, hoping Dean would show and they could take him down to the station for a few questions. Then slap his ass in a cell.

But there was no Dean, and who was this woman?

Russ decided to play dumb for a while and see what information he could get from her. He didn't want to give her the upper hand if she was Dean's partner, though his gut was already screaming that didn't fit. Something was way off, and he had to figure out what it was.

Studying the red-and-purple cubic art print to the left of her head, he rubbed his jaw, proceeding with caution. "You're right. It was seven. Sorry I'm late."

She touched his hand on the table, gave it a soft stroke before letting go. "Can you face me when you speak? I'm deaf, remember?"

Deaf? No, he didn't remember that. He'd never known that. Jesus. Russ snapped his jaw shut. For a split second he wondered if she was lying, but then he realized she had the flat, nasal voice that characterized deaf speech.

Her hand moved across the side of her face in a sign language gesture he didn't understand. "I can't read your lips when you're turned."

Due to quick wit and good reflexes, he only sat there blank-faced for twenty seconds or so. Then even though he didn't know if he was coming or going, he forced a smile onto his face. "I'm sorry, I wasn't thinking. And I'm sorry I'm late." He gave a little laugh that sounded more demented than charming, but he was trying, despite feeling poleaxed. "This isn't a good first impression, is it, Laurel?"

He tossed her name in to confirm what he was already certain of—that it belonged to her. Her lack of reaction to it now told him she really was Laurel. Being this close to her also made it obvious she wasn't plain like Dean's other victims, not by any stretch of the imagination. And as far as he knew, none of the other women had been deaf either. He wasn't sure if that was relevant, but he wanted to know.

If she was a victim, that is.

"You're taller than I pictured," she said, her hands gesturing while she spoke. "And cuter."

Somehow she didn't make it sound like a compliment. Yet she was smiling coyly from under long, thick lashes. There was something about her . . . an innocence, or naïveté, that made him uncomfortable. Which was freaking ridiculous. For all he knew, she was as big a con as Dean. Innocence could be faked.

Deciding to test it, he pushed back the bill of his baseball hat and readjusted it. "Thanks. And you're much more attractive than I expected."

It was true, even though he said it to gauge her reaction.

Laurel didn't blush or stammer or smile flirtatiously. Instead she just looked pleased. And it made him ninety-nine percent sure she was a con artist's wet dream, not his girlfriend.

The situation was worse than any Russ could have envisioned. She wasn't butt-ugly at all. In fact, she was downright hot, and it aggravated the hell out of him. He was trying to think, to concentrate on sorting this new development out, and he was completely distracted by the fact that her leg kept knocking into his. There were showy pretty women, and model-gorgeous women, and then there were women like Laurel. Sweet and soft and sexy, with an innocent sensuality radiating off her pink skin. She was beautiful, damn it.

Her hair was the color of split pine, with lots of darker and lighter streaks running through it, making it interesting to look at. Eyes like lake water, and rich cherry-red lips that jutted forward in a permanent pout. That off-white sweater she was wearing hugged a couple of really nice breasts, and despite the coffee aroma hanging in the air, he could swear he could smell her. Sweet and sugary, like a fresh bag of cotton candy.

If he were scum like Dean, he would string this woman along for a long, long time, taking everything she had to give—emotionally, physically, financially—enjoying every second along the way. So where was the bastard?

"Well, I wanted to e-mail you a picture of me, but I was too chicken. Which wasn't fair of me, since I knew what you looked like. I looked you up in your high school yearbook."

Russ lifted an eyebrow. This just got weirder and weirder. "How did you get a hold of my high school yearbook?" And damn, what had he looked like back then? Bad hair and acne, probably. Arms that looked like they'd gone through the taffy pull, thin and rangy, like his thirteen-year-old brother, Sean.

"Michelle Ganosky gave it to me. Remember Michelle? She's the one who saw your name in the reunion chat and suggested I introduce myself."

"Michelle?" Russ couldn't remember women he'd dated two weeks ago, he sure in the hell wasn't going to remember a girl from high school. Unless he'd slept with her, but he couldn't exactly ask Laurel about that.

Then his memory jogged. "Oh, Michelle Ganosky. Wasn't she that . . ." he trailed off, realizing he'd been about to say "deaf girl." He cleared his throat and unzipped his jacket, uncomfortable. Could he fit his size twelve feet in his mouth?

"Deaf? Yes, Michelle's deaf. That's how I know her. We went to college together for a year before I had to come back home. But I didn't tell you I knew Michelle because I didn't want you to know that I'd started talking to you intentionally, which I did. And I guess now I've told you anyway." She laughed, pushed her hair off her shoulder.

Russ was starting to get a clearer picture of what was going on here. Laurel had met someone in a high school reunion chat room. Trevor Dean. Not as Trevor Dean, but using his name, Russ Evans, the slimy motherfu . . .

"Did you know I'm a cop, Laurel?"

She blinked. "Cop? Is that what you said?"

"Yes, did you know I'm a cop?"

Tense, he waited for her answer. Up to now, they'd had no reason to think Dean knew they were investigating him.

"Yes, you told me."

Laurel's answer shot that assumption out of the water. His anger rose. Dean was playing with the department, dicking them around—or, more specifically, him. And dragging this woman into it.

"You told me a lot of things, Russ." Her smile was flirtatious.

He could only imagine. Infuriated at Dean, Russ shifted and hit Laurel's leg again. He jerked it back quickly, aware of her sharp intake of breath.

"Laurel, I'm not the man you've been talking to online. I don't even own a computer." He'd probably throw the thing out the window if he did. He had trouble sitting still and no patience for technology.

Laurel just frowned at him.

"Do you know Trevor Dean?"

"Who?" She fiddled with the ends of her scarf, over and over, her fingers always moving. They flowed in sign language when she spoke, and when she wasn't talking, they were still wiggling, plucking, fluttering.

He wanted to draw those fingers into his mouth and suck them.

Russ rubbed his eyes. That was nice and inappropriate. *Jesus.*

"I don't know anyone named whatever Dean, and I don't understand what's going on here."

Russ did. Laurel wasn't a sophisticated con artist's girlfriend. She was either fun on the side for Dean, to flirt with online, or she was his next target.

Russ wasn't about to let that happen.

Not on his watch.

Not to this woman.

And maybe Laurel could help him catch a thief.

Chapter 2

Laurel Wilkins sipped her coffee and tried to figure out what in the world Russ was talking about. She wasn't having much luck, so she contented herself with admiring his cuteness while waiting for him to explain himself.

There was a lot of cuteness involved, so she could be looking for a while. He was delicious, like a caramel wrapped around a crème filling. Strong jaw, a baseball cap over his light brown hair, eyes the color of dark chocolate before it melts. Broad shoulders, visible even through his navy winter coat. Hard chiseled muscle beneath a jersey-gray T-shirt. Jeans that had hugged his crotch when he'd walked toward the table. Large hands that could benefit from a good moisturizing lotion, and an earnest expression that was incredibly sexy.

Laurel's whole body went hot and sensitive, moist, like she'd spent too long in a steamy shower.

"Look, I'm sorry, but you've been exchanging e-mails with a man who's using my name. Trevor Dean is a con artist, he rips women off. First he meets them—some online, some around town—then he gets them to trust him." Russ shifted a little, but met her gaze head-on. "He sleeps with them, moves in with them, then cleans them out. The PD has been investigating him for theft and fraud."

Laurel's lovely thoughts of seeing Russ strip to Bruce Springsteen music evaporated. *Theft and fraud?* Had she misread his lips? "What?"

"Theft and fraud."

She took a fortifying sip of her third mocha latte. So much for her wild and wanton plans. "How do you know it's him I've been chatting with?" And exchanging personal thoughts and feelings, and most embarrassing of all, a little sexy flirtation.

She'd told that person she hadn't had sex in six years. He had probably turned right around and tagged her e-mail address as "dumb blonde ripe for the picking."

"We found your name and this appointment among the personal things he left behind at his last victim's house."

Laurel couldn't decide if she was more embarrassed or disappointed. Disappointment was edging out embarrassment by a horny head. But she couldn't admit that to Detective Dream Boat. "This is very embarrassing."

"Don't be embarrassed. Be glad you found out now."

Easy for him to say. He hadn't put on pink underwear in anticipation.

And worst of all, she'd really liked the guy. He was funny and thoughtful, always free with a smiley face in his e-mails. Laurel felt her cheeks pinken, until they probably matched the hue of her scarf. Her mother always said she was too nice, that she'd offer to help a serial killer learn how to tie better rope knots.

That was a ridiculous exaggeration, but maybe she was too trusting. It had never even occurred to her to doubt that Russ Evans was Russ Evans.

The Russ Evans in front of her gave her a stern, paternalistic look. "And you shouldn't be giving out your personal information online, you know. The world is full of crooks and weirdos. And never, ever agree to meet anyone in person like this again."

While she had just come to that conclusion herself, it made her feel like a disobedient child to have him say it. She couldn't stand it when people patronized her, especially not when she could think of better "p" words Russ could do to her. "I'm in a public shop. Nothing could have happened to me here."

His eyes rolled back and his lip curled. "Give me a break. There's one guy working here who probably has more hair than brains. Someone could pull a gun on you, wave it at the clerk, and haul your ass out of here in about thirty seconds, no one to stop him."

Well. That was a cheery thought.

"And don't be so trusting, Laurel . . . you haven't even asked to see my ID. I might not even be a cop, for all you know."

Oh, God, he was right. She didn't know if he was a cop. She didn't know anything, really. Maybe *he* was the con artist, but was talking her into believing he was a cop. Confused, she primly held out her hand. "ID please."

He nodded in approval, extracted his wallet from his pants, and handed it to her. "Never trust anyone."

Laurel thought that was a sad tableau to live by, but she flipped open his wallet and studied the

Cleveland Police Department badge. She glanced at his address, 350 W. 135th, on his driver's license and noticed that the BMV headshot didn't do him justice any more than the high school picture had.

Both her mother's and his warnings resounded in her head. "How do I know what you're telling me is the truth?" she asked, running her finger over the raised surface of his badge.

Russ's mouth dropped open, then he laughed. "I guess you don't. You could call the police department and ask to speak to me to confirm I'm a detective, or you could ask for my boss. He could vouch for me and the investigation."

"The only problem is, I wouldn't be able to hear his answer."

Now Russ looked stricken. "I'm sorry, I didn't think . . ."

He looked so embarrassed, she rushed to reassure him with a smile. It made her uncomfortable when her deafness made other people uncomfortable. "I wasn't criticizing you or trying to make you feel bad. I was just being honest."

But he didn't smile back. He was studying her, resting back in his chair, large fingers playing with the napkin resting on the table. Laurel stopped smiling, deep regret dousing over her. This man, this very attractive and cautious man, was not who she'd been talking to.

And she had rushed up to him, so excited to see him, eager to meet him, grateful he hadn't stood her up. How totally mortifying.

Maybe even worse, Russ Evans wasn't her naughty little secret anymore, her reason to sneak off to her room and check her e-mail, hoping for a message from him. The man she'd been chatting with, he

had been sweet and flirtatious, interested in her—
or so she had thought. And none of it was real.

That man was a con artist, probably out to steal
her money, and the real Russ Evans wasn't the
least bit interested in her.

Oh, God, she wanted to go home and eat a
brownie.

"Well, I'm going to leave then," she blurted.
"Thanks for your concern, I hope you catch the guy
and everything." Laurel bent over to pick up her bag,
purposely lingering facedown so she couldn't see
Russ's answer.

It was a trick she had often pulled as a kid, closing her eyes when she was being punished so she
couldn't see the lecture. Eventually her mother
had started cracking her on the butt when she did
that to force her eyes open. But Russ Evans didn't
know her, or that her avoidance was intentional,
and she just wanted to get out of that shop without
further reprimands from him.

But when she sat back up and turned to pull her
black peacoat off the chair, Russ touched her arm,
held it. She looked at him, wary.

"Did Dean give you any clues about who he is or
where he lives? What interests him?"

Laurel extracted her arm from his hand and
shoved it in her sleeve, not wanting to think about
all the things Dean had said, because that meant
she had to remember all the gushy, naive, personal
things she had written in return. "I don't know. He
said things like he was you. He was a cop, went to
Lakewood High School, likes boating."

"I don't like boats. I'm more into camping." Russ
sat forward, intense, his expression determined, jaw
set, and dark eyes confident. "There could be clues

like that littered throughout his e-mails. Did you save any of them? How long have you been talking to him?"

"About two months. But I didn't save any of them. I do remember he said he lived in Tremont, but he never gave a street."

"Well, what do you usually talk about?"

"Anything. Everything." *Sex.* She was eternally grateful she'd just dumped the trash in her e-mail.

Laurel jammed her other arm through her coat sleeve and fished in her pink purse for her keys. She wanted to leave in the worst way, get away from Russ Evans and his reminder that she was kidding herself, that her life was never meant to be wild and exciting. She was destined to shrivel up like dried fruit, to fossilize into old age never touched by human hands.

Russ Evans just wanted to capture his man, and she felt the need to lock herself in her room and write bad poetry.

"Like what? Can you give me specifics?" Russ seemed oblivious to her discomfort, picking up the wrong coffee cup and idly taking a sip from it, obviously unaware it wasn't his.

Seeing his mouth on her cup, right where her lips had just been, made her snap. She wanted to shock him, to make him really look at her and see more than just the deaf girl who fell for the sweet-talking con. She wanted him to see her as a woman. Just once, she wanted the gorgeous guy to look at her, really see her.

"Sex. We talked about sex."

Russ choked on the frothy sweet coffee, feeling it rise into his nose and sting like hell. Somehow he hadn't expected Laurel to say that. She seemed so sweet, so naive, so *elevated*, that he wouldn't have imagined she would want to talk dirty. The image rose in his head of Laurel whispering in his ear what she'd like him to do to her, and with what, and Russ went hard.

That was professional.

He recovered himself. At least the part above the table. "I see. I don't suppose there are any clues in that, then."

"Not unless you want to know what his sex fantasies are."

Oh, God, just shoot him instead. "I'll pass."

Now if she wanted to tell him her fantasies, he'd be willing to listen.

They both sat silent for a minute, Russ thinking, his mind a mix of perverted thoughts and puzzlement over what Dean was planning.

"Are you sure he's a con man?" Laurel asked.

Because she looked wistful, Russ gave her a harsh answer. He did not want her to do something stupid like hook up with Dean after all. "Yes. Four women, that we know of, have had over a hundred thousand dollars stolen from them by Dean, before their beds were even cold. Got any money, Laurel?"

"Sort of. I have a small trust fund and even though I live with my mother, technically the house is mine."

"Where?"

"Edgewater Drive."

"Lakefront property." Nice. Big money. Dean must be trying to step up in the world.

"Yes." Laurel wrapped her scarf around her neck. "Well, there are other fish in the sea, I guess. Or online."

His head snapped up. He didn't like the sound of that. "Hold it. What do you mean?"

But she wasn't looking at him. She was buttoning her coat. He tapped her arm impatiently. She looked up in surprise.

"Don't meet men online, Laurel. It's not safe. They could be anybody, say anything to you."

"So could people you meet in person."

Damn it, she had him there. But he just couldn't let Laurel leave without understanding the importance of what he was saying. Letting her cruise the Internet alone talking to people would be like sending a bunny out to try and cross an eight-lane highway.

He kind of liked bunnies.

Especially this bunny. Laurel smiled at him. He sighed. He did not want to get involved with her and whatever she was looking for—God knows, he had enough to worry about keeping Sean out of trouble. He couldn't be looking after this woman, too, but he had to extract some kind of promise from her that she'd be smart. He really didn't want to read about her in a future police report.

"Look, there's got to be a better way to meet people. At work, someone your friends know, church or something. There are plenty of nice guys out there looking for a relationship. Just be smart, safe, use protection." And Jesus Christ, he sounded like a squeamish father handing his car keys off to his teenager.

Laurel's jaw had locked, her cheeks pink. It was either from the heat since she had bundled up in her coat, or she was irritated with him.

"I don't want a relationship. I just want to have sex."

Oh, man, *that* wasn't what he'd wanted her to say. "Laurel!" he blurted out, shocked in a way he hadn't imagined was still possible.

"What? It's true." She looked down at the table, the lapels of her coat swallowing the sides of her face. "My whole life I've done what other people have wanted me to do. I've been good, polite, considerate, and most of the time I don't mind that. I mean, I don't want to be *not* nice or good or considerate, but for once I want to be selfish. Wild."

Laurel didn't look wild. She looked cute and fuzzy in her fleece, like the woman you'd take home to your mother, set up on a pedestal and admire from afar as an icon of female perfection. She didn't look like a woman you should get down and dirty with.

Which didn't explain his hard-on.

"Well," he hedged. "How old are you? Twenty?"

Laurel watched his lips intently as he spoke. He thought it was pretty amazing that she knew what he was saying just from reading his lips. But it also meant a lot of times her eyes were on his mouth, not meeting his gaze. Which gave him the sneaky ability to watch her more closely than he could anyone else, without her thinking he was staring.

He liked looking at her, all pretty and pink, a woman very different from any he'd ever dated. Russ dated bold and brassy women because they were good at accepting what he had to offer at face value. They understood what it meant, having a little fun, and leaving it at that. He was committed to Sean first, his job second, and if a woman didn't get that from day one, he wasn't going to touch her with a ten-foot pole, no matter how hot her body was or how interesting she seemed.

At his question, her nose wrinkled in indignation. "I'm twenty-five! Almost twenty-six. And except for one year at college, I've never lived anywhere but with my parents." Laurel's voice was rising, and in his peripheral vision Russ could see the coffee clerk and a plain brunette glance their way. "I don't date, I don't do anything even remotely exciting, I don't have sex."

Whoa, hello, just grab a megaphone and announce that. "Uh, Laurel . . . your voice is getting kind of loud."

"What? Oh, sorry." She peered around him and blushed.

"But just because you haven't dated in a while isn't a good reason to latch onto the first guy you meet. Casual sex has its merits." Hell, he lived by casual sex and its merits. "But you still have to be careful."

"I know that. I may be trusting, but I'm not stupid."

"I never said you were stupid . . ." And somehow he had turned this into an interrogation and had alienated her. *Smooth move, Evans.*

To prove his point, she stood up and reached for her keys. "Thank you for your concern. I'm leaving."

"Wait a second, Laurel." They hadn't resolved anything. She hadn't agreed to stay locked up in her house yet where no men could touch or hurt her. "If Trevor Dean e-mails you again, you need to call me."

"What's his name again? I can't figure out what you're saying."

Russ pulled a pen out of his jacket pocket and wrote *Trevor Dean* on a napkin. Under that he scrawled his own name and both his work and home phone numbers. He handed it to her. "Don't answer him and don't let him know you're onto him. Just call me first thing, okay?"

"Fine." She sighed a little, obviously not thrilled with the situation, but she was polite nonetheless. "Have a good night, Russ."

"Wait." He grabbed her arm again as he stood up. She was shorter than he'd thought, stopping below his nose, and he let go of her slight wrist. "I'm sorry I keep grabbing you. I don't know how else to get your attention."

"You can touch my arm, stomp on the floor, wave. I just don't like it when people stick their hand right in my face." Laurel didn't sound angry, she actually looked pleased that he'd bothered to ask.

Russ felt that something again, that indefinable feeling swirling around inside him that he couldn't let this woman walk out of here alone. He wanted to think it was the cop in him, drawn to her vulnerability, wanting to protect her from harm. But something told him it was more than that, complex. Something that he was going to ignore until it went away, like a toothache.

"Okay. Listen . . . my partner, Jerry, is outside and we have a car across the street. I would really feel better if you let me follow you home, make sure you get there alright. I don't know why Dean didn't show up, but it bothers me."

Laurel chewed her lip, readjusted her purse. "Fine, if you insist. But I only live five minutes from here."

"A lot can happen in five minutes."

Yes, she could have an orgasm just from *looking* at him for five minutes. But she kept her face neutral.

"Promise me, Laurel—I'm serious here—that you won't make plans to meet any more strange guys. That you won't run off and have sex with someone you don't know."

His concern was sweet. It also infuriated her, the straw that broke her good-girl back. "I could have sex with you."

Well, that felt good to say. Liberating. And she hadn't even needed alcohol to work up the nerve to say it.

Russ looked like he'd been liberated of his ability to speak.

Laurel just stared at him, trying to project sassy slut, which admittedly was a stretch. Of about a hundred miles.

"What do you mean?" he finally asked, fiddling with the bill of his baseball hat again.

"I mean, we could have sex. You and me."

Russ looked stricken, and Laurel felt the moment waning. The rush of boldness evaporating, nerve skittering off to hide.

What was she thinking? He wouldn't want to have sex with her when he probably had exotic dancers on speed dial. And she shouldn't have just blurted it out like that anyway, even if she had been half-serious.

"I'm kidding," she lied, rolling her eyes for effect. "My point is, unless *you* want to sleep with me, it's really none of your business what I do or with who."

"I'm concerned! I don't want to see you get hurt, or wind up dead, goddamnit."

That had all the makings of a parental lecture. While it was really nice of Russ to care, it wasn't what she was looking for. Laurel's own father had died, and she wasn't looking to replace him. If she

did, it certainly wouldn't be with a man she wanted
to strip naked and lick.

"Thank you for the warning. But even though it
may surprise you, I can take care of myself. I can
even walk across the street by myself." Laurel turned
and left him sputtering.

Chapter 3

Trevor Dean watched Laurel Wilkins leave the coffee shop and stepped out of his car. Laurel had hung around longer than he'd expected, which was a good sign—meant she was eager to meet him. Or Russ Evans.

Trevor chuckled to himself. That still made him laugh, using cops' names to pick up women. He had a whole laundry list of detectives whose names he used on a rotating basis, and they had no idea. It wasn't identity theft—he wasn't using anything more than their names—but it was a good private joke. Flipping the bird at those screwups, who let him walk around and get away with stealing left and right. Plus, it was an easy system for him to keep track of who he was supposed to be from day to day.

Jill was waiting for him in the coffee shop, probably wondering what was keeping him, so he picked up the pace, tossing his cigarette butt down onto the sidewalk. It was colder than a wart on a witch in Alaska, and his leather coat didn't do squat to protect him. Maybe he should have headed south this year, worked his way down to the Florida Keys.

But that would mean starting over from scratch.

He had a system going in Cleveland, been working it for over five years, and the cops were none the wiser. Three women, at all times. One at the starting gate, one in the race, and one crossing the finish line.

Worked like a charm.

Jill spilled her coffee when he walked in, then mumbled to herself as she mopped it up. She gathered up the wet napkins and pushed them aside, wiping her fingers on her blue sweatshirt.

"Hi, sweetheart." Trevor kissed Jill's forehead and sat down across from her. "Spill your coffee?"

"Yes, I'm such an idiot."

"But a cute one." He winked at her, knowing she'd blush. She did. Jill was easy to figure out. The minute he'd seen her struggling to get her gas cap off at the gas station, her nose red, her hair flat under a knit hat, he'd known she was the next one.

Trevor liked unattractive women. He liked the way they were so damn eager to please, so desperate for touches, so sure he was going to bolt at any minute. He even liked the sex. It made him feel powerful to know he was giving them something no one else would, and the control always rested with him, just as firmly in the bedroom as out of it. He could do whatever he wanted, because in the end, in the dark, it was all about him.

"I was starting to worry about you. I thought you were going to be here sooner." Jill brushed her mud-brown hair back. "I mean, it's not a big deal or anything, I'm not nagging, I was just picturing you in a coma."

That nervous laugh she gave, that worry, made him smile. He had her.

He'd been living in a hotel since he'd skipped out on Rachel on Saturday, so the timing was perfect. "Sorry, babe, I should have called you to tell you I was running late. But I was having a hell of a time with my landlord, trying to reason with him. He raised my rent two hundred bucks a month."

"What? Oh, Pete, that's awful!"

"I don't know how I'm going to afford it." Trevor sank back, let his shoulders slump, a sigh of defeat emerge.

And waited for Jill to pull out of the starting gate.

"And they just cut your hours at the office, too," Jill said, hating the way Pete looked so worried, the corners of his cute blue eyes crinkling up. He was always such an upbeat person, it was difficult to see him like this.

It still amazed her that a man as good-looking as Pete Trevor had looked twice at her, a woman about as exciting as day-old oatmeal. She had plain hair, a plain face, and a plain body, except for overly large breasts that had earned her the high school nickname Charmin. *Don't squeeze the Charmin* . . .

But Pete was so sweet, so good to her. She was pretty sure she was falling in love with him.

"It will be okay. I'll figure something out. I have a little savings." His eyes darted off to the left, and his fingers went into his hair.

He was lying to reassure her, Jill realized with a start. He didn't want her to worry. Her heart swelled, and she spoke before she could think, doubt, talk herself out of it.

"Why don't we move in together?" Jill blushed at her presumptuousness, but forged ahead despite Pete's look of surprise. "I mean, you spend the night with me a couple of times a week anyway, and why should we both waste all this money on rent? If we moved in together it would save us about four hundred dollars a month each."

She held her breath, waited for his response.

"I thought about it," he admitted. "But I didn't want you to think I was freeloading."

"Of course not! We'll be splitting the rent."

Pete gave her a smile, the one that made her insides tumble and burn. "What if living together reveals all my flaws? I don't want to lose you."

It was love. It was definitely love. "You won't lose me. You have me as long as you want me."

He picked up her hand, kissed the back of it. "I'm counting on that."

Russ zipped up his jacket when he stepped outside. He could feel the tension actually lifting and rising into his chest and head, squeezing him, pissing him off, and making him want to grab Laurel and lock her in a room with crime scene photos.

Take care of herself. Ha. Laurel was a bunny in a city full of foxes. Some day she was going to be just hopping along, all soft and sweet, looking for clover, then wham . . . in for the kill.

He had a job to do, and it wasn't protecting naive women from themselves. Laurel was walking west down the street, head down, not the least bit aware of her surroundings. Shit, someone could step right out of that hedge and just grab her and she wouldn't even realize until it was too late, because she wouldn't hear a damn thing.

Take care of herself? Please. She screamed *rich, vulnerable woman alone, take advantage of me.* She was so damn appealing, Russ wanted to take advantage of her himself.

Watching her hit the button to unlock a white Lexus SUV, Russ swore. He jogged the last ten feet to the bookstore and got in the passenger seat of Anders's black truck, keeping Laurel in his view. "Follow that Lexus SUV."

Jerry shifted the truck into gear, but tossed him a petulant look. "Where the hell have you been? You've been gone for thirty minutes. You cheating on me? Got another detective on the side you're hooking up with?"

Russ laughed. He liked working with Anders, who kept the laughs rolling even when they were knee-deep in scumbags—or worse, paperwork. "Come on, Jerry, you know I'd never do that to you. But a good relationship needs to be based on trust, you know."

"You're gone all the time, you don't talk to me anymore, what am I supposed to think?" Jerry stopped at the light behind Laurel's Lexus and shot Russ a grin. "You come home late, smelling like cigarettes and coffee, which I know you don't drink. I think we either need counseling or it's over, man, it's just over."

"Shut up, Anders. You know you're the only partner for me."

"Be still my heart." Jerry glanced around as he followed Laurel down Lake Avenue and onto Edgewater Drive, past stately brick and stone homes built in the twenties as suburban getaways for the rich. "The blonde lives well, huh?"

"Her house, but she lives with her mother. Inheritance, I guess." Russ kept one eye on the taillights of Laurel's car while checking out the neighborhood. "She didn't know who Dean was, never heard of him. Get this. She thought she was chatting online with Russ Evans, her friend Michelle's old high school classmate."

Jerry whistled. "Dean's a smart-ass."

"Who knows more than we thought." He watched Laurel pull into the driveway of a massive brick three-story house, the front flat, its architectural focus the two dozen windows reflecting crisp moonlight back at him. "Jesus, what do you call this kind of house?"

"Expensive."

And more than a family of twelve could ever use. "My whole house would fit in one room."

Jerry idled at the curb, his eyebrow lifted. "Got the lake in her backyard and the world at her feet. Must be nice to be rich."

Laurel's car had retreated into the garage around the back of the house, and now lights were flicking on all over the first floor. There were no blinds at the windows, and even though the house sat back from the street behind a stately yard covered under six inches of snow, Russ could see the outlines of furniture, lamps. Then Laurel, as her blond head popped past a sofa.

He thought about her suggestion that they have sex. It may have been a dig, a way to prove her point, but his body had heard that suggestion and run with it. Worse, he kept imagining her saying that to someone else—and him ripping the guy's face off.

"Wait here a minute." Russ opened the car door.

"Oh, here we go again. Wait here, Jerry, while I flirt with a suspect."

"She's not a suspect, I told you that." He got out of the car. "Call Pam on your cell phone if you're feeling left out. Try and make her remember why she ever thought dating you was a good idea."

Anders called after him, "And while you're hitting on Blondie, why don't you try doing your job and seeing if she'll act as bait to help pull in Dean."

Russ stopped closing the door, catching it with his foot. He knew Anders was right, but the idea of enlisting Laurel's help went against everything he was trying to accomplish. He wanted her out of this. Now. And to stay in her pretty house, protected and innocent, untouched by ugly reality.

"Not this woman, Anders. We put her up as bait, and more than likely she's going to get eaten."

"By Dean or by you?" Jerry gave him a smarmy grin.

"Pig." Russ slammed the door in his face, cutting off a wave of laughter.

As he headed up the driveway, hands stuck in his pockets, Russ wondered what the hell he was doing. There was no reason to be strolling up to Laurel's front door, except that he wanted to make sure she was all right. That she had locked up the house nice and tight, checked all her windows, thrown the dead bolts.

The intensity of his concern bothered him, sent his nerves vibrating, made him edgy. For a man who thought remembering to bring condoms was the height of consideration, he was making too much out of this. He'd met plenty of people over the years on the job—especially women and children—whose eyes had cried for help, understanding, compassion, and he'd felt that pull, that draw deep down in his gut to do something. But he'd always managed to maintain distance, keep a cool head, do his job with sensitivity, yes, but with the hard-ass detachment needed to not go insane or slide into cynicism.

Ringing Laurel's front doorbell couldn't be classified as keeping his distance. And if he was going to breech that boundary, hell, he might as well go all the way.

The landscaping along the front yard was

shrouded with burlap to protect it from the January temperatures and icy snow. Discreet lighting illuminated the brick walk as he walked quickly. He wasn't exactly sure what he was going to say, but he was thinking somewhere along the lines of offering himself up as a sexual sacrifice.

If she was serious about having an affair, why the hell couldn't she just have it with him? That way he would know she would be safe.

And if he enjoyed himself, well, that was only a side benefit. The real important issue was protecting Laurel.

Wasn't he just a Good Samaritan? With an erection.

The front door flew open when he was still five feet from the stoop. "What are you doing?" Laurel stood in the doorway, wearing those hip-hugging black pants, slippers, her white sweater, and that damn pink scarf still draped around her neck. She had pulled her hair up into a ponytail, shaving a few years off her appearance, as if she didn't look young enough already.

"I'm just checking to make sure you got in the house okay."

"What?" She leaned forward, strained her eyes. "I can't see your mouth, the walk is too dark."

Russ stepped forward and onto the stoop, under the blazing lights framing either side of the door. He repeated himself clearly, then capped it off with a charming smile designed to have her melting.

It didn't work. Laurel's lips pursed. "As you can see, I'm in the house, safe and sound." She stared at him, expectantly, waiting for him to leave.

Russ's smile began to feel maniacal. But something kept him lingering on her doorstep. "Aren't you going to invite me in?"

Her eyes went wide, with an innocence that looked insincere, to say the least. "A total stranger? That wouldn't be very smart, would it?"

A grin split his face. Damn, she was sexy. "Good answer."

"Good night, Russ." Rolling her eyes, Laurel stepped back and closed the door.

Russ stood there, listening for the click of the dead bolt. There wasn't one. He waited. And waited. The door jerked open again.

"What?" Laurel shot him a look of impatience.

"You didn't lock the door. I was waiting to hear it click."

"Ahh," she said, and slammed the door with enough force to rattle the brass door knocker.

But he heard the distinct sound of the lock sliding shut.

He smiled at the door, accepting the inevitable.

Distance be damned. He couldn't stay out of this. If Laurel wanted an affair, it was going to have to be with him. He'd keep her safe *and* satisfied.

He'd decided, and that's all there was to it.

Laurel was not an angry person. She never lost her temper, very rarely got mad at anyone, and spent a good portion of her time making excuses for other people's lousy behavior. But right now, she was not particularly happy with Russ Evans. Not that she'd go so far as to say that she was furious, but she was feeling a distinct irritation with the man. The real Russ Evans. The fake one was much nicer, even if he was a lying con artist. At least he treated her like an *adult*.

But Russ had stood there on her doorstep, looking like her every scruffy fantasy come to life. Ooz-

ing sex appeal out his jeans, and he had treated
her like a slightly dim twelve-year-old. He'd done
everything short of patting her on the head.

Of course, she had pretty much acted like an im-
becile in the coffee shop, running on and on about
wanting to be wild. At the time, she had been trying
to make a point. In retrospect, it sounded pathetic.

She was embarrassed, confused, disappointed, and
beneath all those lousy layers, attracted to Russ. Maybe her mother was right—dating was too dangerous. How ironic that both her mother and the man
she'd like to date agreed that she should lock herself up in the house and petrify.

After taking care of the urgent biological needs
three mocha lattes had brought on, Laurel grabbed
a muffin in the kitchen and stomped up the two
flights of stairs to her suite of rooms on the third
floor. When she spotted the array of sweaters tossed
across her bed, evidence of her earlier indecision
over what to wear, she almost laughed.

She could have been wearing a paper bag for all
Russ had noticed. He looked at her and saw nothing
but a naive, trusting, undersexed kid. While he was
right on the undersexed part, the rest was all wrong.
Completely and totally wrong. She knew there were
bad people in the world. She wasn't an idiot.

What he failed to realize is that she had thought
she was meeting a man her friend Michelle had
known for fifteen years or more. It had been a safe
assumption that it was all right to meet a cop your
friend knew in a public coffee shop. There was only
so much you could do to protect yourself without
sealing your house off in plastic and breathing
through a mask. She wanted to be smart. But she
also wanted to live.

Laurel had spent twenty-five years safely enclosed in a bubble-wrapped life, partially because of her mother's protectiveness, partially from her own shyness and fears. But she didn't want to exist like that anymore.

When her father had been alive, he had understood the importance of pushing her to be independent. He had supported her decision to attend a deaf university in Rochester, and he was the one who had encouraged her to communicate both orally and with ASL, American Sign Language. But her father had died of a heart attack at the tail end of her freshman year in college and after she had come home to her grieving mother, she had never gone back to Rochester.

It had seemed just too cruel to leave her mother and return to a school she had never wanted Laurel to attend in the first place. Laurel had taken a temporary job at Sweet Stuff candy store and somehow, without her even being quite sure how, five years had slid by. Cut off from the deaf community she had reveled in at college and isolated from the hearing by her own circumstances.

When Aunt Susan had called requesting help, Laurel had felt seized by the opportunity to get out there in the real world, meet people, enjoy herself. And she was still going to do that, Russ Evans and his ominous warnings or not.

Wiggling the computer mouse on her desk, she watched her kittens-in-a-basket screen saver disappear. Pinching off a piece of the muffin she'd set on a paper napkin, Laurel popped it in her mouth and opened her e-mail.

She had a message from Michelle, and interestingly enough, one from Trevor Dean as Russ Evans. It surprised her to see it there, boldly sitting in her e-mail box with the subject heading, I'M SORRY.

Somehow she had thought she wouldn't hear from him again, that his amusement with her would be over now that he had stood her up.

Clicking the message, it opened as her cat, Ferris, leaped onto her lap and settled his considerable orange bulk. Laurel finger-spelled HELLO onto his back, digging into his rich fur and feeling the vibration of his purr. By herself, she never spoke out loud, but relaxed in the silence, mind drifting, lazy, the way she never could when she was communicating with other people. That required intense concentration, to understand and to be understood.

Dean's e-mail had been sent at 6:47 P.M., when she had already been on the way to the coffee shop.

> *Hi Laurel, I hope I catch you before you leave. Something's come up with work, a case I've got a lead on, and I'm going to have to cancel our plans. I'm really looking forward to meeting you, but can we make it another time? Please, please, forgive me?* ☺
> *—Russ*

If she had read that without meeting Russ Evans, she would have been satisfied with Dean's excuse. She would have appreciated the pleading, wondering about the excitement of being with the police department. She would have thought he was cute, sweet, a good guy.

Now she knew he was a thief and a liar, and somehow next to the real Russ Evans, this e-mail sounded weak and feminine, and nothing like a cop would really sound.

There was nothing left to do but feel like a total schmuck. And while she lamented her schmuckishness, her determination to bust out of the bubble of her narrow existence grew. She liked who she was, enjoyed helping people, but she felt that stuck the way she was in the confines of her sugarcoated life, everything was completely meaningless. Laurel wanted to do something important, make a difference, matter.

Like protect other women from Trevor Dean.

She was lucky. Her heart and her finances were intact. Her pride and her confidence were a little dented, but she'd recover. How must it feel to lose everything you had to a man who'd sworn to love you and didn't?

She was thinking it would feel like crap, and then some.

Russ wouldn't be in the office, she didn't think, so she wouldn't call him there. And she couldn't call his home number because she wouldn't know when the answering machine picked up. She'd call the PD number in the morning, let him know what she'd done. Because for the first time in her almost twenty-six years of unexciting vanilla-pudding existence, Laurel was going to take decisive action.

> *Hi Russ,*
> *I'm sorry we missed each other! I hope every-thing went well with your case—I think it's just amazing how the police can solve crimes. I'd love to make new plans to meet you. Just say when and where.*
> *Ttys*
> *Laurel*

She clicked SEND and stroked Ferris's fur in satisfaction, wondering if the rush she felt was from excitement or the excess of caffeine in all those mocha lattes. Either way, this felt pretty dang good.

She was lying, and doing it well. Her mother would be so proud.

Of course, e-mail worked to her advantage. Face-to-face, she was likely to blurt out the whole truth, then cap it off by suggesting to Dean he get help through counseling.

Laurel clicked on Michelle's e-mail, which was short and to the point.

well??? how was russ? did you bag him? <g>

Laurel rolled her eyes. Michelle hadn't been witness to that look of sheer terror on Russ's face when she'd brought up the whole "Let's you and me have sex" thing. Laurel remembered it all too clearly and was pretty sure she was permanently scarred. Or Russ was.

Though Michelle lived an hour and a half away in Erie, Pennsylvania, they e-mailed daily and were probably closer now than they'd been in college. Michelle was married now, but she liked to participate in chats and loops with people she'd gone to high school with in Cleveland, which is how she'd seen Russ's name.

He no-showed,

Laurel typed quickly. Then added,

But the REAL Russ Evans showed up an hour later, the one from your yearbook. Turns out I was chatting with a fake, a con artist . . . YUCK, huh?

Laurel sent the message, leaned back in her chair, and finally unwound her scarf from around her neck. She tossed it on the bed with the discarded sweaters. Ferris's green eyes looked up at her in rebuke as her movements jostled him.

"Sorry." Stroking his fur, not wanting to toss Ferris to the floor, Laurel just sat there and brooded. It wasn't like her to give in to self-pity, but when faced with a lifetime of celibacy and the realization that you'd spent your twenties sorting Jelly Bellies, it was a little hard to put on a happy face.

And it was all her fault. She couldn't blame her mother for everything. She hadn't been locked in, à la Cinderella, and her room was a far cry from a dreary tower. It surrounded her, pretty and light, full of white furniture, dried flowers, and framed pictures of friends and family. This had been her suite—the trio of bedroom, bathroom, and sitting room—since she was sixteen, yet Laurel was always aware that this was her mother's house, no matter what it said in her father's will. This was her childhood home, not her own. Not a home she'd built herself, decorated and labored over, and gasped when the first mortgage bill arrived.

She was stuck in adolescence, like a female Peter Pan without the green tights.

An INSTANT MESSAGE box from Michelle popped up.

>   *what??? a con artist? that's crazy!!! what does he con?*

Needy women like her, apparently.

>   *He steals money from women, women who trust him, think they're dating him.* :-/

>   *disgusting bastard . . . have they caught him??*

Nope, but the real Russ Evans really is a cop, and he was there hoping this Dean guy would show up. I'm glad he didn't, so I didn't have to see him. I feel violated or something, Michelle, I mean I told him personal stuff . . .

Laurel didn't know what she was so bothered by. She hadn't told him anything important, any deep dark secrets like the fact that she still ate Spaghettios, or had a Britney Spears CD.

did you ever have an orgasm while chatting with him?

Eeew. She sat up so fast, she almost dumped Ferris.

What? NO! ::blushing::

then he hasn't violated you. ;-) just forget about him, let the cops deal with him. But tell me bout the real russ . . . is he still hot? I had it bad for him in high school, but he only dated blondes.

Was he hot? Is the equator hot? Is boiling oil hot?

He's still hot,

Laurel typed against her better judgment.

YOU'RE blonde. LOL.

And puppies were cute, but neither point was relevant. Laurel bit a big hunk of the muffin.

> *Hot, but insufferable. Sort of like the good-looking English teacher everyone has a crush on, but he's oblivious to it because he sees you as kids . . . Russ spent the whole time telling me how stupid and naive I was for making plans to meet a man I don't know.*

And there lay her irritation with Russ Evans, besides the fact that his face had drained of blood when she brought up sex between them. His concern showed her that he was a decent, caring guy who took his job seriously. But she didn't want him to lead her through a preschool Safety Town lesson on the dangers of the big, bad world.

She wanted him to look at her and want her. Want her like a woman. Want to drag her off into a corner and rip her clothes off. She'd come up a little short on that one.

> *well, screw him,*

Michelle wrote.

Laurel licked a crumb off the tip of her finger and groaned. That was the problem. She wanted to do just that.

Shifting Ferris off her lap—she didn't need any more heat down there—Laurel stood up, ripping her ponytail holder out in agitation. Wild. She was supposed to be wild.

It was time to take charge of her own life, her future. Have fun before she needed prosthetic parts.

So what would a wild woman do? Make Russ see her as a woman.

> *Maybe I will.*

She IM'd Michelle. Then added a little devil emoticon at the end for good measure.

Being sweet was overrated. All it had gotten her was a boring wardrobe and a possible place in heaven.

Time to shake things up a little.

Chapter 4

He was starting to fixate on Laurel Wilkins.

A little poking, a little prodding, and Laurel's address had fallen into his hands. One drive-by, and Trevor decided it had been a mistake to stand her up. But his excuse and apology appeared to have been accepted, and they were back to chatting casually again. It hadn't been his intention to keep in touch with her or to reply to her suggestion that they meet again.

But a couple of days later and three more compulsive drives past her mini-mansion, Trevor hadn't been able to resist e-mailing her again. Charming, cajoling, *I promise I'll be there this time, yes, definitely, let's meet. You pick the time and place.*

She hadn't responded yet, and Trevor was feeling unusually impatient.

Even after he moved in with Jill on Saturday, he couldn't get Laurel out of his mind. He'd bet his Cayman Island bank account that house was worth seven hundred thousand. Which meant there could be much, much more to be had in assets.

Trevor stamped his cigarette out in the metal

ashtray on Jill's faux oak coffee table. The room was cold, the windows drafty, and Jill stingy with the thermostat. She was cooking dinner for him in the tiny kitchen, slapping pots around and swearing under her breath at regular intervals. Burnt spaghetti sauce smell hovered in the air, clogging his nostrils.

He was better than this. He deserved more than this.

A million bucks in his pocket, he could leave this frozen city and lounge around Florida, take some time off. Buy some new clothes, a flat-screen TV. Quit living out of his car when he was between girlfriends.

Trevor stood up, reached for his jacket.

It was time to get to know Laurel Wilkins even better.

"Jill, honey, I'm going out for cigarettes. You need anything?"

"Get out of the car."

Russ stared at Jerry as his partner about fell into his lap trying to pull the latch on the passenger door, opening it. "What the hell is your problem? Get off of me."

"Get out." Jerry reached toward his thigh.

Knocking Jerry's hand away, Russ shifted toward the door, a little unnerved. "Anders, touch me and I'll be forced to hit you."

Jerry snorted and unlocked Russ's seat belt. "You can only wish I'd cop a feel off you. Now get out of the car before I shove your dumb ass in the snow."

Russ was clueless as to what the hell was going on. He'd just been staring out the window mind-ing his own business, listening to Anders yap on and on about the hard time his girlfriend had given him over going to a bachelor party, when suddenly he was being tossed out of the damn car. "You want to tell me what's going on?"

"You're making me crazy, that's what. Every day you make me drive by Blondie's house three, four times while you stare out the window, drooling. Get out of the car, knock on the door, ask her out. Get yourself laid, before I smack the shit out of you."

Jerry was giving him a stern look, his jaw set. He'd forgotten to shave, thick black whiskers spattered across his chin and upper lip, and his eyes were bloodshot, the result of the contentious bachelor party. Jerry was the sort of guy who was neither good-looking nor ugly, just a decent build, no major flaws, and a sense of humor that drew your attention away from the thinning hairline.

"You're kidding, right? You don't really expect me to go knock on her door." Though the idea had stolen over him repeatedly during the past few days. He was having trouble shaking it. It stuck to him, like lint.

It had occurred to him, once the altruistic determination had worn off, that he couldn't exactly just stroll up to Laurel and announce that she was going to have sex with him, and it would be for her own good, damn it.

"Yes, I do. It will save us a trip to the ER."

Russ snorted. "Yeah, when they have to revive you when I beat your ass."

"I could take you."

"Bullshit." Russ looked at Laurel's brick house again, poised silently, staring down at him like a rich grandfather. Who disapproved of a cop wanting to put the moves on Laurel. He couldn't tell if her car was in the driveway or not, and he wondered where she worked, what she did with herself.

"See? You're doing it again, mooning over her with that sappy look on your face. What are you waiting for? Afraid she'll turn you down? That is a legitimate concern, since this is you we're talking about."

"Bite me," Russ answered, although he wasn't putting his heart into the mock fight. He did want to knock on Laurel's door. He wanted to assure himself that she was all right. That she hadn't run out and done something stupid like hook up with a guy she didn't know.

And he wanted to talk to her, get to know her, tease her, make her laugh a little. He wanted to tug on her pink scarf, pull her over to him, give her a soft kiss.

Oh, Christ, he was mooning. He was so unfamiliar with it, he hadn't recognized the symptoms. Annoyed, he opened the door a crack and biting air whistled in, freezing the sappiness right out of him.

"I'm just concerned about her, that's all. She's very trusting."

"How brotherly of you." Jerry shook his head. "Get out of the car, Evans. Jesus H. Christ. I never took you for such a wuss."

He was being a wuss. Damn, that pissed him off. He was dancing around the truth of what was going on like a running back dodging a defensive lineman.

What he really wanted was Laurel safe . . . while naked in his bed.

"Shit, I'm going." He stepped out of the car into the street.

"I'm hitting Burger King. I'll see you in an hour."

"Anders!" Russ tried to grab the door, but Jerry was already accelerating, leaving him standing on the curb feeling like a dumb ass.

When he trudged to the front door and rapped on it with his knuckles, he winced at his own stupidity. For hell's sake, Laurel was deaf. She couldn't hear him knocking. Which meant he was going to be standing on the doorstep for an hour until Anders came back reeking like a Whopper extra value meal.

Running his fingers over the door knocker, Russ took in the engraving. *The Wilkins, 1957*. He felt like *The Idiot, 2005*.

He rang the doorbell three times in quick succession, thinking maybe Laurel's mother was home. Turning to observe the quiet neighborhood, he considered banging on the house next door and asking to borrow the phone. His cell phone was sitting on the seat in Anders's truck, the bastard. Nothing stirred, no sign of life anywhere behind expensive drapes hanging in multipaned windows. He could feel the wind racing off the frozen lake, slapping him in the face.

This was what he got for getting involved with a woman. Cold.

That should tell him something. Run for his life before he let every body part but his brain rush him into trouble with Laurel. The door behind him swung open. He turned, prepared to deal with Mrs. Wilkins and explain how he meant no harm to her daughter and was going to save her from selfish bastards who only wanted one thing by taking that one thing for himself.

Instead, he saw Laurel.

She was wearing jeans that sat low on her hips and another body-hugging sweater, this one red. It was advertising, plain and simple. The clothes told a man that underneath there was a curvy and delicious body, which only went and proved his point. She was totally naive if she could put on that tight, teasing outfit and not know that it screamed sex to a guy.

It sure in the hell was screaming to him. *Take me, Russ.*

"Russ." She smiled, did that little tongue thing, licking her bottom lip, baby blues peeking up from under her long lashes.

Man, oh man, oh man, he was dead. There was no way he could let another guy touch her, take advantage of her generosity and innocence. He hadn't wanted to get involved, had enough bullshit in his life to fertilize a field, but how could he let Laurel run off buying trouble?

It sucked to have a conscience.

And hormones.

But if Laurel wanted an affair, he was just going to have to charm her into wanting it with him.

"I tried to call you at work, but you don't have TTY access. I called the main number at the station and asked to be put in contact with you, but all it did was give me your voice mail, I think."

"I'm sorry." Jesus, what an ass he was. He'd given his phone number to a deaf woman. Clearly he hadn't reached detective by his intelligence alone. "Why were you calling?"

Maybe charming her naked wasn't going to be so difficult, if she had been looking for him.

"He e-mailed me. Dean." Laurel reached out, her voice excited, and took his hand, pulling him towards her. "Come on, I'll show you."

"By the way," she added over her shoulder before he could recover from the bizarre yet intriguing sensation of holding hands, "cute shot of you in the police academy on the PD's Web site."

Peeling his eyes off her ass, Russ stomped his feet on the beige rug just inside the door. "I want to have sex with you," he told her back. "Touch you until you squirm with pleasure."

Laurel's head shot around. "What did you say?"

Oh, shit. He had never actually verified how much or how little Laurel could hear. He strove for nonchalance, shrugging his shoulders. "What makes you think I said anything?"

She shook her head, looking puzzled. "I don't know. I could feel it, sense it."

He relaxed a little. "Do you hear anything? Like could you hear the doorbell?"

"I can hear airplanes taking off and thunder when I wear my hearing aid, but that's about it. But I have a light that flashes to let me know there's someone at the door."

Russ followed Laurel up a winding staircase, feeling the rich, smooth mahogany wood beneath his hand. He shamelessly gawked as he looked around the entryway, which was as big as his living room. Bigger. Hell, this hallway alone had three sofas in it, and he only had room for a love seat in his place.

Houses like this made him nervous, and he shoved his hands in his pockets, afraid to touch anything and leave poor-person fingerprints on them. But he did crane his neck around, checking out the details. The ornate woodwork around the doorways, the crown molding, the massive leaded glass window halfway up the staircase. Added together, the furniture probably cost two years' worth of his cop salary. Yet he had to admit it wasn't ridiculous, over-bearing, or Hollywood over-the-top. It was just simple good taste, expensive things in an expensive home.

There were houses like this all up and down the road, all over the lakefront, and these people weren't on the Forbes list, or considered filthy rich. They were what his mother would have called well-off. His father would have called them lucky bastards.

And they were still a world away from him and his two-bedroom bungalow with the fixer-upper metal cabinet kitchen that he hadn't quite gotten around to doing anything with yet.

Laurel turned, went down a hall past a half-dozen doors. Turned again, went up more stairs. Good thing he'd eaten his Wheaties for breakfast.

She paused before an open doorway and smiled. "My computer's in here."

"That's quite a hike," he told her.

"I guess we could have taken the elevator," she said.

Russ laughed.

But she added, "We never use it, so I didn't think about it."

"You have an elevator?" Was she serious?

With a nod she pointed down the hall, and damned if he didn't see a black wrought-iron gate for an elevator. "This house has some crazy stuff. It's a Clarence Mack."

He guessed the name was supposed to mean something to him, but it went over his head.

"He was a local architect who designed luxury homes for the new upper middle class in the twenties. The original owners were bankers and I guess out to prove they had arrived. They put a ton of upgrades in."

"Well, it does have three floors. I guess I can see the practicality of an elevator." If you were a lazy slob.

"Except the third floor was for servants, who wouldn't have used the elevator. Now the third floor is for me. This is my room."

Russ could have sworn a hush fell over the house as he stepped over the threshold.

Chapter 5

Laurel had successfully lured Russ into her bedroom. Not bad, considering she hadn't known he was going to show up on her doorstep before she had finished formulating her plan for throwing herself naked at his feet. Figuratively, of course.

The e-mail from the con artist gave her an opportunity to bring up her quest for sex again. She'd try to be more subtle this time, but she was like a blind bat trying to fly through water. Seduction wasn't her area of expertise.

She wasn't exactly sure what was, unless it was directing a customer to the bin of chocolate Goobers.

That was going to be tough to eulogize someday.

Laurel bent over her computer and clicked on her e-mail. Russ stood behind her, looking large and denim in her frilly lace, girly-girl room. A glance back showed him kicking his boots off on her honey-pine hardwood floor, like he was settling in. It stripped the situation of any businesslike feeling that remained, and Laurel swallowed hard.

"Sorry, I was trailing snow on your carpets."

"It's okay." In fact, if he needed to take anything else off, she was fine with that, too.

He had on oatmeal-colored socks, the kind with the red strip across the toe. Hunting socks, hiking socks, man socks. On her throw rug, shaped like a fat, white daisy with a lemon dot in the middle.

"Here's the first e-mail."

Russ leaned over her shoulder. She knew he was reading the message out loud—she could feel his breath teasing across the back of her neck. She reread it herself, drew in the masculine scent of Russ's aftershave and shivered.

"He sounds so sincere apologizing, doesn't he?" Laurel mused. It was interesting to her, to read the message again, to wonder if she would have trusted the sincerity of it if Russ hadn't told her the truth first. She liked to think that sooner or later natural instincts would have kicked in and she would have sensed that something about the guy was off. But then again, it was just words on a screen, easy to interpret however you wanted to. Maybe in person, she would have seen the lie in his eyes.

Russ's fingers touched her chin. She turned, startled, pulled out of her musings. His face was close. She could see he had a chipped tooth on the bottom left—just a little point missing at the top. He looked frustrated, intense, like he was struggling to stay calm.

Laurel sucked in her breath and tried really hard not to want to kiss him. But her legs trembled, her shoulders shuddered, her breath caught. She wasn't very good at the not-wanting-him thing.

Too bad sex didn't seem to be the first thing on his mind.

"Don't believe him. Don't e-mail him. Change

your address and stay clear of chat rooms. Do you understand me?"

Nope, she could tell he wasn't thinking sex. He was thinking *God save me from dumb blondes*. Laurel didn't want to hear another lecture, not now in her bedroom. She honestly hadn't been suggesting anything other than the fact that the guy was good at what he did. She wasn't such a sap as to still be taken in by him, despite what her mother thought. And she didn't really care one iota what Trevor Dean was doing, not when she had Russ Evans touching her. In a chin lock, but hey, she had to start somewhere.

Then move forward from there. She touched his lip with her thumb, gathered up her courage. "How did you chip your tooth?"

"You're changing the subject."

Absolutely. "I can see it . . . I was just wondering."

His eyes had gotten very dark, like melted chocolate. He hesitated, then said, "My buddy bumped me when I had a beer bottle in my mouth."

"Did it hurt?" Instead of dropping into her lap like a good little hand, her palm slid down his shoulder and held onto his bicep.

For balance, of course. Because she was in danger of falling flat on her ass, blown away by the rising desire she thought she could see in Russ's face.

Not that she was an expert on interpreting sexual interest, but she didn't think that under normal circumstances a man looked capable of tearing a woman's clothes off with his teeth. Russ was getting there fast, and she had the tight nipples to prove it.

"Yes, it hurt." His hand was still under her chin, and he tilted her head a little, studied her. "So are you still planning on going wild and having casual sex?"

Yes. That eliminated the need for her to work sex into the conversation. He'd done it all on his own, and she was truly grateful. Now if she could just swallow her saliva and not her tongue, she'd be all set.

Laurel forced the words out, wondering if they slurred. "I'd like to. But not with just any man." He'd pretty much ruined that. She wasn't going to be interested in any man but him. "Not a stranger, either. But it's hard to meet people. I work in a candy store, and our clientele is not usually single men." She was babbling, saying too much. *Just get to the damn point.* "I would want it to be with someone I could trust."

Russ took her hand, pulled her to a standing position, brushed her hair off her cheek so she shivered when his callused hands swept her skin. "Why just an affair, Laurel? I don't understand."

Neither did she sometimes, so it was going to be tough to explain. She took a deep breath, captured his other hand with hers, and went over to the wild side. "I have a nice life, Russ. I do. But I'm lonely, that's all. I just want a man to touch me."

His eyes went dark, narrow, fierce. She almost forgot to look at his lips, almost imagined she could hear his thoughts in his deep, rich eyes.

"I'd like to touch you, Laurel."

Good, they were completely in sync then. "I was hoping you'd say that."

"And I'd like to touch you now, everywhere, and tumble you back onto that prissy bed of yours."

Oh, my. Laurel glanced at her bed. She wasn't sure if she was ready right this second. It was just past noon on a weekday.

"But I'm on duty, so I can't."

Disappointment and relief collided like cymbals.

"But can I come back tonight? We can go out . . . see what happens."

"My mother is out of town," she said to avoid whimpering in acquiescence.

"Good." His hand went into her hair and his head bent down.

It took her a second to realize that he really and truly meant to kiss her. By the time she was clear on it, he was already there.

It wasn't questing or tentative or polite. It was deep and possessive, wet, and almost rough. Laurel just gripped the edge of her desk and held on for the ride. She could feel his hunger and confusion, which mirrored her own.

But it was still a hell of a kiss, and when he pulled back, she was panting, heart racing, thighs burning, eyes wide.

He wiped her trembling lip with his thumb. "I'm going to be sorry I did this."

"I hope not." She meant that most sincerely. She wanted to please him, wanted him to enjoy her body as much as she planned to enjoy his.

"Are you determined to do this? Even if we regret it?"

She didn't plan on regretting a damn thing. "Yes."

Russ looked a little grim, stoically determined. "Okay, we'll just have to do this together, then. We'll just forge our way through."

He moved his hands forward, mocking completion, and Laurel actually felt all the blood sink out of her face into her chest, then rise up again to set her cheeks aflame. "Forge through? We'll just forge through? You make me sound like a driveway that needs to be plowed!"

Mortified, Laurel watched in disbelief as he had the nerve to look offended. As if he were the one being forged. Why didn't he just cut a path, carve out a solution, and get right on the task at hand while he was at it?

"Well, that's a really crude analogy, Laurel."

Before she could even prevent it, her mouth dropped open and she was laughing. They were having the most bizarre conversation in her bedroom. "You're the one who brought up forging."

He gave her a brief grin, then touched the tip of her nose with his finger. "Shit. I guess that came out wrong. I've just never talked so much about sex. I usually just do it."

That's all she really wanted, too. They had a united goal, which was a start. "Russ, are you doing this because you think you should to protect me, or because you're attracted to me? Because I don't want pity sex just because you're a nice person."

She may be horny, but she had pride.

"Laurel." Russ tugged her hand, pulling her up against the length of him, hard and fast. "I don't have sex with anyone because I'm nice. Getting together with you is all about giving in to the bad part of me—the part that's wanted you since I first saw your hot little ass strolling away from me in that coffee shop."

Oh. Okay, then. Hot little ass was good. She gripped the front of his sweatshirt and adjusted her thighs so she could take better advantage of the erection that was swelling in his jeans. She rocked against him, felt him groan.

"This isn't a test either, is it? To make sure I do the right thing and don't talk to strange men?"

"I don't mean it to be a test, but we need to be clear on that. While I'm with you, you can't be making plans with other guys. I don't like that. When you're mine, you're only mine, even if it's just for one night."

She liked the sound of that. "Okay, I won't talk to other guys."

"Same goes for me. I won't make plans with other women." His hands gripped the small of her back, held her tight against him, and he shook her a little. "And no e-mails to Dean, promise me, Laurel."

She bit her lip. "But I already sent one."

Oh, God, she was going to kill him. Russ fought the urge to sigh, feeling himself sliding deeper and deeper into something he didn't know how to label. He wasn't coming on to Laurel because he felt sorry for her, that was true. But he did feel protective of her, ready to go at anyone who might want to hurt her.

His desire to catch Dean grew tenfold. As did his desire to satisfy Laurel so completely she wouldn't need to look at another man for ten years.

"What did you say to Dean?"

Laurel backed up, gestured to her computer, blinked large blue eyes at him. "Well, he sent me that e-mail apologizing, you know, and I thought that I could help you and the police if I kept an open communication with him. So I, ah, suggested we make plans to meet again."

His head was going to explode. That had to be the only explanation for the crushing pressure he felt at his temples.

"Tell him you've changed your mind." There was no way he was allowing her to act as bait. He couldn't be with her every second, and somehow, some way, he just knew she'd wind up hurt.

Dean had never once shown himself to be violent, but when backed into a corner, rats will attack.

"Why?" she asked, not defiantly, just looking confused.

"Because Dean usually goes for the small potatoes. A couple thousand here, a couple thousand there. He has to know who you are, where you live. He's going to go hard and fast for you."

"All the more reason I should keep in touch with him. All you need is for him to show up, right? Then you can arrest him on the evidence you already have, right?"

"Yes." They could take him in for questioning, fingerprint him.

"How do you know he's using all these different aliases anyway?"

"Once we started piecing together that these women had identical stories, we started lifting prints off things he left behind with the women. Dean had an arrest at eighteen for forgery, so we had his prints. Eventually, we connected him to five aliases. But the problem is, when someone is never using their real name and is sponging off other people financially, it can be hard to find him."

And Dean was good at hiding, Russ had to admit.

"That's why you need me, then."

He needed Laurel for a lot of reasons, all involving the erection he was sporting right now that wouldn't go away. Not for a criminal investigation. "That's sweet of you to offer, honey, but I don't want you involved."

"You don't think I can do it. You think I'll screw up, or panic, or blow your cover."

Oh, hell, now Laurel was glaring at him. This was why he didn't have a girlfriend. He didn't know

what the hell he was doing when it came to understanding women and keeping them happy.

"I don't want you hurt."

"I can't get hurt sending e-mails."

They stared each other down, and damn it, he
was the first to look away.

Laurel smiled and he knew he was screwed.

"Make sure you save everything he sends you."

"I will."

Russ turned and bent to reach for his shoes. "I'll
pick you up at six, then. Tonight."

Laurel tapped his shoulder. "I can't see your
lips."

He wondered how frustrating that must be for
her, yet she never looked ticked off. Just patient,
curious. He was embarrassed that he couldn't seem
to remember that she was deaf.

"Sorry. I said I'll pick you up at six, okay?"

"Okay." She leaned closer to him, so that he
could smell the sweet sugary scent that seemed to
cling to her. "I'm looking forward to it, Russ."

Oh, so was he. More than she could imagine.

Chapter 6

Russ's anticipation was shattered when he stepped through the front door of his house and found Sean lying upside down on the couch, feet up on the wall, a bag of potato chips spilling its contents all over the cushions. Sean was attempting to sing along to a video blaring on the TV, but he was a hell of a long way from American Idol as far as Russ was concerned.

Just seeing Sean set his nerves on edge lately. It was a constant visual reminder that he was doing a lousy job replacing his parents. When they had died in a car accident the year before, Russ had been stunned, dropped into grief without warning, and he'd taken then twelve-year-old Sean immediately, wanting to give the kid the kind of love and stability he'd known with their parents.

Russ was pretty sure he'd screwed that up.

Sean was failing every class in school, had a mouth like Howard Stern, and fought every single thing Russ asked him to do with a determination that Russ would be proud of—if it hadn't been directed at thwarting him.

"Hey, Sean." Russ kicked off his snowy shoes and

treaded across the shit-brown carpet he kept meaning to pull up and replace.

Sean didn't answer him.

"You do your homework yet?" This was a game they played every day. Russ asked, Sean lied, and the report cards showed the real truth.

"Didn't have any."

Sean turned the volume on the TV up even higher, and Russ had to yell to be heard. "Let me see your assignment notebook." It was something Sean's homeroom teacher had suggested. Sean was supposed to write down his homework, then Russ looked over the notebook and signed off when he saw that Sean had completed each item.

A shoulder shrugged towards the floor. "I didn't bring it home since I didn't have any homework."

Russ's temples started to throb. He knew Sean was lying, but he didn't know what the hell to do about it. What he knew about kids could fit into a shot glass. He did remember at that age he hadn't been such a wiseass, so bold in his rebellion. But then his parents had been alive when he was thirteen.

Sean had gotten a raw deal, no doubt about it.

Deciding to leave the fight about grades for tomorrow, he picked up the mail that had fallen through the mail slot to the floor and started flipping through it. "I'll order you a pizza for dinner, then you're going next door. I have plans tonight."

That got Sean's attention. He turned himself upright, wiping his greasy hands down the front of his basketball shirt. "What? No way, man, screw that."

"You're going, and that's all there is to it." His next-door neighbors, Maria Rodriguez and her daughter, JoJo, helped him out quite a bit when he needed someone to sit for Sean. Together, they were raising JoJo's two-year-old son, and they needed the money. Russ needed the peace of mind that Sean wasn't alone when he was off working crazy hours.

"I don't need a babysitter. I hate going over there. It smells like diapers all the time, and Maria slaps my hand when I swear." Sean looked indignant as he crumpled a potato chip and scattered the pieces over the couch like confetti.

"You're going to vacuum that up," Russ said, feeling his blood pressure rising as he pointed to the couch. "And Maria has my permission to slap your hand whenever she thinks you deserve it. If you'd stop being such a wiseass, you wouldn't have to worry about it."

"That's fucking child abuse, man." Sean glared at him, then deliberately picked up another chip, smashed it, and tossed it on the floor in defiance. "I'll call the cops on you."

"I am the cops, punk." He took a deep breath and ripped the bag of chips out of Sean's hand before more wound up ground into the carpet.

"Give me those!" Sean tried to grab the chips back, got one corner of the bag, and they ended up in a tug-of-war over the damn barbeque potato chips.

Russ gave one last violent yank and stuffed the bag up under his sweatshirt. He couldn't force Sean to do his homework or stop swearing like a pissed-off trucker, but he could keep him from crumbling potato chips, damn it.

Sean gave up the fight and sank back on the couch. "What are you doing tonight anyway? Working a case?"

Before the car accident had shattered Sean's life, he and Russ had shared a pretty decent relationship, given they were seventeen years apart and had never really lived together. They had hung out, played video games, talked sports and movies, and when he got older, girls. Sean had been curious about Russ's job, and for the most part, they'd enjoyed each other's company.

Russ wanted that back in the worst way. He wanted Sean to stop seeing him as his jailer and remember the good times, before everything had gone south. "No, it's not work. I'm just going out to dinner with a friend." And hopefully a lot more.

Sean's reaction was typical. "What? A friend? Please. You've gotta be kidding me. I have to go and be babysat so you can run off and get laid?" He pushed himself off the couch. "This sucks."

Russ couldn't argue with that. Mom and Dad dying definitely did suck, in the biggest way. As did his own parenting skills.

"You know what, Sean? Get over it. I'm entitled to go out with a woman once in a while."

Sean stood up and headed down the hall. "You get to do whatever you want and I get stuck going to school and hanging with old ladies and babies. It's not fair."

"Who the hell ever told you life was fair?" Russ called after Sean's retreating back. "And it's not like school is hard for you—you're not doing anything!"

The only reply was the slam of Sean's bedroom door.

Russ headed for the kitchen and a beer, telling himself he had nothing to feel guilty about.

So why did his chest hurt and his head pound?

He tossed the mail and the chips on the counter. Then he yanked open the refrigerator and told the milk, "I hate being a grown-up."

* * *

The doorbell light flashed in Laurel's room, and she panicked. Russ was here. And she wasn't wearing pants. Not a good combination if she wanted to: (a) retain her dignity and not jump him, and (b) answer the door before he gave up and left.

This was the problem with not asking him where they were going for dinner. She'd spent an hour trying to find something to wear and in the end had on only black panties and a gray twin set.

Grabbing the black skirt she'd discarded as boring, she stepped into it, then swiped black knee-high boots off the floor and ran. At the top of the stairs, she jammed her feet into the boots and zipped, then almost killed herself when she tried to dash downstairs on the little spiky boot heels. As she hit the hardwood entry, she missed the bottom step and stumbled.

Breathless and overheated, she finally flung open the door and smiled nervously at Russ. "Hi."

"Hi," he said, though he didn't smile. He looked like he had the other two times she'd seen him, casual and sexy, though he'd left the baseball hat at home. His hair was thick and flattened like he'd either shoved it that way after a shower or just ditched the hat moments before.

She should have worn jeans, like he was.

"You look . . . amazing," he said, his eyes running up and down over her.

"Thanks." Laurel felt better about her outfit as he visually devoured her, her body reacting to his heated possessive gaze. Her nipples pebbled in the twin set and he saw. She knew he did, because he lingered there, and his head went back and forth slowly.

"I was going to ask you if you wanted to just order something in, but then I saw your outfit and thought you looked too good to keep at home." He stepped inside the front door and closed it behind him. "Now I changed my mind again. I think we'd better stay here."

Laurel didn't back up, not even when he filled her space and stripped off his jacket. "Why?" she asked, wanting to hear him say it, heart pounding and palms sweating, body aching.

"Because we both want to go upstairs, don't we?"

That was putting it mildly. "*I* do," she told him, truthfully, flushed with excitement and amazed at her boldness.

"Good. Because I do, too." Russ tossed his jacket in the direction of the steps and it slid onto the floor.

Laurel moved to pick it up, thinking to at least hang it on the post at the bottom of the banister. She bent over and let out a squawk when Russ touched her. There. On her butt.

It wasn't a light tap or a friendly pat or a spank. It was a caress, slow and intentional, moving across the skirt, his thumb tracing the panty line under the wool.

She stood up, jacket in hand, and couldn't mask her look of surprise.

"What?" he asked, eyebrow lifted, mouth struggling to contain a grin. "I was just trying to get your attention to tell you to leave the jacket alone, I don't care about it."

"I said you could tap my *arm*." Not that she actually minded, but a little warning would have been nice so she could have given a better response than leaping like a cat whose tail's been stepped on.

He shrugged. "Your ass was closer." He moved towards her, and Laurel backed up until the banister collided with her back. "Besides, those boots, that skirt, bending over—it was too incredible to pass up."

There was no response she could think of that didn't involve whimpering or stammering.

He stopped right in front of her. "Do you like Chinese?"

"What?" Lipreading wasn't an exact science, and there were times she doubted her interpretation.

"Chinese food. We could just order some and stay in, if that's okay with you."

It was very okay with her. In fact, she wanted to skip the food and head straight up to her room and rip Russ's shirt off of him. He had muscles under there that she wanted to explore. One at a time.

"That sounds good. But you'll have to make the call. My mom keeps a list of take-out places in the kitchen." She waved her hand in the general direction of the kitchen and licked her lips. If only her mother knew she was using her neat and tidy take-out list for nefarious purposes. She wasn't sure if her mother would be happy or horrified.

Russ nodded. "That will work. Lead the way."

Laurel felt his eyes on her as she headed down the hall, walking slowly, mindful of the heels. It wasn't every day she wore knee-high boots, and she had to adjust her gait a little so she didn't trip or take little shuffling bird steps. The built-in desk in the kitchen had a drawer that was filled with pens, paper clips, spare keys, and take-out menus. Laurel pulled out House of Hunan and turned to hand it to Russ.

It struck her how odd he looked in her kitchen—

how masculine and overpowering. He was wearing a green crew shirt that was hanging loose over his waistband. His jeans were worn soft, faded, and about to give at the left knee. Those hiking boots had seen better days.

It had been six years since her father had died, and Laurel saw how, in the intervening years, his male influence, however slight, had slowly been removed from her mother's decorating. Whereas the kitchen had once had a black-and-white floor, keeping with the era of the house, it was now a warm terra-cotta ceramic tile. The cabinets were lighter than they'd been when her father was alive, and the counters were bursting with floral arrangements in milk jugs and spicy-scented kitchen candles.

Russ looked out of place, and yet, so very, very appealing.

"What do you want to eat, Laurel?" He flipped through the menu. "Sweet and sour pork? Cashew chicken?"

"Number seven." She pointed to the chicken with snow peas. "Do you want anything to drink? Wine? A beer?" There was some beer in the back of the fridge from her mother's Christmas party. She didn't think beer went bad, and Russ looked like a beer kind of guy.

"A beer's good." He glanced around, then reached for the phone resting in its cradle next to the oven.

Laurel stuck her head in the fridge and unearthed a Heineken from the very back. *Glass or no glass?* she wondered, then questioned why it mattered. She popped the top on the bottle and set it on the counter next to Russ, watching him while he spoke into the phone. His lips were obscured by the mouthpiece, but she liked watching the sensuous curve of his mouth, the strong determined line of his jaw, the soft way he formed his words.

She didn't have any trouble lipreading Russ. Some people were a struggle, and there were always a few she could never understand a single word they were saying. But she caught almost everything that came from Russ's lips. His words were never rushed, just calm and steady and dependable, like she imagined he was.

Disturbed with where her thoughts were going, straying into personal territories, she got herself a glass of red wine and sucked half of it down before he turned back to her.

"Fifteen minutes."

"Great." They stared at each other.

"Here's your beer." She picked it up so quickly it sloshed over the top onto her hand, forming an amber puddle.

"Thanks." He took the bottle of beer and brought her hand along with it. Before she could think to object, he sucked the beer droplets off her wrist, his tongue trailing across her damp flesh.

Her eyes fluttered shut as the warm, wet feel of his mouth sent a sharp kick of desire to her inner thighs. When his tongue wandered between her thumb and index finger, she shuddered, wanting to squirm. He sucked hard, then slid back up, resting his lips on her pulse point. Laurel could feel her heart thumping, eager and anxious, goose bumps racing across her sensitive skin.

God, it had been so long, just so long since she'd been with a man. And then it had really been a boy—they'd both been nineteen—unsure of themselves, fumbling, overeager, rushed. Russ was a man. A very strong man, rough around the edges, all worn jeans and five o'clock shadow.

He wasn't in a hurry as he licked her flesh and moved over and over her with excruciating randomness. Here and there, and she never knew where his tongue was going to land. Without warning, it moved away, then a second later landed on her mouth, covering her with a gentle teasing kiss. Laurel's eyes flew open, and she saw Russ watching her with arrogant, knowing eyes, a smile turning up the corner of his mouth.

"Can I do that again?" he asked, looking sure of her response, reaching around to the back of her neck.

She nodded, and before the motion was completed, he had pulled her head forward so their mouths collided. This kiss wasn't light, sweet, questing. This one was hot, urgent passion, desperate groping hands, his tongue sliding along her bottom lip seeking entrance.

Laurel moaned when she watched his eyes roll shut in want. Everything inside her ached and burned, and she slid her hands to his neck, kneading the thick, knotted muscles there. Her chest was pressed to his, her breasts heavy, nipples taut and yearning, and she lost all sense of balance and proportion. She wanted everything he could give her, right then and there, and when his hot tongue touched hers, Laurel dropped her hands to the loops of his jeans and brought their bodies together hard.

She was met with a thick, hot erection straining his jeans.

His grip in her hair tightened, their mouths feverish, grinding for more, a deeper taste. Russ tasted like the beer he'd sucked off her hand, and his unshaven chin scratched her cheek, rubbed it raw with his jerking movements. Laurel ran her fingers into his thick hair, tugging on it in surprise and pleasure when his hand moved down to cup her behind, aggressively and without reserve.

This is real, this is real, she told herself in a frantic chant. She held onto him with curled fingers, afraid he'd come to his senses and stop.

But Russ walked them back a step, ditching the beer on the counter. Then with both hands free, he had her sweater set pushed up far enough so his hand could slip underneath. Laurel was drowning in desire, flushed and wet, amazed at how fast she'd gotten aroused, how close she was to coming in her mother's kitchen.

He murmured something against her skin, his breath and lips tickling her, teeth nipping through the lace at her breast. Laurel leaned on him, forcing him back against the cabinets so she could spread her legs. Relinquishing her hold on his jeans, she worked her skirt up a little so her knees could rest on either side of his thighs. Then she couldn't resist bumping against him. She thought Russ approved, since he kneaded his hand into her backside and ground her forward onto his very obvious erection.

She knew she whimpered, and she just didn't care.

Then his hand slipped under her skirt, his tongue still swirling around her nipple, dampening her bra. It was so fast, so unexpected, so good, Laurel clung to his shirt. He bit her nipple, lightly, and her knees buckled. Russ held her tighter and stroked the front of her hot, wet panties.

Laurel knew the minute that his rough finger shoved under her panties and met her hot inner flesh, she couldn't hold back. She was going to come.

Russ ground his teeth and tried not to pant. Jesus,

Laurel was coming apart in his arms and it was the sexiest damn thing he'd ever seen. She was making a little humming sound of approval, something she probably wasn't even aware she was doing, and it stroked and rolled over him, making him so hard he hurt. It felt incredible to hold her, to see her desire, smell it, sink into that silky wetness between her thighs.

He hadn't meant to slip a finger in there, but her skirt had worked up so high. He'd known he'd find her slick and ready behind that satin and he wanted to feel it, know it, own it.

She wanted him bad and it was a huge fucking turn-on. He wanted to give it all to Laurel, over and over, until she was loved so thoroughly she couldn't walk. He stroked inside her, tight muscles clinging to the two fingers he'd worked into her.

And then she came. With little shudders, eyes glassy as they rolled back in her head, and Russ held her, smiling at how incredible she looked. Her blond hair was mussed, lips swollen, prim little sweater set shoved up past her breasts, creamy flesh spilling over the top of her bra. Her legs, encased in those sexy black boots, were spread, her skirt almost at her waist.

"Damn it, Laurel, that was so hot."

She didn't answer, but clung to him with wide eyes. Her cheeks were pink. "Wow. That was unexpected."

"Not to me." He had come here tonight to see that. And since he hadn't been smart enough to capture it on film, he was going to have to do it again.

Her head turned a little and she jerked back, nearly stumbling in her heels. "Oh, God, the delivery person is here."

Russ heard the faint ring of the doorbell at the same time she pointed to a light flashing next to the phone. "I'll get it." Since he was the one still dressed.

But he tugged her sweater down as he gave her a quick kiss. She just blinked and rubbed the flat of her hands on her skirt, looking dazed as he turned in what he thought was the general direction of the front of the house.

He almost got lost on the way to the front door, taking a wrong turn at the dining room and winding up in a pantry before he backtracked. "Damn museum," he muttered, though he wasn't really annoyed.

Horny was a more accurate description at the moment.

Dispatching the delivery person quickly with a larger tip than was necessary, Russ made his way back to the kitchen. He hoped they were going to eat in here. One peek at the dining room had him worrying that he'd drop an egg roll on the Persian rug. Not that the kitchen was really any better. It was all feminine and expensive, gleaming stainless steel appliances, and so many flowers it looked like a mail order bulb catalog had puked in Laurel's kitchen.

Not that he had a problem with flowers, but it just made him uncomfortable that everything was so perfect. Not that he wanted his kitchen to stay the homage to ugly it currently was, but he also didn't think he'd be bringing Laurel back to his house anytime soon.

Laurel was sitting at the table in front of the big floor-to-ceiling window that looked out over the backyard, and, somewhere in the dark, the lake.

Plates were on the table, along with cloth napkins and her wine. His beer had been poured into a glass. She shot him a nervous smile when he sat down across from her, unrolling the top of the paper bag.

Embarrassed. She was clearly embarrassed, her hands folded primly in her lap and her knees locked together as if to deny they'd ever been spread wide apart. Russ had figured on ditching the food in the fridge and heading right upstairs to her lacy big bed, but now he saw he needed to tread carefully.

He'd gone too fast, too soon. No matter that she'd been trying to climb onto him, and when he'd touched her she'd been dripping wet. He should have slowed down, finessed her a little.

Like he'd ever been Mr. Charming.

Pulling a container of rice out of the bag, he popped the top. "So, I hope you're hungry. There's always too much in these things. You open this little tiny box and like twelve portions fall out. It's amazing."

She laughed, though it was stilted.

"Tell me about this house, Laurel. If the Wilkins moved in, in 1957, how come you live here with your mom? Your parents divorced?"

Get her relaxed, that was the strategy.

She took a deep breath and pushed her plate towards the box of rice he had hovering in offering. "No. My dad's parents bought this house in '57, then they passed it on to my dad when they retired and headed to Florida when I was a baby. I grew up here. My dad died when I was nineteen."

Russ's gut clenched. "I'm sorry. Damn, I know how that feels."

"You do?" Laurel held her hand up to stop him from giving her any more rice.

"My parents died last year. Car accident." It hurt to even talk about it.

"Oh!" Her hand flew to his and she squeezed his fingers. "I'm sorry, Russ, that must have been awful."

"It was. Is," he corrected himself. "But I'll get over it, I mean, I'm thirty years old. But my little brother, Sean, is the one who's lost out big-time. He'll be fourteen in March, and he's stuck with me. A lousy replacement for our parents."

Laurel forgot to be embarrassed over letting Russ yank her skirt up fifteen minutes after he'd arrived for their first date. The pain on his face moved her. Dejection swam in his eyes and she wanted to comfort him, give him the confidence he was already giving her.

"He's lucky he has you. Without you, it would be a lot worse."

He laughed, but it was joyless. "I'm not sure about that. I don't know anything about kids, Laurel. He's so angry all the time, and cocky, and stubborn."

"Aren't all teenagers?"

Russ poured noodles onto his plate. "Maybe. But I don't know what to do about it."

"Maybe nothing right now. He's still grieving, and kids deal with death differently. When my father died, I just retreated. I stayed in the house and did nothing but eat and watch movies."

"When did you get over it, start acting more like yourself?"

"I think about five days ago when I got up the guts to go meet Russ Evans in a coffee shop."

Russ dropped his disposable chopsticks onto his plate. "Laurel, tell me something before we go upstairs." He pinned her with a stare, so intimate and knowing, she felt a flush rising on her cheeks.

She needed to learn how to stop blushing. It wasn't going with her new image.

"What?"

"Are you a virgin?"

Chapter 7

The embarrassment came back for another visit, and brought its cousin, humiliation, with it.

"No! I'm not a virgin." Technically she wasn't, though no one would ever recruit her to star in an instructional video.

Russ looked relieved. "Okay, that's good."

Wondering how much of a novice she appeared, Laurel chewed a pea pod, then reassured him, "I've had sex six . . . no, seven times." But the seventh practically didn't count because her college boyfriend had lost his footing and fallen out of the saddle before completing the ride.

She looked up from her plate long enough to see his jaw drop.

"What? That's almost as bad." He rubbed his chin, looked panic-stricken.

The cozy feelings she'd been experiencing towards him evaporated. "Well, I'm sorry if I disappointed you. And I thought men liked virgins, that it's a fantasy or something."

"Not for me," he said shortly. "I don't have the time or patience for instructions, understand?"

Point made and then some. He liked bimbos.

"This can't be a total shock to you. I told you it had been a long time for me." Appetite gone, she pushed her rice around.

"I'm sorry, Jesus, I'm sorry. That sounded completely wrong." Russ stood up, came around the table to her. "I'm not trying to be a prick."

Could have fooled her. Laurel pulled away, leaned towards the window.

He stopped her by putting his hand on the arm of the chair, surrounding her with his masculine scent. He touched her chin, forced her to look at him. "I just need you to be sure this is what you want."

Where the heck had he been? This was exactly what she wanted. "I'm sure."

Regret crossed his face, and she didn't think it was her imagination.

"Because this is all I can give you. Pleasure—lots of pleasure—but nothing else. Sean takes all I've got, and then some."

Pride made her lock eyes with him, lift her chin, square her shoulders. "I never asked for anything else."

He studied her as if he wasn't sure he could believe her. "Okay, then. If you're sure this is what you want, if you're cool with everything."

"Russ, it sounds like you're the one who's not sure." Laurel pushed her chair back towards the window, trying to escape him. If this was it, and he was going to leave now, she didn't want to be that close, didn't want to have to smell him, see him, or be tempted to touch him. "I'm sorry if I upset you earlier, I didn't mean to . . ." she could not say *have a rip-roaring orgasm* out loud. "It's just been a while, like I've said, so if you don't want to deal with my inexperience, that's fine. I understand."

She put on her polite smile, the one her mother had taught her to use in awkward social situations. "I had a lovely evening, thank you."

He stood up. His eyebrows shot up towards his hairline. Hands on hips, he told her, "Well, that sounded damn pretty the way you said it, but I'm not ready to leave yet."

Her breath caught, and she had to clamp her thighs together to quiet the ache there. "No?"

"No. Let's go upstairs and make this evening a whole lot lovelier."

Oh, my. "If you're sure."

He grinned. "Let's make a deal. The next one who asks if the other person is sure gets smacked. We both want to be here, don't we? We both want to take this upstairs, don't we?"

"Yes."

"Okay, then." Glad that was settled, and they could get on with it, Russ closed up all the food boxes, stacked them, and pulled open her refrigerator. It was frighteningly clean and filled with skim milk, little yogurts, and baby carrots. He set the boxes in front of the egg substitute and added to his mental list cleaning out his own fridge. He still had ham from Christmas in there.

Done with the task, he turned and found Laurel putting their plates in the dishwasher. She was kind of on the tiny side, thin despite those curves that made him drool. She was so pretty in such a natural way, nothing artificial or false about her. Russ was equal parts eager and terrified to proceed.

She'd only had one lover in college and had led kind of an isolated life. What if he scared the shit out of her? He didn't think he'd whip it out and she'd scream or anything. But he was used to women who gave as good as they got, who knew where to yank pleasure from, and he didn't worry with them. They just got naked and went at it. That wasn't going to work here, and he felt bumbling and blue collar, which pissed him off.

He'd just have to take it slow, make sure she was okay with whatever he did. She had passion. That was clear from the way she had shattered on him before dinner, but that didn't mean she was up for anything and everything. So while he had the urge to pick her cute little body up and settle it on his waist, he resisted.

But he did lift the hair off her neck and kiss her.

She sighed, a soft little sound of surrender. Russ nibbled her ear, breathing in that sweet sugary smell that seemed to be part of her natural scent. Her hair tickled his nose, her fingers gripped his leg.

Then she turned fast, startling him back. "I want to go upstairs, Russ. Now."

Hot damn. She looked ready to devour him, inch by inch. "Lead the way, gorgeous."

Laurel took his hand in a way that he was starting to kind of like, and tugged him towards a set of back stairs off the kitchen. Servants' stairs, he guessed. Though thoughts of using the elevator flitted through his mind, by the time he decided he'd really like to do it with Laurel moving between floors, they had rounded the curve on the second floor and were starting up to the third.

So he readjusted his thoughts to her ass and what it would look like if he lifted that skirt and she had nothing covering her but panties and those sexy, dual-purpose boots. Businesswoman by day, hooker by night, is what he thought of whenever he looked at them.

Inside her room, Laurel turned to him, her blue eyes sweeping down, shy. Her ankle rocked on the boot heel and she folded her hands together, like she didn't know what to do with them.

Russ reached behind his neck and stripped his shirt off. Might as well set the tone.

She gasped. Then gawked. Her tongue popped out and swept her lip.

He tossed the shirt to the floor, enjoying the hunger stamped on her features. Kicking his shoes off, Russ closed the distance between them. Coaching himself to go slow, he took her hands, pressed them to his bare chest.

Laurel groaned, eyes fluttering shut for a brief second. Then she ran her fingers lightly over his skin, pausing to touch his chest hair, before running down his stomach. Now he was the one groaning, aching at her innocent touch, the eager way she dived towards his waist, skimming beneath the waistband of his jeans and darting back up to knead the muscles on his sides. She brushed over both of his nipples simultaneously and Russ ground his teeth.

Locking his hands behind her back, he brought his mouth to her eyelid, kissed the fragile flesh there, felt her eyelashes flutter over his rough lips, before he moved to the other and did the same. She was soft and didn't wear makeup, which he liked. He could kiss her anywhere and not worry about his lips coming back with pink or gray or brown powder all over them.

Her hands were driving him nuts stroking all over his chest in fascination, and Russ decided it was time to slip that sweater off of her. Except that he had the oddest feeling that someone was watching them. Disturbed, too many years on the PD behind him, he swept his eyes around the room.

And met the hateful glare of the fattest cat he'd ever seen in his life.

"Uh . . . Laurel?" He tapped her shoulder, then pointed. The cat was inches away from them, standing on Laurel's dresser, white paws out in front, mounds of furry flesh spilling out on either side. Somebody had been hitting the wet food too much lately.

Unbelievably, her face lit up. "Oh! Ferris, there you are, my big boy." She reached out and rubbed fat furry ears. "I thought you were taking a nap."

No wonder this cat looked pissed off and ready to take names. No self-respecting feline would want to be called Ferris or big boy.

Laurel had stopped speaking out loud, but continued a dialogue with her cat in sign language. Russ liked watching her sign, enjoyed the fluidity of her hands, the expressions on her face, but it also baffled him. He didn't see how anyone could ever learn something that looked so complex.

Whatever she said to the cat, he responded by hopping down off the dresser, stretching his back legs, and trotting off towards the couch, his belly fat swinging on either side of his hips.

Russ wondered if humans were forced to walk on all fours, if more middle-aged guys would cut down on the pork rinds and beer. That was nasty looking.

Somehow Ferris made it onto the couch and settled down, body curved. He still eyed Russ with disdain, chin on the cushion.

"I don't think he likes me."

"He's just not used to half-naked men in my room." Laurel smiled.

"How about all-the-way naked men?"

Her breath caught and she shook her head. "Huh-uh."

"He's going to have to get used to it." Trying to

ignore the feeling of cat contempt being aimed at him, Russ took the edge of Laurel's sleeve and tugged it down, freeing her right arm.

He did the same with her left, until the sweater fell to the floor, leaving her in a matching gray sweater with no sleeves. Damn it, he hated layers. He'd been hoping they were connected to each other and she'd be standing in her bra now.

Impatience rising, he jerked the second sweater off over her shoulders, then whistled in appreciation. Her blond hair was mussed from his careless yank of the sweater, her lips were ripe, wide open, her breasts rising and falling in the black bra.

Remembering he wasn't supposed to startle her, he brought her to him for a long, sweet kiss, deep but not urgent. She relaxed and clutched his biceps as he undid the zipper on the back of her skirt. Laurel shuddered as it fell off her hips and down to her ankles. Russ kissed her again, slowly walked her back to the big bed with the fluffy white pillows and girly blankets.

He pushed her gently down, wondering if they were supposed to turn down the sheets or something. The bed looked too perfect, too innocent to just climb on top and lay Laurel out. The covers needed to be mussed, unmade, crumpled before he'd feel comfortable on it.

Laurel was on her back, blinking up at him, waiting, her creamy white skin flushed pink with anticipation. Her skirt was still at her ankles, and he dropped it to the floor. And there she was, lying there, waiting, ready for him, in nothing but a black bra, a scrap of black panties, and black high heel boots.

"Oh, Jesus Christ," he said, giving his cock a shove as it rammed painfully into his zipper. Inexperienced, practically a virgin with as little as she'd done, and yet he'd never seen a woman look sexier or more fuckable than she did right then.

But she bit her lip. "What's the matter?"

She started to sit up, and he realized she'd taken his desperate prayer the wrong way.

"No, no, stay there." He put his knee between her legs, a hand on her shoulder holding her down. "You just look amazing. So beautiful."

Her mouth went into a little O.

He lifted one of her feet up, stuck it on his chest, the heel biting into his flesh. The little black panties fought the good fight, but gave it up and slid over, falling into the dip between her cheeks and revealing the curve of her ass on one side.

Russ swallowed hard and tugged down the boot zipper. It went with excruciating slowness while she laid still, her chest rising up and down, her fingers clutching the bedcovers. Laurel didn't bother to move the strand of hair that had fallen across her face and stuck to her lip.

He stepped back, took the boot with him, and her bare toes fluttered before her leg fell to the bed. Russ flung it behind him, enjoying the hard sound it made hitting the floor. It fed his urgency, but he took a couple of breaths, ignored the hot throb in his pants, and reached for her other leg.

Laurel was ready with it this time, lifting for him. This one went quicker as he strained to control himself. He threw this one even harder, farther, watching it skid across the room and slam into her desk with a satisfying thud. It helped to release his excess energy, his shaking, burning need to just rip those panties down and sink into Laurel hard and fast, pumping until he came deep inside her.

He reached for her hand, steadier, pulled her up, ignoring her questioning look. Ripping the white lacy blanket off the bed helped him redirect, too, and he sent it to the floor with the violent flick of one wrist. Then followed it up by tossing aside decorative pillows shaped like hearts and sausage links.

That was better. It looked more like a bed and less like a magazine photo shoot for *House Beautiful.* Laurel just stared at him, but before she could question his destruction, he covered her mouth with his, poured all his passion and need and want into that kiss until they were both shaking and he ached everywhere.

Russ unsnapped his jeans, unzipped them, pulled a condom out of his pocket, and tossed it onto the bed. Then he put his arms behind her back, urged her down onto the bed. Laurel went without a sound, her knees clamped together and her hands splayed across her flat stomach. Balls tight, cock throbbing, he got rid of his jeans, turning the legs inside out as he ripped them off.

Despite his need to do otherwise, he left his briefs on, and climbed up alongside Laurel on the bed.

He was reaching for her bra when he got bit.

Chapter 8

Laurel was lying on her torn-apart bed, quivering, mentally urging Russ to hurry up and get the show on the road, when he jerked back, his face a mask of pain and surprise.

"Russ? What's wrong?"

He had sat up and was leaning over the side of her bed. While it gave her a very nice view of his tight buns in navy blue underwear, things were not progressing in the way she'd like them to. The underwear should have been long gone by now.

Laurel scooted to peer over to where he was propping himself up on the floor, reaching under her bed. She tapped his shoulder. "What are you doing?"

He turned, twisting his back so she could see his mouth, and his face was red from bending over. "Your cat bit me."

"What? Ferris bit you?" Laurel stared at him in shock. Ferris had never bit anyone. "Where?" Maybe it had been something else. *Like what?* she wondered ruefully. A spider? A mosquito in January?

"On my leg."

Laurel glanced down past the beautiful buns

and saw on the back of his calf an angry red welt
that looked like . . . teeth marks. She covered her
mouth, half-horrified and half-amused. It seemed
Ferris didn't like having his domain entered by another male.

"Oh, I'm so sorry, Russ! But what are you doing?
You're not going to hurt him, are you?" Laurel
dropped on her stomach and bent over the bed,
peering into the darkness under her dust ruffle.

Ferris blinked at her, looking perfectly innocent. "Come here, boy." She clicked her tongue,
held her fingers out. He edged out, sniffed her fingers.

Dropping to the floor, Laurel scooped him up
and stood, using both hands to support his ample
weight. She turned to Russ. "I'll just put him in the
bathroom."

"I wasn't going to hurt him," Russ said, looking
offended. "I was just going to have a little man-to-
man with him when I was tossing his furry ass out
in the hallway."

"Okay, sorry." Really, she couldn't imagine Russ
hurting an animal, but it had been an instinctive reaction. Laurel reached out to squeeze his arm, let
him know she hadn't meant it as a slur. But before
she could, Ferris slapped his paw across Russ's forearm.

Fortunately, he didn't have any front claws, but
it still startled Laurel, almost causing her to lose
her grip on him. She adjusted her hold and looked
down at her cat, who had done a one-eighty, per-
sonality wise. He was normally so sweet.

Russ glared at Ferris. Ferris glared back.

"He hissed at me!" Russ looked so affronted that
Laurel laughed.

It was while she was laughing that she realized

she was standing there in her bra and panties, and Ferris's fur was tickling her bare belly. It had her turning quickly to the bathroom. Good Lord, she had an almost-naked detective in her bedroom and a cat that was more determined to pull the plug on her sex life than her mother.

With less gentleness than she would have normally shown, she dumped Ferris on the bathroom floor, avoided catching a glimpse of herself in the mirror, and pulled the door shut.

Now to turn around and walk back to the bed. It shouldn't be that hard. But her heart was pounding, her throat was dry, and her left breast was in danger of popping out of the top of her bra. Hand hanging onto the bathroom doorknob like it was glued there, Laurel tried to get herself to move. She wanted this. So what was the problem?

The problem was it was damned embarrassing.

She felt the vibration as the floorboards gave under Russ's tread. He had a heavy walk, and on the hard wood, she could feel the movement.

She sucked in a deep breath and turned just as he reached her.

"Where were we?" he asked with a delightfully wicked smile.

"On the bed," she answered, wishing they had never left it.

Russ towered over her, the breadth of his shoulders making her feel petite, feminine. He was large, muscular, skin dry and darker than hers. Caramel-colored hair emerged from the waistband of his briefs and traveled north. Laurel felt very soft, very small, very sexy when he looked at her like that.

"Then let's get back to it."

With one hand on the small of her back and another on her thigh, he hauled her up into the air, shocking the heck out of her. Laurel clamped her legs around his butt so she wouldn't tumble to the floor, and grabbed onto his shoulders.

Her breasts rammed his chest. Her lips hovered tantalizingly close to his. The juncture of her thighs rested right above his straining erection. Laurel relaxed her body. Her damp panties collided with him, and she tossed back her head in abandon. This was perfect, everything she'd been waiting for—a hot, sexy man driving her wild with lust and want.

Russ carried her to the bed, laid her down, put his thumbs in his briefs. "I'm going to take these off now. If you think that might unnerve you, look away."

She thought he was joking, but to play along, she smiled innocently, looked away. Right into the mirror over her dresser, which gave her a perfect shot of the front of him. And gripped the bedsheet in fascination when he dropped his briefs efficiently, stepped out, and put a knee on the bed.

Oh my word, and then some. Time had dimmed her memory of Geoffrey naked, but she was fairly certain he hadn't been sporting anything quite like Russ had. She would have remembered that kind of skyscraper.

"Umm . . ."

He locked eyes with her in the mirror. "It's okay, Laurel. We'll take our time."

She nodded frantically, terrified. Terrified that he'd use that on her, terrified he wouldn't.

In self-defense she closed her eyes, then decided that was a lousy idea. If she couldn't see him, or hear him, she wouldn't have a clue what he was doing. The front of her bra yanked down and his tongue flicked across her nipple.

See, that just proved her point. She had been

completely unprepared for that. With a cry, she opened her eyes and watched the top of his head as he bent over her. Laurel caught glimpses of his pink tongue moistening her nipple, sucking the tip, while she squirmed beneath him.

There were tricks a woman who wasn't currently dating anyone had, to keep herself satisfied and back from the edge, but nothing could ever replace the feeling of a man's hot tongue sliding over her body. Trailing between her breasts, over her nipples, down into her navel, cruising over the front of her panties . . .

"Russ, please." She forced the words out, reaching for him, dragging him back up for a quick, hot kiss.

Foreplay was overrated when you'd been waiting six years to have sex.

Russ took the kiss she gave him and popped the hook on her bra at the same time. And proving he was talented at multitasking, he cupped her breast, lavished nips and sucks on her nipple, while his other hand tugged her panties down.

He felt around until he found the condom he'd tossed, and then his fingers probed the opening in her damp curls.

Laurel lay on her bed in frantic anticipation, his hands and tongue everywhere, spinning her desire way out of control, hitching her breath, robbing her of reason. Russ had surrendered his hold on her breast so he could roll the condom on with one hand, teasing her with little strokes with the other. She wanted to reach down, touch him, feel him, help him, but nothing seemed to move.

She was frozen, insensate, drowning.

Russ rested on his knees and struggled with the condom, looking down so Laurel couldn't see him swearing at it. "Stupid piece of latex shit. Get on there before I tear you and make you completely useless."

It wasn't cooperating and Laurel was waiting for him, ready for him. He took a deep breath. He counted to three, not willing to go any higher.

Russ rolled the condom on, fitting it in place correctly this time.

He prayed for patience to do this right.

Then, locking eyes with Laurel, he held himself up with one arm, used his fingers to coax her apart, and eased into her. He groaned as he felt the pleasure seep all the way to his toes.

Her thighs drifted farther apart, her lashes fluttered open and closed. Russ rested inside her, halfway there, wanting more than anything to plunge and take, and knowing he owed it to her not to. This woman trusted him, and he wanted to give her the best.

Jaw locked, teeth clenched, he sank a little deeper, felt the stretch and pull of her tight inner muscles. She made a low murmur of approval, and emboldened, in control of himself, Russ started to stroke. Long, slow, steady thrusts, in and out, gentle, loving touches that just about cost him his sanity.

He wanted to fuck Laurel, but knew you didn't fuck girls like that. You made love to them, sweetly and softly, and beat back your base instincts. Or tried to, anyway.

It hurt to hold back, but he did, stroke after endless stroke, minute after minute. She moaned, wrapping her legs around his thighs, her fingers plucking at the pillow, her hair spilling across the side of her flushed cheek.

Russ decided he'd met the most beautiful woman on the face of the earth.

And the thought was racing through his tight and tense body, making him burn harder and harder, when her eyes widened in shock and her back bowed. Her orgasm was graceful, flowing, silent, as she went up, then down, body clenching onto his.

Not trusting himself, knowing how desperately he wanted to pound into her, he pulled almost all the way out, then slid deep, and allowed himself to come in tight, pulsing jerks.

Instead of an explosive burst, it dragged on and on and Russ held his whole body still the entire time, marveling that pleasure could be so intimately mixed with pain. He was dying. Laurel was so damn hot and it was killing him not to have her the way he wanted to.

But she ran her fingers over his back, smiled up at him in shy satisfaction, and he knew it was worth it.

And he had enjoyed himself—he just wanted more and then some. He felt capable of coming about twelve more times. Being a nice guy was a bitch.

He groaned and pulled out before he was tempted to toss all his prior nobility out the damn window and drive into her with pounding thrusts.

Dropping a kiss on her swollen lips, he settled next to her, rested an arm idly across her breast. "You okay?"

"I'm fine."

Russ stirred to look at her. *Fine?* Fine didn't sound right. Where were the mewing sounds, the lazy satisfied yawns, and the declaration that six years of celibacy had been worth that moment?

"How was it?" Well, that was a first, asking a woman to rate his performance.

"It was fine." Laurel played with the front of his hair and smoothed his eyebrows.

She was smiling, but he knew he was scowling. What was fine? Fine was fucked. There was no fine. There were fine lines and fine wine and fine dining. Work was fine and having pizza for dinner was fine, but when it came to sex, nothing should ever, ever be fine.

"What's wrong?" He went up on his side, found himself cupping her breast, rolling her nipple.

"Nothing's wrong." Laurel arched in approval, pushing her nipple into his touch.

"Then what's this fine bullshit? If you didn't like it, tell me, and we'll fix it." Male pride already had his cock swelling, on tap for another round.

"Well . . ." Laurel blushed. "I just thought . . ."

"What?" Damn it, he was getting a complex here. And as if to prove he was capable of driving her wild, his hand moved down between her legs and stroked her.

"I just thought that it would be, well, *harder.* Deeper, or something."

Holy shit. Russ shook his head in shock, fighting the urge to laugh. She wanted it *harder?* Here he'd about blown a testicle trying to hold back, and she wanted to get down and dirty.

Clearly nervous she'd offended him, Laurel stroked his arms. "I mean, it was good, Russ, really it was. Maybe I just have unrealistic expectations."

That wasn't going to soothe his ego.

She covered her face. "Oh, I'm making it worse, aren't I? Don't mind me, while I curl up and die of humiliation."

Russ did laugh. Hell, she wanted it harder, he'd give it to her. With pleasure.

He pulled her hand off her face. "Laurel, I'm not upset. Truth be told, I was worried about you being inexperienced. I held back. A lot."

When he sank his finger inside her while talking, she let her breath out with a *whoosh*. "Really? You mean, you could . . . ?"

Oh, yeah. He sure in the hell could.

He pulled the finger out of her. She whimpered. Russ took her hands and jerked them straight up over her head. "Hold onto the bed, Laurel. You're going to need it."

Her mouth opened as she clutched the white headboard, like she was going to ask a question.

Russ didn't wait to hear it.

Spreading her legs with his knees, he drove into her, fast and *hard*. Her head snapped back, a low moan ripping out of her, and Russ felt a surge of triumph. He could, would, please her.

Before she could suck in another breath, he pulled back, thrust again, deep enough to send her slamming back into the bed frame. Yes, yes, yes, damn it, she looked so good, so aroused, so intrigued. When she would have turned her head to the side, Russ caught it, held her so she had to look at him as he pushed inside her hot, eager body over and over.

Laurel held onto the bed, her shoulders squished, her eyes trained on the lustful expression on Russ's face. This was better than fine—this was incredible, fabulous, mind-blowing. He took her with uncontrolled urgent pushes, and she reveled in it, felt pleasure wringing out of every inch of her body, spiraling out her limbs and wracking her with gratitude.

"Oh, God, Russ, yes," she said, not sure if the words came out loud, or in the whisper that sometimes rolled off her lips.

He was pushing so hard against her that she couldn't draw her legs up and around him, but lay

slack on the bed, taking it, squeezing her inner
muscles as if she could hold his swollen erection
inside forever.

"Like it?" he asked, shaking her chin to get her
attention. "Like it hard, Laurel?"

"I do like it, I love it . . ." Laurel glanced down,
saw her breasts heaving with the motion, looked
farther, saw Russ's tuft of body hair. Saw him thrust-
ing in and out, the slick shaft rising and falling
deep inside her spread thighs.

The orgasm swept over her, a powerful, passion-
ate wave that stole every thought from her head
and sent her body jerking upward. He didn't stop,
didn't slow, and she pulsed and ached and moaned,
feeling ripped apart, shattered.

Her hands slipped off the bed, limbs useless, slack,
as he kept pounding and her body continued to
contract around him. She saw the difference, felt
the force of his orgasm this time as his face
scrunched up, his shoulders jerked, and he poured
himself hot and reckless into her.

That look, that feeling, was incredible. Laurel
watched him in awe, her own body replete and satisfied. Now *that* had been worth the wait.

Though she sincerely hoped she wouldn't have
to go another six years, she figured this would
hold her if she did.

Russ collapsed on her, his upper lip sweaty as it
brushed her skin. Damp bangs fell over his forehead, onto her breast. He closed his eyes, breathed
hard, and Laurel watched him—gratitude, pleasure,
and something else rising in her chest.

He had held back for her. He had respected her
inexperience, even when he had said he didn't have
time for instructions.

Russ Evans was a very sweet, sexy man and she

had better watch her step, or she was going to be falling for him. And that wasn't fair to him or to her. She had meant what she'd said about relationships—she wasn't necessarily looking for one. She had just wanted a man in her bed.

She'd gotten one.

Opening his eyes, his mouth turned up in an arrogant grin. "Better?"

She nodded. "Never better."

"Good." He peeled himself off of her, leaving her chest damp and chilly.

As goose bumps raced across her, he brushed back her hair and pulled the sheet over her. "I can't spend the night, honey."

Laurel wasn't sure he'd actually called her *honey*— it had looked more like *bunny*—but he couldn't possibly be calling her bunny, and she wasn't about to ask him if he'd just called her honey, in case he hadn't. She decided to just assume he was, and enjoy it.

"That's okay, I understand."

"It's my brother. He's with a babysitter, but I need to get home."

There it was again, that strange feeling rising up in her and making her want to do a cartwheel. "It's a big responsibility. You're a good brother, Russ."

"I'm trying." He sighed and sat up, pulling the condom off. "Can I see you again? How about Friday?"

That was a really long four days away, but Laurel was pleased to see he wanted to extend this beyond one night. "That would be great."

"I'll see if Sean can spend the night at a friend's house." His eyebrows rose up and down suggestively as he stood up, facing her in all his naked glory. "Want to have a sleepover here with me?"

Russ in her bed, all night long. Let her think about it.

Hell, yes.

She nodded. "I'd like that a lot."

He grinned. "I think you would. You're getting that hot look on your face again, the one that makes me so hard I can't walk."

A glance below his waist proved the hard thing. Laurel sat up for a better look, pulling the sheet with her.

"So, you, me, and absolutely no Ferris." Russ turned and yanked open the bathroom door. Ferris tumbled out, paws up, like he'd been scratching the door.

Which she realized, he probably had been. "Has he been scratching the door?"

"Nonstop, for twenty minutes. I mentally blocked him out, but Friday he needs to ship out to the first floor."

"I'm sorry, I didn't know he was being such a pest." As if to verify that he was, in fact, annoying, Ferris strolled past Russ and took a swipe at his ankle.

"Ferris!"

Russ said something to her cat that she couldn't hear, but she didn't think it was "here, kitty."

While Russ disappeared into the bathroom, Laurel pulled her panties back on, then grabbed a sweatshirt from her drawer and a pair of worn-in jeans. She wanted to walk Russ to the front door, and it was a long hike in a sheet. Running her hands through her hair, she sat down to pull on the jeans, feeling a wonderful soreness between her legs.

She felt fabulous. Absolutely incredible. When Russ had stopped holding back, Laurel felt like he'd stopped seeing her as a naive almost-virgin and had seen her for the woman she was, with a woman's wants and needs.

When her head popped through the hole of her sweatshirt, Russ was in front of her in his briefs, reaching for his jeans. "Hey, Laurel?"

"Yes?"

"Did you ever get an e-mail back from Dean?"

"Not yet. But I haven't checked my mail today."

"Remember what we agreed on. Don't make plans to meet him. Just let me know if he contacts you."

They hadn't agreed on that. He had told her that when he had been in "listen to me, stupid girl" lecture mode. Not wanting to spoil the afterglow with a discussion over semantics, she just nodded. "I'll let you know."

She was going to help Russ catch that guy whether he liked it or not. She was the only woman in a position to play both sides and lead the cops to Dean, and she was going to do it.

Russ didn't really have a say in the matter.

Chapter 9

Russ was feeling damn good as he pulled into his driveway.

Laurel had been, well, just amazing.

He wanted Friday to arrive right now, so they could continue to discover all the various pleasure points on each other. And he thought he'd really like to sink his tongue into her hot flesh and taste her.

Adjusting himself before hopping out of the car, Russ shook his head in amusement. Laurel Wilkins—fuzzy, fleecy, bunny Laurel—was a hot tamale.

Russ knocked on the Rodriguez's front door gently so he wouldn't wake up JoJo's little boy, Mario. As he waited, he shifted back and forth, thinking he needed gloves. He'd lost his somewhere in his coat closet.

Sean opened the door, and without a word, streaked right past Russ to their house, opening the side door and slamming it closed behind him.

"Well, hello, how was your night?" Russ watched in disgust, his good mood souring. He stepped into the Rodriguez's and waved to JoJo, who was on the couch, remote in hand.

"Hey, JoJo. How bad was Sean tonight?"

JoJo looked up from the TV and flipped her curly black hair over her narrow shoulder. She was wearing a sweatshirt that was about six sizes too big for her one hundred pounds.

"Have you talked to him about condoms and stuff like that?"

Russ closed the front door and tried not to develop an ulcer. "Why? What happened?"

"He came on to me."

"What! What do you mean?" Russ kicked the snow off his shoes and took the navy easy chair across from JoJo. He felt the need to sit down. *Jesus*. JoJo was twenty-five, a hell of a long way from Sean's thirteen. Maybe she had misunderstood.

"We were watching a movie and he turns to me and asks me if I would ever date a younger man. I'm thinking he means like two or three years, you know, so I say, 'sure, whatever.' " JoJo folded her arms across her chest and smirked. "Then he says, 'so how about you and me, babe? The bedroom's right down the hall.' "

Oh, my God. "He was joking, right?"

"I thought so, definitely, so I say, 'sure, cutie, whatever.' " JoJo shook her head. "Then I swear to you, Russ, he tried to kiss me."

"No way." His brain hurt. "Oh, shit, I'm so sorry. What did you do? Smack him upside the head?" That's what Russ wanted to do.

"No, I told him, you know, that I'm a mother, and with him being underage and all, I just couldn't risk it. They'd take my kid away." She shrugged, tugged her shirt over her knees. "I thought I'd let him keep some dignity, you know?"

Why? He'd certainly lost his sanity. "Well, that

was nice of you, but I think the head smack would have been more effective."

Russ couldn't even begin to imagine why Sean would think trying to kiss JoJo was a good idea. Granted, at nearly fourteen, kissing under any circumstances probably seemed like a good idea, but Russ didn't see where the balls to try it on an adult came from. When he had been thirteen, he wouldn't have even looked twice at a woman that *old*—relatively speaking, of course.

But Sean clearly wasn't coming from the same place he had at that age.

"You need to take it easy on him, Russ, he's just kind of a mixed-up kid right now. He misses your folks." JoJo reached over and patted him on the knee, which somehow made him feel ten times worse.

"I know he misses my parents." The question was, what the hell was he supposed to do about it? He couldn't turn back time or raise the dead, and given those limitations, he was at a loss. "I guess maybe we should go to counseling or something."

"Those shrinks don't know what they're talking about." Maria emerged from the kitchen, slotted spoon in her hand, and waved it at Russ, her thin arm vibrating violently.

He wondered what exactly she was cooking at nine o'clock at night. "No? Then what do I do, Maria?"

"Get married."

"Oh, Jesus Christ." That would add a heap of problems to the ones he already had. And he didn't know any woman he would ever consider attaching himself to for life.

Except for maybe Laurel.

No, that was his dick talking. He didn't even know Laurel. He'd only met her a week ago, and she wasn't cop-wife material. Too trusting and too rich.

Maria crossed herself, reaching for the cross dangling between her breasts over her red turtleneck. "Watch your mouth, or I'll smack you like I do your brother."

It was time for him to go before he took a spoon to the wrist. Russ stood, dropped some money on the coffee table, and headed for the door. "Thanks, ladies. Have a good one."

"Think about the marriage thing, you'll see I'm right."

"Yeah, whatever."

"And you wonder where your brother gets his smart mouth from."

Russ laughed and headed out the front door. Crossing the five feet between their walkway and his drive, Russ watched his breath hover in front of his face and pondered what to say to Sean. Besides, *knock it off, dumb-ass.*

Sean was leaning on the kitchen counter eating a packaged brownie. Russ ached just looking at him. Even standing there eating Sean looked sullen, unhappy. Physically, it seemed, he was changing daily. He'd grown four inches in the year he'd lived with Russ, and had gangly arms and legs that seemed to be waiting for his metabolism to slow down so they could add some bulk. He had shaggy hair that got on Russ's nerves, that sort of retro-seventies lion mane that a lot of the under-twenty set seemed to be sporting.

Russ thought it looked stupid. But then he wasn't exactly appearance-conscious himself.

And Sean's appearance wasn't the problem.

Russ would gladly cough up a thousand bucks if someone could tell him what the hell Sean was thinking at any given minute.

"Hey."

Sean nodded from behind his brownie. "You have fun? Get laid while I was off in Diaper World?"

Though his temples started to throb, Russ decided to treat Sean's crude comment as an opening. "Speaking of getting laid, what do you know about it? Because if there's anything you want to know, you can ask me. Chances are pretty good I'll know the answer."

Sean snorted. "So this is like our birds-and-bees talk? Wow, cool. Let me see. Ask you anything I want?"

Russ felt a tremor of alarm. "I'm here for you, man. Anything you want to know."

Chocolate crumb dangling from his lip, Sean crossed his arms over his bulky yellow sweatshirt. "Okay. So where does the word *fuck* come from?"

What did he look like, a linguist? "I don't know. I don't think anybody knows that."

Obviously not impressed, Sean turned and opened the refrigerator door. "You know, I've been wondering, who has to be on top when you're doing a 69?"

Did it matter? Russ was glad Sean wasn't looking at him, because he could swear he was actually blushing. He wondered if he should even be answering this, before he said carefully, "It can go either way. It's based on the preference of the individuals involved."

"Oh, okay." Sean emerged with a soft drink and popped the top. "How do you find a girl's G-spot?"

Russ raked his hand down his chin, scratching his whiskers, and reconsidered Maria's suggestion.

If he were married, he could make his wife have this conversation, and that alone might be worth the rest of the hassles of marriage.

"First of all, I'm canceling cable. Second of all, you don't need to know that unless you're having sex." Trying not to hyperventilate, he asked Sean in his cop interrogation voice, "Are you having sex? Tell me the truth."

Sean, who had been looking relaxed and mildly curious, suddenly slammed down his soft drink can, his face contorting. "No, I'm not having sex. God, how stupid are you? You have to have a girlfriend to have sex, and in case you hadn't noticed, jerk-off, I don't even have any friends!"

Sean rushed past him, knocking him in the shoulder, sending him stumbling a foot to the right. Russ reached out for the wall, held it. Oh, man.

He was right. No one ever called for Sean. No one invited him anywhere. There were no drop-offs at a friend's or the mall, unless it was his old friends at his old school, from before he'd moved in with Russ.

His little brother had no friends and he hadn't even noticed.

Trevor nudged Jill's arm off his chest and slipped out of bed. Grabbing the blanket that had tumbled to the floor during sex, he tossed it around him— Jill still wouldn't turn up the heat—and headed down the hall.

He was feeling impatient, and damn it, he didn't like that. It was a bad feeling, a feeling that led you to stupid mistakes, a feeling that could land you in a cell instead of southern Florida.

Lighting a cigarette, he pulled his laptop computer out of his backpack in the coat closet and plugged it into the phone jack in the living room. Wrapping the blanket tighter around his legs, he dialed up an Internet connection.

Searching through public records, he had found that Laurel Wilkins was the actual owner of that big money pile on Edgewater, which made Trevor's plan all the more palatable.

He just needed a little more time and a little more information.

Patience was what he needed.

But there was no harm in chatting with the lovely Laurel.

Or in meeting her.

Laurel woke up feeling muscles she hadn't even known she had.

Shifting Ferris off of her feet, she stretched, yawned, smiled. She had slept with Russ Evans and it had been *fine, honey.* Plus she got to do it all over again on Friday.

Life was good, and she had to go to work.

But before she jumped in the shower, she couldn't resist going into her e-mail and sending a quick message to Michelle.

I bagged him.

With a laugh she sent the message, wishing she could see Michelle's face when she got her e-mail.

That's when she noticed there was an e-mail from Dean in her inbox. The subject said "Thinking of you."

When she clicked on it, Laurel held her breath. She really wanted to be able to help Russ catch this guy. She had to do this right, use the right tone to convince Dean that she was still interested in him.

> *Hi Laurel,*
> *Thinking about you and hoping we can make plans to meet again. You busy Saturday?*
> *Russ (holding his breath)*

Aside from the fact that it was really starting to bother her that he was calling himself Russ, Laurel pounded her desk in triumph. He wanted to meet her again, and she would happily agree.

Then greet him with the very police detective whose name he was defacing.

Laurel was hauling her last case of Bottlecaps candy back into the stockroom when the store's assistant manager, Catherine, touched her arm.

"What's up with you today, Laurel? You're like, giddy, or something."

She was. She couldn't help it.

Giddy and full of energy. She had restocked sixteen varieties of candy and had pulled a fund-raising order together. They were a wholesale candy distributor as well as a warehouse-sized retail store. They had every kind of candy imaginable and specialized in nostalgia candies.

She liked her job. It was fun, it was easy, and it kept her communication skills sharp from dealing with the customers. It wasn't saving the world, but her boss treated her well, she got along with all of her coworkers, and it was close to home. Occasionally she got a pang or two that she should put her talents to better use, but then an assessment of her talents led her to the conclusion that she liked working with people and she had nothing to be ashamed of. She was a damn good candy store employee, and if that's what she wanted to do, well, everyone would have to get over it.

Not that anyone but her really cared. She seemed to be the only one who had a problem with it.

But Laurel was starting to think the problem wasn't with her life, it was that she'd forgotten how to be independent. Or maybe she'd never known how. Since her mother had gone out of town and she had found the courage to walk into that coffee shop, she had been thinking it was time to stop hiding out in her house with her mother. Maybe she didn't need to be wild, she just needed to live a little, on her own.

Maybe it was time to get her own apartment.

She shifted the Bottlecaps to her other arm. "I'm just in a good mood, that's all."

Catherine was a couple of years older than Laurel, but her little finger alone was probably more adventurous than Laurel. Cat had black streaks in her blond hair, had every piece of loose skin pierced, and was fond of sprawling tattoos wherever jewelry couldn't be displayed.

"You're always in a good mood. You're like our Susie Sunshine."

Normally that comment might have bothered her. But today she didn't care, especially not since she was leaving Sweet Stuff in ten minutes and going over to the police station to find Russ so she could tell him about Dean's e-mail. And why was she always so defensive about being nice? What was wrong with being pleasant and happy all the time anyway?

Did that make her a schmuck, a fool, a naive idealist?

No. It made her a nice person, that's all.

"Service with a smile," she said to Catherine.

Catherine laughed and shook her head. "I keep telling you that you need to come out with me. We'll go clubbing. Guys will absolutely love you in a tight skirt, with that sweet angelic look you always have on your face."

All the reasons Laurel had refused to go out with Catherine in the past were still there. She couldn't hear the music—could just feel the beat—making dancing sometimes difficult. With strobe lights and dark alcoves, lipreading was next to impossible. Pounding music made her breathy speech harder to understand. And she didn't have a nightclub wardrobe.

But then again, she'd never given it a chance. Who knows? Maybe she'd have a great time and wish she'd done it sooner. "Maybe I will go out with you. What night do you usually go?"

Catherine's jaw dropped, and she reached to the metal storage shelf for support. "Did you just say yes?"

Laurel laughed. "Yes." She shrugged. "Why not? If it's horrible, I just won't go again."

Catherine grabbed Laurel's hands and started to jump up and down, vibrating Laurel from finger to shoulder. The chain connecting Catherine's ear to her lip bounced. "Oh my God! This is so cool! We'll have so much fun."

That was debatable, but Laurel was willing to give it a shot.

"Okay, okay, let me go. I have to finish putting this stuff away so I can leave."

"Saturday." Catherine released her, but pointed her finger at Laurel. "I will pick you up, so you can't back out. Wear something black."

"Got it." Maybe somehow she could sexy up those black knee-high boots. Russ had certainly seemed to like them—at least, pulling them off and flinging them across the room while she had laid on her back on the bed in nothing but a bra and panties.

Laurel experienced an unexpected surge of warmth in her khaki pants. It seemed her body wanted her to be flat on her back again, and she had to agree.

Certain that GOT LAID LAST NIGHT was stamped on her forehead, Laurel turned and shoved the candy onto the shelf and wiped imaginary dust on her pants. "So, later in the week you can let me know what time. I've really got to go now."

She took off before Catherine, who could sniff out any conversations, jokes, or even a person's thoughts about sex from seventeen feet away, figured out what had caused her good mood.

But in her haste to get out of the store, she forgot to ask someone to call the police station for her and ask if Russ was available. So when she arrived fifteen minutes later, and spent another ten minutes trying to communicate with the front desk clerk, whose mumbling made it near impossible to read his lips, she was frustrated to find out Russ wasn't even there.

"Do you know where I can reach him?" she asked.

The clerk, a big man with quivering jowls and a

mouth that was almost motionless when he spoke, shrugged. He said something that she didn't catch, and Laurel tried not to sigh in frustration.

"Is there someone else I can speak to? Another detective who understands the fraud case Detective Evans is working on?"

The guy scratched his head, looked put out. Then he held up his finger for her to wait, overemphasizing by pulling it back and forth, like she was braindead instead of deaf. He turned away from her, picked up a phone.

Hoping he was calling someone she could actually understand, Laurel shifted on her feet in the lobby and waited. The clerk hung up the phone, turned his back on Laurel. She waited, wondering how long she was supposed to stand there before she accepted that he'd given up on her and no one was really coming.

But a minute later a man with dark hair and a muscular build appeared in the lobby. He was rubbing his unshaven chin and looking curiously at Laurel. "You're Laurel, aren't you?"

"Yes." She smiled and stuck out her hand, no clue who he was. "Laurel Wilkins. It's a pleasure to meet you."

The man was staring at her openly, giving a quick cruise up and down, a grin splitting his face. He shook his head a little. "Oh, man, Evans is dead."

"Excuse me?"

He let out a laugh. "Nothing." He shook her hand, held it too long. "I'm Jerry Anders, Russ's partner. Come on back and tell me what's on your mind."

Laurel had never actually been in a police station before. It was a disappointing experience. She had expected half-dressed hookers and crazed addicts flinging their arms around. There were just a few men and women in uniform, and some in just jeans and sweatshirts, moving around a windowless maze of cubicles and tiny offices. A guy in a gray suit was eating Corn Pops out of a single-serve box, his plastic spoon overloaded as it lifted to his mouth.

Jerry gestured for her to sit down in a metal folding chair next to a desk covered with pictures of himself and a woman with high-volume black hair. "So what's up? You're looking for Russ, I know. But is it personal or police business?"

Laurel unwound her scarf and dropped it in her lap, feeling a rush of embarrassment. She wondered what Russ's partner knew about her and if it involved her being naked in any way. "Police business. I got another e-mail from Trevor Dean. He wants to meet me on Saturday."

Anders didn't move from his relaxed slouch back in his chair. "Well, now that's interesting. Russ will definitely want to know that."

"Can you call him and tell him? I can't use the phone." She tapped her ear in an unconscious gesture.

"Sure. Or you could just stop over at his house on the way home and let him know. 350 West 135th. Just five minutes up the road. I know he's home, I just talked to him."

"Oh, I don't think he'd like me just stopping over." Laurel was very tempted, curious what Russ's house looked like, wanting to meet his little brother. But she was very aware that her showing up uninvited could be perceived as pushy on her part.

They'd spent the night together, they had plans for the coming weekend. She didn't want to blow that.

"Sure he would. He's got it bad for you, Laurel."

Astonished, she gaped for a second before recovering herself. Enough to stammer, "I don't think so . . . I mean, it's not what you think . . . I just want to see that Dean gets caught, and Russ said not to e-mail him back without talking to him first."

"So see, perfect reason to go over there. I'll call him and tell him you're on your way." Jerry leaned forward on his desk. "It will piss him off if you don't tell him."

He was probably right. Laurel chewed her lip. "You'll call him and let him know I'm coming over?"

"Absolutely."

"Okay, well, thank you." Laurel stood up, clutched her purse, still not sure this was such a hot idea. But she didn't know what else to do. Russ didn't have e-mail at home, and if he had it at work, he'd never mentioned it. She could come back to the police station tomorrow and have another go-round with the front desk clerk, or she could wait until Friday when she saw Russ.

But Dean wasn't going to want to wait for her reply until Friday.

"It was nice to meet you, Detective Anders. Thanks for your help."

"You too, Laurel." He stood up.

She waved him down. "No, that's okay, I can see myself out. Good-bye."

Squaring her shoulders, she reminded herself that she was independent. She was going clubbing. She was sleeping with a cop.

She could handle a little impromptu visit, no problem.

Jerry watched Laurel walk, a natural, sensual sway to her hips. She wore conservative clothes, but couldn't completely hide curves that clung to her pants and sweater. When you paired that with her innocent, wide-eyed expression, it was an interesting combination—and hell, a turn-on.

Evans was a lucky bastard.

He reached for his phone, which he'd left lying off the hook on his desk. He could never figure out the damn phone system and whenever he tried to put someone on hold, he always managed to hang up on them. He'd done it to Pam so many times she'd threatened to withhold oral sex if he did it again.

Not wanting to risk losing his blow job privileges, he'd just started leaving the phone off the hook when he got interrupted.

"Hey, babe, sorry about that. You still there?"

Pam sounded suspicious. "What did you just do? Whatever it was, it sounded wrong."

"What?" He'd done Evans a favor. He'd sent Blondie right to him, special delivery. Save Russ twelve drives by her house tonight. "It's police work."

"Yeah, right. It sounded like you setting Russ up with someone."

"He's got it so bad it's disgusting. He's drooling, he's mooning, I can't stand it. I'm just speeding things up." Jerry dug into his desk drawer, pulled out a breath mint. He was frickin' starving. Chewing it hard, he added, "Come on, if I've got to be stuck with a girlfriend . . ."

Before the thought even finished, he realized that was a stupid thing to say, joke or not.

Pam's "Excuse me?" confirmed it. As did the subsequent dial tone in his ear.

Shit, it looked like he'd lost his blow job privileges anyway.

Chapter 10

Russ pitched the chicken he'd meant to cook two months ago into the industrial-strength garbage bag he'd hauled out to clean his refrigerator. Shifting things around, and digging deep, he'd discovered certain items that could qualify for science experiments and a veritable salmonella breeding ground in that chicken. It was safe to say this chore was overdue.

"Hey, Sean, you need a science project? I've got some cheese that's eight shades of green and has more fuzz than Grandma's upper lip."

Peering over his shoulder, he waved the package at Sean, who backed up.

"Nasty. You need like a maid or something."

"Yeah, a cop who can afford a housecleaner. Love to see that."

Sean spit out his sweatshirt drawstring, which he'd been sucking industriously. "You've got money. You sold Mom and Dad's house, remember?"

Russ clunked his head on the fridge door when he stood up, startled. Where the hell had that comment come from?

"What do you mean? That money's to send you to college, not for a maid." Of course, Sean wouldn't be qualified to mop the floors at any college if he kept screwing his grades up the way he'd been.

"Forget it." Sean turned and headed into the living room. "The doorbell's ringing."

"Sean!" Russ threw the cheese in the bag and kicked the fridge door in frustration. He didn't want to forget it. He wanted to get to the root of what was bothering Sean, and there was clearly plenty.

He had sold his parent's house, almost immediately after they had died, because he hadn't been able to deal with either the memories or the size of the house and yard. They'd had an old house that needed tons of maintenance and drafty windows that sent heat bills soaring every winter.

Russ didn't have the time, money, or patience to deal with any of that. His tiny house, with a yard so consumed by the driveway and the deck that it took six minutes to mow, was just perfect for him.

He hauled out creamer with a six-month-old expiration date on it. He didn't even remember buying creamer. Curious to see what it looked like, he popped open the top and was hit with the most foul odor he'd ever encountered outside of a jail cell. "Oh, shit."

Trying to force the soft, sticky carton closed again, he wasn't paying attention when Sean came back in the room.

"Hey, Russ?"

"Yeah?" He gave up, dropped the carton in the bag, and hoped like hell the plastic would hold.

"There's someone here to see you."

"Huh?" He glanced over his shoulder. And damn if he didn't see Laurel standing behind his brother.

"Laurel!" *Oh, Jesus.* He was up to his eyeballs in spoiled food, and Laurel had popped into his kitchen. Kicking the bag aside, he pulled the ties tight to keep the stink in and slammed the refrigerator door closed. A quick glance around the room confirmed the worst.

There were dirty dishes in the sink, the newspaper spread all over the kitchen table. The vinyl floor was cracking, and the cabinets were dented and rusting at the hinges, looking tired, old, and metal.

He wiped his hands on his jeans.

"I'm sorry if this is a bad time." Laurel bit her lip nervously and fiddled with her scarf.

God, what he wanted to do with that damn scarf. One of these days he was going to take that, wrap it around her hands, and attach her to her bedpost.

Now he was a poor cop with a dirty kitchen *and* a hard-on. That was sure to impress.

"No, no, it's fine, I was just . . . cleaning."

Sean snorted, the little shit. "Did you meet my brother, Sean? Sean, this is Laurel Wilkins, she's, um, a friend."

Sean shot him an incredulous look. Russ arched his eyebrows at the garbage bag, hoping Sean would catch on and help him out here.

"She introduced herself." Sean took a long, drawn-out second, but ambled over to the garbage bag. Then opened the back door and tossed it onto the deck. Nowhere near the garbage can.

But Russ wasn't going to argue. At least the odor originator was gone.

"I'm sorry, Russ, I thought Detective Anders was going to call you and let you know I was on my way here. That's what he said he'd do when I spoke with him at the station."

That ripped him out of his cleaning concern. "Why? What's wrong? Did Dean get nasty with you or something?" He crossed the room and brushed her hair back, studied her face.

She looked worried. And damn cute.

He kissed her softly. She let him, even brushed her lips back over his. But then she pushed gently on his chest and darted her gaze in Sean's direction, clearly worried.

Russ was thinking nothing could corrupt Sean at this point, given the experiences of the night before, but he pulled back anyway. He kept his hands on the small of her back, though.

"Dean e-mailed me," she said, sticking her hands in her deep coat pockets. "He wants to meet on Saturday night. That's all his message said."

Russ hoped this was the break they were looking for. They could make arrangements to pick Dean up wherever he wanted to meet Laurel. "That's good, bunny, really good."

"I'm telling you first before I reply." She looked a little bitter about that fact, so he kissed the frown lines on her forehead, kneaded the flesh under the waistband of her sweater.

The phone rang. He ignored it.

"Thank you, you did the right thing." He moved to her temples, running her eyelashes across his lips. She gave a sweet sigh.

"I hate to bust up your make-out session, but Jerry's on the phone." Sean waved the phone at him.

Russ turned, glared at Sean, who grinned, and grabbed the phone from him. He intentionally walked towards the back door, so Laurel couldn't read his lips.

"What the hell, Anders? Thanks for warning me

Laurel was coming over. I was up to my ass in rotten food, cleaning out the fridge."

Jerry choked back a laugh. "Sorry, I meant to call you, but I got distracted. Got the financial reports back on Dean's last victim. Miss Morgan forgot to mention to us that she added Dean to all her bank accounts two months ago. Technically the bastard didn't steal a dime of that twenty grand—he had her permission to be in those accounts."

"Oh, man, you're kidding me." Russ rubbed his eyebrows. "So, what, we've got him for forging a check nine months ago, and identity theft without actually stealing from the person who's identity he borrowed, and his word against four disgruntled ex-girlfriends that he took their money. That isn't going to get us shit in court, is it?"

"Nope. Get Laurel to stall. We can't pick him up yet."

"Damn it. I don't like that. Laurel's not exactly a good liar."

"Tell her what to say, I don't know. We've got to do something. Time to keep digging and hope something surfaces."

"Alright, thanks, man, talk to you soon."

Russ turned and found himself alone. Alarmed, he sprinted into the living room. Laurel and Sean were setting up a card game on the coffee table.

"Uh . . ."

When he walked in front of them, Laurel glanced up and smiled. "Sean's going to teach me how to play gin rummy."

Okay. Sean was shuffling the deck, and Russ wasn't sure what the hell to say. So he turned on his heels and went back into the kitchen. He filled the sink with soapy hot water, wondering how he felt about Laurel sitting in his house, feet on his shit-brown carpet, playing a card game with his brother.

He either really liked it or he hated it. He wasn't sure which.

When he was halfway through the mound of dirty dishes, Laurel came into the kitchen. "Sorry," she whispered, as she came and leaned on the counter next to him. "I didn't want to interrupt your night like this, but I didn't want to tell Sean no. He's a sweet kid."

This was why Laurel needed to be locked in her house behind armed guards. If she could think Sean was a sweet kid, she was capable of believing anything.

"It's fine. He could use the company." Russ rinsed a pot and laid it on the dish towel that served as drying rack. "And I needed a reason to force myself to do these dishes."

She laughed. "So what do you want me to tell Dean? Where should I say I'll meet him?"

Russ turned off the water and wondered how to tread delicately through this. Then he figured, what the hell, he didn't know a damn thing about being delicate, so he just came out with it. "Laurel, you're going to have to tell him no. We don't have the evidence we need to take Dean in, so there's no reason for you to meet with him yet."

Laurel had taken off her coat, and rubbed her arms. She was wearing another one of those high-neck, tight sweaters she favored. This one was red with white snowflakes trailing across her breasts. He wanted to catch one on his tongue.

"That's terrible! What should I say to him?"

"Tell him you're busy Saturday night—you have to work or something. Suggest maybe a week or two from Saturday. Do you want me to write the message?"

She actually rolled her eyes. "I can handle it. Besides, you don't sound anything like me."

No, that was true. She always sounded kind of classy and sweet, and he pretty much sounded like a bachelor cop.

Deciding not to comment, he dried his hands on his pants and touched one of her snowflakes. The one that rested on her nipple, which he stroked, feeling his cock swell.

Laurel yelped. "Russ!"

Man, she felt good. Friday was a long time away. "I want you," he told her, in case she hadn't figured it out. "I could send Sean next door . . ."

She smacked his arm. "I'm leaving, and you should be ashamed of yourself."

He grinned, noticing that while she looked outraged, she was trembling and wasn't pulling away from his finger. "I'll let you know when shame kicks in, but right now that's definitely not what I'm feeling."

Laurel bit her lip, gave a shuddering sigh, and took a step back. "I'll see you Friday."

Russ watched her leave, then went back to the dishes, his boner hitting the cabinet, making him wince. It had been a really long time since he'd wanted a woman the way he did Laurel. Maybe he never had. But if he had thought that sleeping with her would ease the ache, he had been dead wrong. He had been preoccupied with her all damn day. She made the funniest littlest noise when she came, her eyes widening, lips trembling . . .

"I like your new girlfriend." Sean, who couldn't go twenty minutes without eating, went digging in the freezer.

Russ liked her, too, enough that he'd just been fantasizing about her. But she wasn't his girlfriend, would never be that. "Thanks, but she's not my girlfriend. We're just casually seeing each other."

"Whatever." Sean pulled out a frozen burrito. "Are you going out with her on Friday?"

"Yeah." Russ stuck the last newly cleaned glass on the precarious tower of drying dishes. "And you've got your choice—you can go next door or I can drive you to Grandma's."

"What? Are you serious? I thought I wouldn't have to go next door anymore!"

Drying his hands, Russ studied his brother's outraged face. A suspicion rose. "Oh, really? So are you telling me that you pulled that Don Juan crap on JoJo because you thought I wouldn't let you go over there anymore?"

Sean blushed, sullenly studying his burrito, beating it on the edge of the counter rhythmically.

Russ had his answer, and it pissed him off. "You little manipulator! Don't think you can pull that garbage with me. Jesus, and you wonder why I think you need a babysitter."

He paced the kitchen, angry, wanting to just grab his brother and shake him. "No TV for a week, you got it? And you can walk yourself next door and apologize to JoJo."

"Fuck you," Sean said, so succinctly that Russ blinked. Who taught the kid this crap?

Sean stomped past him, threw himself on the couch, and picked up the remote. Defiantly, he clicked on the TV and turned the volume up to thirty, rocking Russ's eardrums. Sean set the remote down, and Russ went over and grabbed it.

Blocking his brother's view, he turned the TV

back off and was about to ream Sean, when Sean rushed him, trying to snatch the remote back.

Sean reached behind Russ's back, grabbing for the hand holding the remote. "Give it to me, asshole!"

"Knock it off, Sean." Russ switched from left hand to right, passing the remote back and forth while Sean dodged around him, making growling sounds.

Russ actually laughed, not in amusement but out of frustration, but either way it probably wasn't a good idea. Because the next thing he knew, Sean was leaping on his back, tugging at the hood on his sweatshirt. Russ staggered forward, off balance from Sean's weight, prying at the neck of his shirt. Damn thing was digging into his flesh and cutting off his windpipe.

"Give it back!"

Shoving the remote down into his waistband to free his hands, Russ tried to toss Sean off without hurting him. "You're strangling me, Sean, damn it, let go." Since he could talk, he knew he wasn't really being strangled, but it was uncomfortable.

Sean slid off his back and reached around his middle, groping for the remote.

And then the front door opened so forcefully it hit the wall. "Russ! Sean!"

It was Laurel, horror stamped on her face. "What are you doing?"

Sean took advantage of the distraction to twist Russ's arm behind his back.

"Oww, damn it, knock it off!" Russ smiled sheepishly at Laurel. "We're just having a disagreement. We haven't worked out all the kinks in our relationship yet."

"I think that's an understatement."

Red-faced, Sean said venomously, "Russ, you are such a prick. A total dickhead, shit-face, asshole."

He had probably been called worse, but coming from his brother, it didn't make him feel all that great. Nor did he want Laurel reading those words coming off Sean's lips.

So he grabbed Sean's head and shoved it forward, down to waist level, so she couldn't see what he was saying.

Sean slapped up at him, struggling to stand. "Damn it! Let me go! Cocksucker."

That was a new one. "Promise me you'll shut up, and I'll let you go."

"Fine."

Trusting Sean was probably a mistake, but he couldn't hold him there all day. When he let him go, Sean stood up, fixed his hair. They were both breathing hard, and Laurel looked at them both like they were drunks urinating in the street.

He'd always had a way with women.

"So, what brings you back so soon?" Russ strove for casual as he put the remote in the pouch on his sweatshirt.

Laurel wasn't going for it. "I forgot my purse. Then when I came up the walk, I saw you in the window. I thought you were choking or something!"

Choking? Sean and Russ exchanged a look. Sean shuffled his feet and bit back a grin. Russ scratched his jaw, picturing Sean giving him the Heimlich. Then they locked eyes again, and both started laughing. God, they must have looked like idiots. Sean slugged his arm.

"Sorry, man."

"Yeah, me, too." He grabbed Sean under his arm and rubbed his hair with his knuckles, wondering if just maybe he and Sean had reached a new level if they could laugh together again.

Laurel rocked on her feet impatiently and watched Russ and Sean grinning like they'd won the lottery. What exactly was so funny?

They had been *assaulting* each other. "Well, I guess I'll just grab my purse."

She started towards the coffee table, where she'd set her purse down and forgotten it.

Sean touched her arm, still locked in a wrestling move with Russ. "Hey, Laurel, we were just about to go get a pizza. Want to come with us?"

She glanced at Russ. His grip on Sean's neck had tightened, but he nodded. "Come with us. Please. So we can prove we do actually have manners."

Mainly because she was curious about their behavior, and because the other option was eating a salad at home by herself, Laurel nodded. "Sure. Thank you for inviting me."

The brothers—one gorgeous, and one gangly, but growing towards gorgeous—grinned at her.

At that moment, Laurel thought that she had fallen just a teeny tiny bit in love with both of them.

Ten minutes later they were sitting in a booth with a slick plastic tabletop, both Russ and Sean sitting across from her so she could see their mouths. She started to unwind her scarf, but Russ reached over the table, grabbed one end, and pulled until it snaked across the table and landed in his lap. She was about to ask him what the heck he was doing, when Sean tapped her wrist.

"So, have you always been deaf?"

Russ nudged him.

"What?" Sean looked puzzled.

"It's okay, Russ, I don't mind," Laurel answered. "I wasn't born deaf. I had meningitis when I was three, and when the high fever receded, I was left deaf."

"Bummer."

She shrugged. "I don't know. It's not such a big deal . . . being deaf is part of who I am now."

"So can you teach me to swear in sign language?"

Laurel laughed. "Actually, I don't think I know any swear words. I didn't learn sign language until I was ten, and even then it wasn't pure ASL, but English word-signed. In college, I was pretty busy trying to learn ASL grammar, keep up with my classes, and hang out with my friends, but that was six years ago. If I learned swear words, I don't remember them."

Sean chewed the straw that had been given to him by the waitress, dunking it in and out of his glass to saturate it with soft drink before sucking again. "That's too bad. I figured I could tell off teachers without getting in trouble."

"Sorry."

"So where do you live?"

"On Edgewater Drive in Lakewood."

Sean brightened up. "Cool. I grew up in Lakewood. We lived on Andrews. I was supposed to go to Lakewood High next year, but I got stuck moving in with him." He jerked his thumb at Russ, whose color had suddenly leeched from his face. "Now I have to go to John Marshall, and it *sucks*."

Laurel struggled to find something to say, but Sean didn't wait for a reply. He said, "Isn't Russ's house a shit-hole?"

Then Sean shifted, looking uncomfortable.

"Sorry, um, I didn't mean to say *shit*. I just mean, it needs a wrecking ball or something."

Russ looked offended. "It's not that bad, it just needs a little cosmetic work. It's structurally sound."

"What did you think, Laurel?" Sean asked.

"Well," she said, striving for diplomacy. "It could use a little updating."

"See? Just a little updating," Russ repeated to Sean, nudging him.

"She means it's ugly, but she's too polite to say that."

"Tell me the truth, Laurel. I can handle it."

Picturing the mud-brown carpet, the dingy off-white walls, the tired-looking sofa, and the lack of absolutely anything decorative, Laurel cleared her throat. The kitchen was a relic from the 1950s, and not in a cool, retro way. More like no one had given a darn in fifty years.

"I think maybe you're a candidate for a *Queer Eye for the Straight Guy* makeover show."

Sean tipped his head back and laughed.

She hastened to qualify her statement. "There's nothing wrong with the house, it's just not really warm, or personal. It doesn't tell me anything about you."

Fortunately, Russ looked amused. "Except that I'm a slob?"

He took a sip of his beer and looked at her with dark, thoughtful eyes that reminded her of the night before when he had been sliding into her, slow and sure.

Laurel hid behind her napkin, flustered. "You're not a slob, you're just clearly a little too preoccupied to worry about your décor."

He laughed. "Well said, Laurel."

Something was passing between them, something hot and intimate, that made Laurel want to squirm.

"Can I have some money to play the video games?" Sean held out his hand and gestured towards the row of games across the pizza parlor.

Russ reached into his pocket, giving Laurel a nice shot of bulging bicep. He gave Sean a ten. "Stay away for a while."

Sean rolled his eyes. "No kidding. But once the pizza gets here, I'm coming back."

When Sean walked away, Russ stretched his legs until they hit hers. "I thought he'd never leave."

Laurel moved away from the temptation of his hard thighs and crossed her legs. "You don't mean that."

"I'm glad you two are getting along. I'm glad Sean's not being a total pain in the ass for a change. But I do want to be alone with you, and I'm thinking that Friday can't come fast enough to suit me and my raging hard-on."

That set her face aflame. Good grief. Laurel pictured his pants under the table, denim straining to hold back Russ's impressive . . . part. She licked her lips.

Russ groaned, shifted on the bench. "I love it when you do that—look so sweet and innocent, and yet so curiously aroused at the same time. Damn, it's embarrassing to feel this turned-on in a pizza parlor."

"No one knows but me."

"At least until I stand up."

"I guess women have the advantage in that regard, don't we? We can hide our interest."

Russ zeroed in on her chest. "Not entirely." His eyes darkened. "Nice snowflakes."

Oh, boy.

Laurel fanned herself and decided to steer the conversation to less dangerous topics. "So how long have you been a cop?"

He took a long swig of his beer. "Nine years already. I just turned thirty in January. I started out on the beat at twenty-one, then moved to detective two years ago. Our department handles fraud, theft, forgery. We get some white-collar criminals, but mostly a bunch of idiots on the street who think they can cash their next door neighbor's paycheck."

"Do you like it?" Laurel would be scared to even hold a gun, she couldn't imagine undertaking the risks the police did every day.

Russ paused, ran his finger up and down his beer bottle, then nodded. "Yeah, I do. I really enjoy it. Feels like I'm doing something worthwhile, you know?"

"Yeah, I know what you mean." Laurel slumped back in her seat. "I used to want to do that. I wanted to be a teacher at a deaf school."

"Why didn't you?"

"Because my father died of a heart attack and I came home to help my mom. I never went back to college, and I always thought it was for her, that I felt guilty about leaving my mother alone." Laurel stared at the bubbles rising in her soft drink. "But you know, I think it was a good excuse for me, too. I was afraid that year I was away at school. Oh, I was having a great time, but I was also terrified. Scared I wouldn't fit in, that I would always be a girl caught between the hearing and the deaf. I was scared I couldn't handle the coursework in ASL *or* English, and that everyone would figure out I was just a know-nothing phony."

Instead of feeling horrible, Laurel felt a huge, overwhelming relief that she had finally admitted to herself what she had suspected all along. "So I came home because my dad died, but I stayed because I was afraid." She looked at Russ. "That's very pathetic, isn't it?"

He shook his head. "No. No, it's not. Everyone knows what it's like to be afraid. I'm terrified right now I'll screw Sean up. It paralyzes me the way your fear did you."

"I would never be able to tell." Laurel glanced over at Sean, who was energetically driving a steering wheel on a video game. It was obvious there were problems between Russ and Sean, but it must be difficult for both of them to shift from a brother/brother relationship to that of parent/child. "I think Sean will be okay.

"And I don't want to be afraid anymore, Russ. I want to try anything and everything I ever wanted, and if I fall flat on my face, so be it."

Russ gave her a wicked grin. "I think your decision to have sex again was definitely a great one. And you proved to be a natural at it."

When she gasped, he laughed. Laurel picked her glass up, thought better of it for fear of choking, and fussed with her paper napkin. She could not look at him or she would slide under the table in mortification.

The pizza appeared in front of them as the waitress set it on a stand in the middle of the table. Sean instantly returned, hovering behind the plump woman, waiting to reclaim his seat.

Laurel was grateful for the interruption. She felt raw, intimate, with Russ Evans in a way that she shouldn't. She was in danger of allowing herself to like him too much, to want for something that she couldn't have.

Wild women had hot affairs that lasted a week

or two, then they walked away with no regrets and no backward glances.

But Laurel had never been a wild woman, and she strongly suspected it was too late to change now.

Chapter 11

The instant he pushed the door open to Sweet Stuff to pick Laurel up for their date, Russ could smell the candy. It flooded over him—an over-powering mix of chocolate and sugar, artificial fla-voring, and nuts.

"Oh, my God," he said out loud, before he caught himself. This place was incredible. An olfactory orgy.

He had never seen so much candy in his life—ten warehouse-sized aisles packed with a colorful ex-plosion of bright wrappers and shiny, glossy candy. And there, in the midst of it all, was Laurel, her back to him as she rearranged candy hearts on sticks in a vase, moving them this way and that. She belonged here, to this store, to this sweet scent and lush vi-sual display.

She leaned. Her jeans strained, cupping her ass.

Russ went hard in less time than it takes to dot an "i."

Heading towards her, he was momentarily dis-tracted by the twenty canisters of jelly beans with their individual scoopers. He'd have to grab some grape ones before they left. Man, what an awesome place to work. Maybe Laurel got a discount.

He was almost to the counter, and she still hadn't turned around. He had in mind reaching out, stroking that bare spot between her shirt and her jeans, but he'd probably scare the shit out of her.

"I'll be with you in a second, Russ."

Staring at her back, ripped out of his erotic thoughts, he drew up short. How had she known it was him?

Laurel turned, gave him a smile. "I'm almost done. Do you mind waiting a minute?"

"No, I'll just walk around and pick out all the stuff I'm going to buy. Do you get a discount?"

"Thirty percent."

Score. "Cool. You got shopping carts?"

She laughed. "Yes, but you're joking, right?"

"Only a little." She was three feet away and a counter was separating them, but Russ couldn't stand it any longer. He checked for customers in the immediate vicinity, found none, and pulled her to him for a quick kiss. "How'd you know it was me?"

Laurel pushed him back, a cute flush rising on her cheeks. "You have a heavy walk—I knew someone was there because the floor moved a little. Then when you got closer, I smelled you."

Russ lifted his arm and checked his pit with a quick sniff. The only thing she should smell was the soap from the shower he'd just taken.

Laurel laughed, spinning the stick of a chocolate heart in her hand. "I don't mean like that. I mean, you have a certain scent that's just yours . . . sort of woodsy and fresh." She shrugged. "Maybe it sounds weird but I know what your skin smells like."

It wasn't weird. It was sexy as hell. He fought the urge to haul her over the counter and kiss her senseless. "If anyone should know what my skin smells like, it's you."

Her breathing hitched. She got that little *yes, yes, what comes next?* look on her face. The look that said whatever he might be inclined to do, she could probably be talked into it. Because Laurel liked it *hard*.

He wouldn't make that mistake again tonight. This time he'd indulge himself, touch and taste and lick every inch of Laurel's body like he wanted to. He'd take her to the edge over and over, until she squirmed and begged . . .

They were staring at each other, Russ gripping the counter, Laurel holding that chocolate so tightly she'd probably melt it.

"Finish up," he said in a low growl.

"I'll hurry."

"Good."

Russ turned and attempted to distract himself by shopping for his sweet tooth. He lifted a lid on a jar and pulled something out. "Hey, a Pixy Stix." He had fond memories of those. He used to just tip his head back and dump the whole thing in his mouth.

It was an incredible rush. Like cocaine for six year olds.

Temptation twice in the space of five minutes was too much for him. He couldn't toss Laurel on the counter and go up her sweater, but he could have a Pixy Stix. He ripped open a purple one and poured the powder into his mouth. The sugar exploded all over the inside of his mouth, sending his salivary glands into overdrive.

His eyes watered. Damn, that was intense. He clutched the empty wrapper and moved his tongue around to catch more of the powder. That tasted absolutely incredible, like packing all the pleasure of candy into one sharp kick of sensation and leaving him drooling, ready for more.

"Don't forget to pay for that."

Laurel was watching him, amused, her coat over her arm.

"What are they, like a nickel?" Russ wiped sugar crumbs from his lips and glanced back at the jar. "Holy shit, these things are fifty cents apiece! What a rip-off."

"Inflation."

"I guess." Russ spotted Boston Baked Beans, grabbed a box, and shook it. "Hey, these things rock! And Big League Chew, and Slurpy Sticks. Whoa, this is seriously cool stuff."

Laurel handed him a plastic shopping basket from a stack by the door.

"I don't think I need a whole basket," he protested.

Ten minutes later he had it full. At the cash register, he plucked one of the chocolate hearts and handed it to Laurel. He wanted to say something romantic and poetic, but he wasn't that kind of a guy. The best he could manage was, "Sweet like you."

Her eyes widened and she suddenly spun on her heels, clutching the heart, and bolted across the room.

His words must have looked even stupider than they had sounded.

"Okay . . ." He set his basket on the counter and wondered what he was supposed to do now.

At a loss, Russ grabbed a strip of candy buttons and picked at it, placing six pink dots on his tongue. Yuck. They tasted like paper and old-lady lipstick.

He sighed and picked them off his tongue, wondering if he should go and apologize to Laurel. Then he questioned what the hell he would be apologizing for.

It wasn't like they were headed for a relationship or anything. This was about some fun sex, nothing more, and if she wanted fancy words, she'd picked the wrong guy.

Russ flicked the candy buttons off his finger and back onto the paper, suddenly feeling very pissed off.

Laurel took off across the room like a ninny, slamming the swing door to the storage room, and paused to catch her breath. Leaning against a pallet full of Gummy Fish, she clutched the chocolate heart Russ had given her to her chest and wished she did know foul words in ASL so she could sign them to herself.

God, what an idiot she was!

When Russ had handed her the silly little, red foil-wrapped candy, and told her it was sweet like her, she had almost completely lost it. She had felt a soft yearning emotion swell up in her chest, and she'd gotten the hell out of there before she had either said something stupid or Russ had read her feelings on her face.

Shit, shit, she was falling for him.

That wasn't possible.

Well, clearly it was, but she couldn't let it. If she went all needy on him, he'd do a fifty-yard dash out of there. And she didn't want to stop seeing him, not yet, not when she hadn't even had a chance to get really good at the whole sex thing yet.

A hand touched her arm.

Laurel jumped and turned, relieved to see Catherine staring at her in concern. "Hey, you okay? You look sick or something."

Wonderful. Laurel waved her hand and drew in a shaky breath. "I'm fine, I'm just losing my mind."

"Welcome to the club. Glad you could join the rest of us." Catherine pushed up her black glasses. "There's a guy waiting at the register, so I need to go out there, but I wanted to check on you, make sure you weren't hurling back here on the stock."

"Thanks, I'm fine. And that guy is with me. Can you ring him up with my discount, please?"

Catherine's eyebrows disappeared under her spiky bangs. "With you? As in, hey, he's my cousin/uncle/practically brother, or as in, with you like boyfriend/date/sex partner?"

"The last one."

"No, shit." Catherine looked impressed. "No wonder you've been so cheerful. Okay, let's go ring up your beefcake."

Laurel followed Catherine, momentarily distracted by the thought of telling Russ he was considered her beefcake. Somehow she didn't think he'd take to the idea of being a female plaything.

Russ was pacing in front of the register, looking very big and broad. He was wearing another baseball hat, and he shoved at the bill, pushing his hair back before resettling the hat.

He was too good-looking for her.

Too sexy. Too bold.

She wasn't his type, she didn't think. She'd never entered a wet T-shirt contest, drunk beer out of a can, or had sex in the woods.

Not that any of that mattered, since they were sticking to casual sex, nothing more.

Russ looked up and watched her so closely that Laurel found herself slowing down, afraid to face him. Afraid he'd see her need written all over her face.

Catherine must have spoken to him because he looked over, answered her, and starting tossing his mounds of candy on the counter. While Catherine started ringing everything up, Laurel stepped next to Russ and set her purse beside his empty shopping basket and tried to pretend she hadn't just run out of the room.

Russ touched her chin, turned her so she could see him. "You okay? She said you almost got sick."

It felt like lying, but she nodded. "My stomach just . . ." Laurel was distracted by his mouth, so close to hers, those lips so warm and talented. "I think I'm hungry."

Now that was a lie. But it sounded better than the truth, which was that she liked him so much it made her want to throw up.

His thumb rubbed her jaw. "You should have said something. Here I am wasting time buying all this crap and you were starving."

"No, it just snuck up on me." Laurel set the chocolate heart down on the counter so he wouldn't read the dishonesty that was probably blazing all across her face.

But while he released her chin, he didn't let go of her. In fact, he pulled her against his side, wrapped an arm around her, kissed the top of her head with a fleeting touch.

"Eat a piece of chocolate to hold you over." Russ unwrapped a chocolate nugget and pushed it into her mouth, his finger lingering in the moist heat before she pulled her head back a little. His eyes had darkened and Laurel squeezed her lips shut, heart thumping, and looked away. Right at Catherine, which was a mistake.

Her friend was gawking, twisting her thumb ring. And grinning like crazy. "So, you're Laurel's friend? I don't think I've ever seen you in here before."

Laurel chewed the rich chocolate viciously, glaring at Catherine, hoping she'd take a hint and zip it. Despite her burning curiosity, she refused to turn and watch Russ's response. It didn't matter what he might say about her.

In fact, she didn't want to see what embarrassing things Catherine might say either, so she busied herself putting her coat on and adjusting her scarf around her neck. By the time Russ paid and took his plastic bag full of sugar, Laurel had her gloves on, coat buttoned, and purse on her shoulder.

She waved to Catherine and gratefully headed towards the front door. A stinging cold wind worked its way under her coat and sent a shiver running through her. Russ's truck was close, and he opened the door for her. When he hopped in the driver's side and turned the car on, Laurel brushed her hair off her face and tried to figure out what to say.

Russ beat her to it. He frowned. "Are you really going out with that girl? She looks like she lost control of her staple gun and pierced half her face."

"Catherine's nice. She's just trying to shock a little with her appearance."

"She said you're going clubbing together. Laurel, are you sure that's such a good idea? I mean, have you been to those places before? Her crowd is probably pretty rough."

Confusion swirled inside her, stomach acids

churning in angry hunger, like she actually could get sick. Part of her loved that Russ seemed concerned, and the other part resented the hell out of it, because it meant he saw her as incapable of taking care of herself.

"It's just a dance club. How rough can it be?"

He didn't answer. With a jerk of the stick shift, he pulled out of the parking spot.

"Where are we going?"

If he said something, she couldn't see it. Laurel sighed and pressed her head to the window glass. Maybe she should ask him to take her home and they could just call the whole evening off.

Before she wound up doing something stupid, like fall in love with him.

Russ didn't even know where the hell he was driving to. When he'd asked to see her Friday night, he had been thinking they could grab a quick dinner, maybe rent a movie, snuggle up on the couch in her bedroom, and get naked.

Now all he could think was that a woman like Laurel deserved more than that. She was probably used to nice restaurants, where they had real linen tablecloths and wine that didn't have a screw top. He should take her to the ballet or the art museum or something, but that wouldn't be a good idea, either. He had no interest in men in tights, and if he had to stare at paint splattered on a canvas, he'd probably fall asleep standing up.

Eating in a nice restaurant was out of the question because he was wearing his usual jeans, T-shirt, baseball hat. If he went home to change, it would be an hour and a half before they ate, and she was so hungry her stomach was upset.

Jesus. Russ pulled into a gas station and parked, annoyed with himself.

"Laurel. Do you want to eat in a classy restaurant and then go to the art museum?"

She blinked. "Not particularly. Do you?" she asked doubtfully.

He shook his head.

Laurel smiled, that sassy little good-girl-turned-bad tilt of her lips. "I was just hoping we could get some sub sandwiches and go back to my place."

It seemed the one thing they had in common—their powerful lust for each other—was more than enough for now.

"Good plan, bunny." He touched the tip of her nose and drove twenty miles above the speed limit, more than prepared to whip out his badge if they got pulled over.

This was an emergency.

He was going to die if he didn't get to have Laurel.

Russ ate his sub while looking at her like it wasn't the only thing he wanted to eat.

Laurel was glad they'd decided to just sit down in the sub shop, because if they had taken the sandwiches home, she thought it was likely they'd go to waste. And while she'd been lying earlier about her upset stomach, she did need to eat at regular intervals or she got queasy.

Trying to ignore the lascivious looks he was shooting her, she picked up a stray shred of lettuce and popped it in her mouth. "You haven't even asked me about Dean."

"I don't give a shit about Dean right now."

Laurel believed him. Russ was much better at

compartmentalizing things than she was. All week she'd been preoccupied with thoughts of Russ and what it had felt like having him push inside her. Plus thoughts of Trevor Dean and worries that he'd be angry with her when she cancelled their plans. All tied up with concern over Russ's little brother Sean and the hostility he seemed to be carrying around.

Russ didn't seem to have any of her concerns. He just looked horny. Laurel thought in her next life she might want to be a guy.

But then she thought about dragging those testicles around all the time and thought better of it.

"I don't think he liked it when I cancelled. He took a long time to respond, and then he was kind of snippy."

"Snippy?" Russ took a big bite of his Italian sub.

"Yes, like he said that we had plans first, but he understood. It was snippy."

"A con artist who gets snippy. I can't wait to meet this guy in person."

"So how long do I have to hold him off?"

"Until we can get together some more evidence. If you think it's getting too difficult, just stop answering him. I don't like you talking to him anyway."

"It's fine." Laurel protested just because it seemed like she should. It put her back up every time Russ suggested she couldn't handle a few e-mails with a con artist.

Whatever he said was lost around his sandwich, which was just as well, because she had a sneaking suspicion it was a swear word.

"By the way, where's Sean tonight?" What she was really asking was, *How long are you staying? All night, please?*

"He called one of his old friends and is spending the night there."

Oh, yeah.

"I realized I shouldn't have cut him off from his old friends. I wanted him to move in with me, make new friends, just slide into a new life. But he hasn't made any friends, and even though it will be a bit of a pain in the ass to cart him back and forth to see his old buddies, I figured it's important."

She wanted to kiss him right then for being such a good brother, such a good man. "I think that's a great idea, Russ."

He balled up his wrapper. "Now let's get the hell out of here."

Even better idea.

Chapter 12

When they walked through Laurel's garage and wound up in a mudroom off the kitchen, Russ couldn't wait another sixty seconds. He grabbed Laurel by the lapels of her coat, cut off the cry that came from her mouth, and kissed her with all the passion and frustration he felt.

She went slack against him immediately, her fingers fluttering over his waist, her tongue trying to keep up with his. He didn't wait, didn't let her adjust to him, just took her mouth with hot, urgent, demanding kisses that fueled his need and had him throbbing everywhere.

Damn, she was delicious—a sweet hot rush better than that Pixy Stix, and just as powerful.

Russ trailed his tongue across her plump bottom lip, nipped it, enjoyed the startled groan of approval she gave. Still holding her coat, he shoved the sleeves down, let it drop to the floor.

"Bless you for wearing a shirt that buttons." She had a necklace in the shape of a cursive L on, nestled above her breasts. The breasts he caught a fleeting glimpse of when she put her hands on her hips.

It was just a white shirt, nothing spectacular, but that little hint of cleavage, that necklace dangling enticingly, those buttons pulling and straining a bit when she moved, had Russ as intrigued as if she were on the table doing a striptease.

Okay, that was an exaggeration. He almost passed out picturing Laurel gyrating in heels and lingerie. But he was still very, very, interested in unbuttoning her shirt.

But first he buried his head in her neck, smelled her light perfume, licked the graceful curve, felt her shiver. Then he dipped lower, lower, until he moved past the necklace and kissed the swell of her breasts, popping the top button on her shirt.

Her fingers tightened on him, gripping the waistband of his jeans.

"Shouldn't we go upstairs?"

"In a minute." Not that she could see his answer, given that it was spoken to her breast.

Russ sucked the skin that hovered over her bra, undid another button. He grazed his lips back and forth over her bra, a sheer material that showed the darkness of her areola and the tight round pink of her nipple.

Oh, man, she was beautiful. It was a good thing she couldn't see his lips, because he didn't have any words for how incredible she looked, felt, tasted. Laurel was like . . . a gift. Something he didn't necessarily deserve, but that he was so glad he'd gotten.

He finished off the buttons. Parted her blouse. Undid the front hook of her bra. And took both her full breasts into his hands while she gave a little cry of distress.

"Russ, please. I don't want to . . . in the mudroom."

He'd forgotten where they were. There was a row of shoes on a braided rug. A washer, dryer, ironing board. A little bench with an orange cushion stood in the corner. He straightened up, tugged her shirt closed.

"I'm sorry, I'm sorry, but you look so good . . . feel so good." He ran his fingers through his hair, saw that her shirt gaped open again, and reached out and did the middle button with trembling fingers.

"It's okay, it's just, I'm not sure how much I can take. I don't want to have a, you know, in the mudroom."

Her words were slurred, her eyes slumberous, goose bumps on her chest where her skin was still exposed.

Tossing his jacket to the floor and kicking off his boots, Russ grabbed her hand, and on impulse, his bag of candy.

Laurel giggled. "What do you need your candy for?"

"Some people like cigarettes after—I like candy. Now where are the stairs?"

Laurel pointed to the left at the same stairs off the kitchen they had used before. Russ knew the way from there, and jogged, tugging her with him, running so hard that they were both laughing, breathless, by the time they reached the open door to her room.

Russ leaned down to give her just a quick kiss, but Laurel put her arms around his neck, wrapped a thigh around his, and did an intriguing little tongue thing across his lip.

Groaning, Russ pulled back. "Whoa. Hold on, bunny. First things, first." He scanned her room for orange fur. "Where's Ferris?"

"I don't know." She glanced towards her couch. "He's usually on the couch or my bed when I'm not here."

Russ spotted the cat slinking along next to Laurel's desk, trying to make a break for the bed, where he was no doubt planning to hide underneath and attack Russ at the right moment. With a quick lunge, Russ caught the cat by the hindquarters and scooped him up. While his fur was soft and well-groomed, he was one big kitty. "Isn't he kind of heavy for a cat?"

It was awkward even holding his bulk, especially since he was kicking his back legs into Russ's gut.

"He's a little overweight."

Russ raised an eyebrow at her, even as his fingers fell into the creases between Ferris's fat rolls. "A little? This guy is packed solid."

Laurel played with the ends of her hair. "He has an eating disorder."

She had to be fucking kidding him.

Planning on taking the cat all the way downstairs and locking him in the first-floor bathroom or the pantry, Russ swore when Ferris caught him with a claw on his wrist and leaped to freedom. Ferris skittered off down the hall and Russ slammed the bedroom door shut, hoping the cat would stay the hell away.

"How does a cat get an eating disorder?" And what did you do about it? Cat counseling?

"When Ferris was a kitten we found him trapped in a drainage ditch. He was starving, scared to death, and we figured he had been there for a week or so. When we brought him home, he developed an obsessive interest in food because of his tragic experience."

He was sorry he'd asked. "Maybe he needs to get more exercise."

"How do you get a cat to exercise? Throw in a Pilates DVD?"

Russ laughed. "No, wiseass, that's not what I meant."

He didn't care what he'd meant. He didn't care about her cat.

Russ hooked his finger on the one button of her blouse that was in place and wiggled it back and forth. "Is your bedroom a better place to, uh, you know?"

She blushed when he repeated her words back to her. But she also stood her ground. "Yes, this is a better place to, uh, you know." Then she licked her lips and whispered, "It's the perfect place to come."

Damn. Russ felt the force of that sexy statement in every inch of his desperate body. His finger twisted, tightened, tore. Her blouse fell open, right along with her cute little mouth when she realized he'd popped the button right off.

She hadn't redone her bra, so her breasts were bare, round and smooth, her nipples taut and teasing him. Stopping himself just short of diving onto her, he leaned forward and took her into his mouth, sucking and licking her nipple, her warm flesh firm beneath his touch.

Laurel grabbed his arms, squeezed. Russ licked a path from one breast to the other, wanting to taste and feel every speck of her. He pushed her blouse and her bra straps down her arms, where they pooled at her wrists. She jerked her hands off of his, shook the blouse free, then aggressively yanked his T-shirt right out of his jeans.

"You go, girl," he said, running his lips along her clavicle in pleasure. Russ loved women's bodies, the way they were so smooth, so soft, so free of hair—the exact opposite of his. Laurel's was especially smooth and soft and with every glide across that satin flesh, he was reminded that only one man had been there before, touched her in those intimate places, and that had been so long ago it couldn't be much more than a distant memory.

He was the one touching her now, the only one. The only one to give her pleasure, to pull her passion out of the closet she'd been keeping it in, and to enjoy the benefits of all she had to give.

And he'd seen, felt, reveled in all she had to give and wanted more.

Russ undid the button on her jeans, tugged her zipper down. Kissing her neck, sucking at the pulsing vein there, he worked his hand into her jeans, cupped her hot mound through her panties. The satiny fabric was a cloudy pink, like a swirl of cotton candy, and her flesh gave beneath the pressure of his hand.

"Mmm, that feels so good," he said, stroking his thumb back and forth while he just held her, felt her heat and explored the contours of her inner thighs. He heard his own breath hitching in excitement, felt the tightness growing in his cock.

Laurel ran her hands over his stomach, his chest. Her lithe, little, inquisitive fingers caught on his chest hairs and tugged, a reflexive jerk in response to his slipping beneath her panties. Russ allowed himself one indulgent pass over her swollen clitoris, one dip down into her to confirm that she was aroused, slick and pulsing, before removing his hand.

Even when she whimpered in protest, squeezed his chest, he didn't continue to touch her. He wanted her naked, he wanted to see and touch and taste all of her, and he especially wanted to run his tongue over her right between her legs. He stepped back, pulled his shirt off, and helped her tug down her jeans with rough, impatient jerks.

He was urgent now, wanting her with a desperation that was foreign.

Laurel sat on the bed, kicking at her jeans, trying to force them off. Russ went down on his knees, between her legs, and pulled the waist of the pants so they came off inside out. He unrolled her socks, no longer taking the time to explore her, just wanting everything off so he could be on her, in her.

"Laurel, damn, you look so good." Russ had his fingers on his snap, about to shuck his jeans, but the way she sat there, tits thrust out at him, hair flowing over her shoulders, knees falling open, expression bright and eager, made him pause.

Then while he stared in true appreciation, she shocked the hell out of him.

Laurel lifted her hips off the bed, and inches from his very excited eyes, she skimmed off her panties, displaying her dark blond curls and luscious pale skin.

"Oh, yeah, baby, that's beautiful." He wanted to touch, but he couldn't move, couldn't breathe.

And she made it even better by pushing those panties down past her knees, bringing her delectable mound within inches of his mouth. Russ grabbed her hips and sank his fingers into her flesh hard to hold her in place.

"What are you doing?" she asked, trying to bring her knees and bottom back down.

Russ gave her an answer by closing the gap between them and burying his mouth in her hot moist flesh.

Ecstasy exploded in Laurel's body, smothering the shock and embarrassment that had swept over her at the first feel of Russ's tongue. She wasn't totally clueless—she did watch *Sex and the City*—but it was safe to say that until now she'd never really understood eyes-rolled-back-in-the-head, hot, desperate, give-it-to-me-now kind of sex.

Russ cupped her backside firmly with his hands, and his tongue just did the most marvelous innovative things across her clitoris, down over her throbbing folds, and inside her. Laurel watched his head, watched him move, watched the tip of his tongue stroke, stroke, stroke. She felt the pleasure rush through her, tightening her muscles, gripping her fingers, clenching her teeth, forcing her eyes closed.

Everything wound tighter and tighter, forcing her hips higher, forcing his tongue deeper inside her until she shattered like glass—splintering, cracking, and scattering.

Yes, yes, yes, she thought in her head, not knowing, not caring, if the words left her lips.

The orgasm was hot, hard, quick, like rushing down the high hill on a roller coaster—flying, frenzied, exciting.

Her legs collapsed, and even Russ holding her couldn't keep her hips suspended any longer. She fell to the bed, heart pounding wildly, head turned to the side. She couldn't look at him, couldn't see those deep dark eyes watching her from between her thighs. Couldn't see his sexy caramel hair falling over his forehead.

It was too much, too raw, too intimate. Laurel

hadn't understood when she'd said she wanted an affair, hadn't understood how close and hot and slick their bodies would become, hadn't realized how much she would enjoy the bond of fantastic sex. She hadn't known that her heart and mind would betray her and take too much pleasure in what was meant to be fleeting, flirtatious fun.

She swallowed hard, sucking in air, shivering as Russ moved back, leaving empty space and a slight breeze between her thighs. Her inner muscles throbbed from her orgasm, but also lusted, pleaded for more.

A second later, Russ turned her head, forcing her to look up at him. It wasn't a gentle touch, but a rough shake. A demanding *look at me*. He was moving her legs apart with insistent knees, and Laurel felt a jump of excitement intermixed with trepidation. She wasn't sure she could take anymore, she wasn't sure her body could handle it.

"Watch me while I take you," Russ said, and with one swift sure thrust, sank deep inside her.

Pleasure snapped like a sharp whip, and Laurel grabbed the duvet cover for support. Russ hadn't torn apart her bed this time, and they were on top, naked and urgent. His thrusts were hard, demanding, nothing like that first time when he'd tried to go easy on her.

Now he just pushed and pounded, and Laurel watched his face, the way his eyes narrowed, jaw locking. The tension in his shoulders as his muscles moved quickly, desperately. She let go of the bed, pulled her legs up. Locked them around him. And moved.

When she met his thrust, her flesh colliding with his, her clitoris ground against him, and she gave up a soft moan. *Ohmygod, this was really something amazing*. This was everything she could have asked for, times twelve.

He said her name. She glanced up, saw it bursting off his lips with violence at the same exact moment he came inside her. Laurel instinctively clenched her inner muscles around him, holding on as he pulsed, and found herself tumbling into her own orgasm.

It was more relaxed, longer, languid, compared to her first, and she rode it out, pressing herself against him, digging her nails into his back.

Russ didn't fall on her, but rolled a little to the side, pulling her with him so they were still joined. He was shaking his head, swallowing hard.

"Damn, Laurel. I keep meaning to go slow, then you look at me and I can't control myself. Watching you come was amazing."

"Which time?" she asked, resting her head on her pillow and trailing her fingers down to his butt. He had a great behind, firm and compact.

He laughed. "Both."

"You know, before you, I've never actually had an orgasm while . . ." Her words failed her, but her hands continued on with the sign, the flat of her palms smacking together twice, fingers in the V sign.

Russ glanced down at her hands. "What does that mean?"

She chewed her lip and felt a blush creep over her face, even as her hips wiggled a little to ensure he'd stay inside her. "It means intercourse, sex."

"Show me again."

This time she lost her balance a little since she was lying on her side, and the sign wasn't crisp, but Russ repeated it back to her with precise accuracy.

Oh, Lord. Just seeing him signing was sexy enough, but with that grin, and with what he had said, Laurel felt hot and tingly over every inch of her body. And she almost cried when he shifted and pulled out of her.

"I might need to know that sign," he told her, "when I'm begging you for sex some day. It might help win you over."

Like he'd need to beg. Before she could think through the repercussions, she brushed her fingers across his jaw. "You've already won me over."

Russ lay on his side, watching the warm wonder on Laurel's face, and he felt good. Damn good. He liked being with her. She was a respite from all the other bullshit in his life. Being here was sweet and safe. And sexy. Jesus, was she sexy.

She could make him come just by tossing him that quivering give-it-to-me look she got.

He couldn't think of a damn thing to say that could convey anything of what he was feeling, so he kissed her swollen, plump lips, and wrapped his arms around her. Russ rolled onto his back, hauling her with him so she was splayed over him, the press of her soft body delicious against his.

She wiggled her breasts as she adjusted and settled her head on his shoulder. Russ scooted backward until they were at the headboard, and fell back onto the pillow with a sigh.

Only he hit something hard and solid.

"Oww, Laurel, what the hell's under your pillow?"

"Hmm?" She looked up at him as he reached his hand behind his head and started feeling around under the lace pillow.

"What's under your pillow? I almost knocked myself out."

"Oh, it's my vibrator."

Russ stopped groping. "Your *what?*" Holy crap,

she kept one under her pillow? That was just shocking . . . and sexy. Russ pictured her alone in her bed, fingers between her thighs, stroking herself until she was damp and squirming. Then rocking herself onto a vibrator . . .

"My vibrator. Here, I'll show you."

Well, he didn't really need to see it. In some cases the fantasy might be better than the reality, or he might just find himself jealous of a little machine. "That's okay, really, it's fine, I . . ."

Laurel pulled out a rectangular object that looked nothing like any vibrator he'd ever seen. Not that he'd really seen any, except in an occasional porn movie in his younger days. But he didn't really think that thing she was holding could work on any human he'd ever met.

She rested it on his shoulder and turned it on. Russ almost jumped off the bed. Jesus, he didn't want to *use* it, whatever the hell it was.

"See? It's my alarm clock. It vibrates instead of making sound."

Russ sank back on the pillow and laughed. Shit, he was such a pervert. She'd been talking about her alarm clock. The little machine buzzed on his shoulder, creating enough motion and sensation that he could easily picture it pulling him out of a sound sleep.

"What's so funny?" Laurel looked puzzled as she turned the vibrator off.

"I thought you meant a different kind of vibrator. The kind you buy in an adult store."

Her mouth dropped open. "Oh . . . *oh.*"

"I had all kinds of interesting pictures running around in my head."

Still did. He let his hand splay across her ass, brushing back and forth with teasing strokes.

"I don't have one of those!" she said to the wall behind his head, with a blush so vibrant he strongly suspected she was lying.

"That's too bad. I was enjoying the idea of you here, pleasuring yourself." In fact, he was getting hard all over again.

"Where do you keep it, Laurel?" Russ reached over to her white nightstand, pretending like he was about to pull open the drawer. "In here?"

"No!" She grabbed his arm and held it back with more strength than he'd ever have given her credit for.

She tussled with him, which he found both funny and startling. Especially when he put up a mock protest, not allowing her to pull him away, and she only dug in deeper. Laurel leaned farther, yanked harder, got desperate. The book that had been lying on the nightstand fell to the hardwood floor with a loud thwack as their hands jerked back.

"Please, don't," she said in a breathless, pleading voice.

Russ let his hand go slack, sorry he'd caused such panic in her when he'd just been playing around. "I won't. I'm just teasing, bunny." He kissed her chin, the only thing he could reach. "You can let me go, I promise."

So she wasn't ready for sex toys. He wasn't, either. He wanted her just the way she was—all his, all warm and eager and relaxed.

With sugar on top.

Laurel let go of his hand.

"Where did I drop my candy, Laurel?"

"By the door." She looked at him like he was crazy. "You really want a piece of candy?"

"I'm hungry," he lied. "And I burned a bunch of

calories. I need a sugar boost." He patted her behind, hoping to encourage her to shift off of him so he could go get the bag.

"I'll get it."

Laurel moved off of the bed and padded across the floor, her arms over her chest, like she was either cold or a little shy. Maybe both. Russ didn't look away. Couldn't. She had a pretty little room, with lots of white furniture and way too many flowers jumping at him from every angle, but he liked it. The ceiling sloped, since it was the third floor, and her windows were tucked into the eaves and covered with white shutters. The lamplight cast a soft glow around the room, and her computer hummed on her desk.

The room surrounded her, looked like her, smelled like her.

She belonged here.

Laurel had a beautiful body, with the right amount of curves, just enough muscle to look healthy, and a natural grace that made all her movements fluid, stark, complex, like the sign language she spoke. Russ propped his arm behind his head with a groan and gave an appreciative, "Hot damn," when she bent over, giving him a phenomenal shot from shoulder to ankle. "You have no idea what you look like, do you?"

Her back arched and her ass bowed out towards him, giving him a teasing, aching hint of the apex of her thighs. For a second he swore he saw her soft curls from behind.

Then she stood up, plastic bag in hand, and came towards him. The view from the front was even better than the back. Her nipples hardened under his scrutiny and her hips rolled. He wanted to part those folds hiding behind her curls and see if she was still wet. If she still wanted him.

Laurel climbed up next to him, pulled the covers back on the bed, and slipped under, setting the candy between them.

"Cold?" he asked.

She nodded. "Maybe I should put some clothes on."

Oh, God, no. Anything but that.

Russ quickly got under there with her, pulling her close to combine their body heat, of which he had plenty after her little naked stroll. And he had every intention of getting things even hotter between them.

He dumped the bag of candy on top of the covers. A wide array of shiny sugar-filled treats greeted him. He picked a Pixy Stix. A pink one, since that color reminded him of Laurel.

She was watching him with amusement, clearly no idea where his sick mind was heading.

Pixy Stix in his teeth, he tore the top off.

Turned it over, and spilled the powder all over her nipples, where it clung like frosting on a cupcake.

And he wanted a lick.

Chapter 13

He had dumped Pixy powder on her nipple.

Laurel stared down at her breast in shock. She had thought Russ was going to toss the candy in his mouth, like he had at the store, not pour it all over her naked body and—oh, good Lord—lick it off.

He was lapping at her, his tongue elongated as it curved towards her, lifting flecks of candy off her nipple, wetting her, the powder, and his lips until all three were shiny and sticky and covered in deep pink sugar. Laurel grabbed onto the bed, tried to move back away from his questing mouth, but he resisted, held her in place.

It wasn't that she objected, or it didn't feel good. The problem was, it felt too good, so shocking and intimate and wild that she was overly sensitive, anxiously aroused. And maybe, still just a touch embarrassed.

Maybe other people doused each other in kiddie candy and licked it off on a regular basis, but she had no experience with this sort of thing.

She kind of liked it.

Now that the powder was wet, it clumped together in little crystallized balls, and pricked and pulled at her skin as Russ closed his mouth completely around her, taking in her nipple, areola, and a good portion of her breast. She groaned, the sweet scent of watermelon overwhelming her nostrils.

When he pulled back, he glanced up at her, a satisfied smile on his face. "Mmmm, I really like the pink ones."

Russ's tongue darted out to do a thorough circle around her nipple in a final cleanup.

Laurel sucked in her breath. Her nipple hovered wet and aching in front of his mouth. Her thighs shifted restlessly below the sheet, wanting in on the action. Russ was waiting for her response. What she said would either send him into a retreat, or to more traditional means of seduction, or she could give him permission to continue with whatever he had in mind.

Her hesitation lasted only a split second. She trusted Russ. She wanted Russ.

"Is pink your favorite?" she asked, rolling onto her back so her breasts rose enticingly—she hoped—in front of him.

Given the way his nostrils flared, chances were pretty good he agreed.

"I'm not sure I have a favorite. Let's test it." His hand shot out, grabbed a handful of Pixy Stix.

"Purple." He tore it open and dropped it on her other nipple. Then he licked a path across the top of her breast, avoiding the powder. "It will stick better if I wet it first." He tapped his finger on an opened red stix, dropping powder on the damp flesh.

He repeated the process on her other breast, laying out green and orange on patches of flesh he'd moistened first, until Laurel couldn't decide if she wanted to laugh or have an orgasm.

"Russ . . ." she murmured, to what purpose she hadn't a clue.

He took a tentative lick of each color, in such quick, rapid succession that she barely felt him. "Hmm, I couldn't tell, Laurel. I'll have to try again. Do you mind?"

She shook her head, closing her eyes in anticipation of his tongue flickering across her in that teasing little touch and retreat.

Only this time, he licked, he bit, he sucked all over everything, blending flavors and powder until her skin was sticky and slick, an exotic fruity smell clogging her nostrils, sending her salivary glands into overproduction. Laurel panted, pushing herself forward when his mouth left.

A glance down showed him pulled back, studying the glossy shine on her skin, his finger rolling across her nipple, playing with it. Laurel liked the way he fit over her, the way his muscular arms could hold him hovering above her, making her feel secure, desired, comfortable.

He seemed to be thinking, tongue pulling a stray fleck of candy from the corner of his mouth.

"I like it all, Laurel, every last lick."

But even while he spoke the words, even while she felt a longing rising up from between her legs, even while he blew on her breasts to dry them, he was reaching his left hand to the pile of candy.

Laurel went wet in anticipation, then blushed at her own reaction.

Russ only had a sheet of candy buttons, and here she was imagining all sorts of desperate and horny things.

He popped one in his mouth.

Which just proved she was ridiculous. He was only hungry, and what did she know about sex? Obviously as much as might fit on the top of that little yellow candy dot he was ripping off the paper.

Russ stuck the candy button to the tip of her nipple.

Hello. Laurel jerked in surprise. "What are you doing?"

"Playing with the best pair of tits I've ever seen."

Carry on, then. She arched her back, tried not to think about how bizarre she must look, and decided not to ask any more stupid questions. She was just going to enjoy this.

And while she wasn't sure her breasts qualified as the best he'd ever seen, she knew she had a good body, was comfortable showing her bare flesh to him, and pleased he got pleasure from it. He cupped her flesh in his hand, his eyes half-closed, amused. He kissed her mouth, a soft languid kiss with a caressingly playful flavor, the taste of the overly sweet candy mixing between them. When he broke the kiss, he leaned over and pursed his lips, then sucked the candy right off her nipple and crunched it.

She laughed at his grin. "Are you finished?" She was going to need a shower to wash off all the sugar that clung to her in a sticky sheen.

"No." Russ was groping around again. "Close your eyes."

Half-excited, half-scared, Laurel did. She could feel his hands stroking over her, down past her breasts, shoving the sheet until she was exposed to the hip bone. He trailed a thumb over her mound, slowly, then jerked it away, like he was wrestling with himself.

Laurel arched her back, wanting him the way she had never wanted anything. Wanting him deep inside her again and again, rocking her into the bed and letting her feel feminine, powerful, desirable.

She opened her legs in invitation. Russ pushed them closed. Laurel sighed in disappointment, yet anticipated whatever he had planned to tease her.

It wasn't what she was expecting. He pressed on her stomach, around her belly button, sticking more of the little candies on her skin from the feel of it. Then his finger trailed up a little, found the flat plain below her rib cage, and moved in a slow circle, forming an O. Then lifted and dropped down again, tracing another pattern on her.

He was spelling out a word, she realized with a jolt. O-P-E-N. He was spelling out *open*. He wanted her to open her eyes, and he'd found a way to communicate with her without sound, without spoken words.

Laurel snapped them open, heart thumping too fast, emotions rushing over her in all directions, so rapid, so confusing, she didn't know what she was feeling.

Then she looked down to where Russ was tipping his head, nodding for her to notice. And saw that he had drawn a heart around her belly button in pink candy buttons.

Oh, God. Her gut clenched, her heart jumped, her lip quivered. He wasn't supposed to do this. He wasn't supposed to be sweet, funny, caring. He was supposed to be a cool, efficient, sexually experienced cop who gave her a poke and a jab and went on his way.

Because if he acted like this, she was going to have trouble keeping her heart in check. Already had. Everything rushed and pulsed and pushed inside her, and she felt something she was never supposed to feel for this man.

Laurel froze, tears pricking her eyes, pain in her

chest. She didn't say anything—couldn't—afraid her lips would part and shuddering sobs would rush out.

He cocked an eyebrow, looking a little puzzled. "You don't like it?"

Realizing she wasn't giving him the right impression, she just nodded and tried to find a way to convey what she was feeling. How grateful she was to him for treating her like she mattered. If only for tonight, she mattered.

Russ bent and started to brush away the heart, his cheeks a little ruddy, like he was embarrassed. Laurel reached for him, grabbed his shoulder. "Russ."

He looked up and swore. "Shit. I dropped one in your belly button."

She could have never predicted he would say that. Laurel stared at him, then burst out laughing, relieved to have the serious moment pass. "You're kidding."

With a somewhat wobbly grin, he stuck his index finger in her belly button. "No."

"You'll make it worse," she warned, grabbing his wrist. She felt the candy now, and it was an odd invasion wiggling around in there.

He pulled his hand back but instead of moving away and letting her deal with it, he stuck his tongue in and fished around. For a second Laurel thought about protesting, but then she realized that this was disturbing. This was sexual. This was an exact imitation of something else they could be doing.

Her body went hot. Her lips parted on a moan. Her head fell back.

Russ's grip on her hip tightened, pressed. He moved in between her thighs, nudging her apart, and continued to lick around her stomach, down lower and lower. His erection grew thick and hard against her leg, a bead of fluid trickling onto her skin.

She wanted to make love to him again, feel him deep inside her body, holding her down with his thrusts.

But she also wanted to touch him, taste him, show him that she appreciated the care he took with her.

"Did you get it out?" she asked him, knowing he hadn't, hoping she wouldn't wind up in the ER trying to explain that one, but simultaneously not caring right at the moment.

"No. I think you should roll over and shake it out."

There was an image.

But Laurel just sat up, pushing Russ back a little to give her some space and with a quick swipe of her index finger, plucked it out. "What do these things taste like anyway?" She pulled a blue one off the sheet and rolled it between her thumb and finger.

"They actually taste lousy," Russ admitted, resting on his side, the sheet pooling on his upper thighs.

His erection was still prominent, the hard shaft jutting out from between his muscular thighs, and Laurel took a deep breath, stared at it. Hesitated.

Russ touched the tip of her nose. "Whatcha looking at, honey?"

"Your . . ." She gave up trying to speak and stuck the blue candy button right on the head of his penis, where it stuck in the clear fluid hovering there.

Russ's mouth dropped open. "What the hell are you doing, Laurel?"

But he didn't look upset. In fact, he was grinning, and if she wasn't mistaken, that penis got even bigger.

"I'm going to taste the candy," she said and flicked her tongue over the dot, making sure to grab a taste of the flesh underneath.

Russ about lost it right then and there.

He'd never seen anything so sexy in his whole goddamn life.

Laurel's tongue wasn't skilled, but what she lacked in experience she made up for in enthusiasm. She played with that damn candy, licking back and forth, around and around, until she finally closed her lips around his head and sucked it up.

He fell back on his elbows, groaning in desperation. Laurel's blond hair bent over him, tickled his gut, as he watched her deep cherry lips roll up and down on his swollen cock. Her eyes were half-closed, her breath urgent little gasps from her nostrils. She gripped him enthusiastically with her hand down low on his shaft, her fingers brushing against his balls, driving him crazy.

"Oh, yes, that's it, baby." Russ was tense everywhere, caught between holding back and just letting go and pumping hot come into her mouth. He never did that—hadn't since he was a randy teenager with premature ejaculation. It had always seemed to him that once you came in a woman's mouth, you owed her something, and he had never wanted to entangle himself that way.

But watching Laurel had him seriously considering it, as she filled her mouth with him, slicking up his burning flesh and sucking in her cheeks so she surrounded him like a hot, wet glove.

Everything was different with Laurel. Sweeter,

sexier, and in some ways, simpler. Being with her just felt good. And he wanted to keep that, carry it on, see where it went.

But right now he needed to stop her before he tore the sheet in two pieces. He touched her hair gently, not wanting to startle her. Laurel made a cute little "mmm-mmm-good" sound and took him deep. *Oh, shit.* He grabbed her head, tried to yank her off, but she resisted, looking at his cock like she'd never tasted anything so good in her whole goddamn life.

Russ groaned, gave it up, enjoyed the feel of her sliding over him, one hand on his thigh holding him, the other massaging his balls. He tightened his grip on her hair, needing something to anchor him so he didn't suddenly levitate from ecstasy. And of course, once his hands were clamped on her skull, and her mouth in front of him, such a willing hot hole, he found himself taking over, pushing himself inside her mouth with hard, demanding thrusts.

Laurel looked shocked, eyes widening, mouth clamping down. He should stop, should let her breathe, but damn, it felt so good, every inch of him tight and desperate, all focused on that amazing pleasure her mouth was giving him, and he let himself grunt, groan, and swear his approval.

He let it ride to the last possible second of no return, then he jerked back out of her, fumbling around on the bed for the condoms he knew he'd left somewhere in that pile. Laurel was breathing hard, wiping her shiny wet lips, nipples tight, flesh pink, and his cock pulsed and throbbed, begging for release.

The condom went on with trembling fingers. Laurel was on her knees on the bed, brushing her

hair back, waiting for him. "Lay down," he told
her, before he grabbed her and tackled her with
his one hundred and eighty pounds of lust.

"No."

"No?" Russ only managed not to growl by sheer
willpower. "Why the hell not? I'm dying here,
Laurel."

"You lie down." Laurel pushed his shoulders, a
not-so-innocent gleam in her eye.

Well, hell. She wanted to take charge, did she?
Fine by him. "Since you asked so nicely."

Russ dropped back, stuck his hands behind his
head, and watched his cock reach for the sky. Laurel noticed that too, since she was bold-faced staring at it, licking her lips a little and generally looking
so damn eager that Russ had to fight the urge to
grab her and flip her on her back.

Laurel settled her thighs on either side of him
and sat her hot little mound right on top of his
cock. The wet opening teased him, making him lose
all desire to look calm, and he grabbed her hips
hard, ready to shove her down onto him.

But she shook her head. "Not yet." And pro-
ceeded to drive him crazy, sliding herself around
on him, moving the tip of his cock between her
swollen inner folds to her clit, then back again.

"Oh, my," she said on a pant. "This feels good."

Russ gritted his teeth. Laurel could dick-tease
with the best of them. *Damn.*

It seemed she was teasing herself, too, because
without warning, she came, her back arching and
her head snapping forward. She gave frantic little
gasps as her body shuddered on his, her hands
slipping off his erection to land on his waist.

It was a beautiful thing to watch—her shock,

her pleasure—and when her shoulders drooped at the tail end of her climax, Russ shifted a little, dropped her down onto him.

They groaned together as he filled her deeply, and he lay still, absolutely certain that if he moved, it'd be over. He swallowed hard, held onto her hips like she'd leave if he let go. Laurel clearly didn't understand the urgency of his predicament, because tentatively at first, a little bolder a second later, she started to move on him.

Up and down, her body clinging to him, squeezing him, as her breasts tumbled and her breath caught.

Hair in her eyes, a dewy shine to her skin, she rode him hard and fast, and Russ let go.

His orgasm bucked him up, ripped a groan out of him, sucked everything he had and then some, as she held on and took it.

Something hit the floor with a bang, and Russ didn't give a shit. As long as they weren't being shot at or the house wasn't burning down, he wasn't moving. Of course, he was thinking that even if he did die right that second, he could go a happy man.

This was hot sex. This was fine, and then some.

Laurel collapsed on his sweaty chest, sighed. "Wow."

Wow was good. He'd take it. He kissed her forehead, knowing she couldn't see his mouth. His plan was to just lie there for the rest of his life, buried in Laurel. But she rolled off of him, falling into the pile of candy. A second later, she stood up and started across the room.

"I'd better open the door or Ferris will scratch and wake you up."

Russ didn't care about the cat. He cared about the swell of her breasts, the swollen plumpness of her lips, and the way her hair swung over her bare back as she turned.

Then he dropped his gaze to the curve of her backside, lazily enjoying the view, and burst out laughing.

Laurel had three candy buttons stuck to her ass.

"What's so funny?" She frowned at him as she came back to the bed and crawled up beside him.

Russ leaned over her, picked the candies off her butt, and held one up for her to see. She blushed.

"I should take a shower."

"Later. Just lie here for a minute." He pulled her down on him, kissed her. Holding her lightly by the small of her back, he closed his eyes in contentment.

And fell asleep.

Chapter 14

Russ jerked out of sleep, the pressure on his chest so intense he thought he was suffocating. He saw the sloped ceiling, the lamp they'd left on casting a soft glow around Laurel's room, and he remembered they'd fallen asleep after having an orgasm that had shot him into orbit.

The weight on his chest must be Laurel, relaxed in her sleep. Only he'd felt just about every inch of Laurel, and she didn't have hair this thick anywhere on her.

Russ glanced down and met the unblinking gaze of Ferris. The cat was sprawled across his chest, stomach, left arm, and waist, tail flicking along Russ's hip.

"Get off of me."

Ferris lifted a paw, licked it.

"Move it, furball." Russ tried to lift his chest, to buck Ferris off, but the cat just stared at him, clearly unconcerned.

"Laurel." Russ turned his head and tried to get Laurel's attention by brushing his fingers along her thigh, but she didn't even move in her sleep, her lips parted as she breathed softly in and out.

His arm was asleep, and his lungs collapsed. He didn't want to hurt her cat, but it was time for someone to get tough with the thing. Ferris didn't need counseling, he needed someone who wasn't a sap looking him in the eye and telling him the way it was going to be. Russ figured that someone would have to be him.

"Listen, Ferris, here's the thing. I'm going to be here whether you like it or not, so you might as well get used to it. And I'm not like Laurel, I won't fall for that 'I was traumatized, I'm starving' bull-crap."

Ferris lifted his head, narrowed his light green eyes.

"So while you have Laurel wrapped around your paw, I'm just telling you I'm not a pushover. We can get along, we can be friends, but only if you understand the score. And that means get your furry ass off of me. Got it?" He gave Ferris the look he gave to smart-mouthed punks.

The cat blinked, then stood up and stretched, pressing his paws into Russ's chest and nearly puncturing a lung. Then he leaped to the floor with an agility that contradicted the bulk he was carrying.

Russ pulled in a deep breath, grabbing the oxygen Ferris's weight had been depriving him of. "Alright. There we go. I think we have an understanding."

He got out of bed, intending to use the bathroom, but he found himself staring down at Laurel as she slept. She was beautiful awake. Asleep, she was almost ethereal, like a fairy, curled up on the bed, hands under her cheek in a praying position. One foot was kicked out, but her hip covered her triangle of hair and her arm shielded most of her breasts. She looked tantalizing, fragile, untouchable.

Russ shook his head at himself. Man, he'd gotten stupid over her. He could feel himself falling into something with her that he couldn't handle, didn't want. But hell if he could stay away from her.

Goose bumps trailed along her skin, since most of the blankets had fallen to the floor during their enthusiastic sex. Candy was scattered all over the place, along with condom wrappers and the powdery confection of a burst Pixy Stix. The whole scene was seductive, and satisfying.

He was giving Laurel pleasure, and that pleased him more than he would have thought possible.

As he brushed the candy and wrappers to the floor, he kicked something hard with his toe. Bending over, he saw one of the boards supporting her box spring had fallen to the floor. He grinned. Nothing like bouncing the bed so hard you break it.

He pulled the blanket over her, tucking it in on either side of her shoulders, and gave into the impulse to kiss her there, where her shoulder rounded to her arm.

On his way to the bathroom, the computer gave him pause. He was curious to see all the e-mails from Dean and what exactly he and Laurel had been saying to each other. Both now, and before she'd known he was a con. But he didn't know jack shit about computers and didn't think he could maneuver his way through her e-mail. And of course, he trusted that Laurel was telling him everything.

She wasn't the kind to lie or withhold part of the truth.

For that very reason, he was worried about this investigation. He wanted her out of it, away from Dean. As bad as he wanted the guy caught and strung up by his testicles, Russ wanted Laurel safe more.

So they'd just have to catch the bastard without Laurel being involved.

After using the john, he pulled on his briefs and slapped his thigh. "Come on, Ferris, let's go downstairs and get something to drink."

To his amazement, Ferris jumped off the couch and fell into step beside him.

"Alright." He grinned at the cat. "You're not so bad after all. You think I can train you to fetch me a beer?"

Ferris shot him a look of pure disdain as they padded down the steps, the only sound in the big house that of a grandfather clock ticking somewhere in the deep recesses of the first floor.

Russ laughed. "Don't push it, huh?"

Ferris rubbed against his leg, and Russ gave up all thoughts of murdering him.

"Are you sure about this?" Laurel looked at her reflection in the mirror and tried not to panic.

"Yes! If you change, I'll never switch shifts with you at work again." Catherine stood next to her, looking remarkably like Johnny Depp as Edward Scissorhands.

The wild erratic hair, the ripped clothes, the long fingernails—it was all there. Cat had the additional embellishments of blond streaks and a rose-

and-vine tattoo trailing over her pelvis where the shirt was torn and her pants were too low to cover.

It worked for Catherine. She looked confident, sexy.

Laurel felt like a slutty schoolgirl. Which was exactly the look Catherine had been going for, she supposed.

"Look, we can't totally change you, that wouldn't work. You have to be true to yourself, but we had to kick it up a notch. You have that whole good-girl thing going on, so now you're a good girl who could be talked into doing something naughty."

Which was a pretty apt description of the way she'd been behaving lately. She still blushed when she pictured waking up that morning, still sticky from candy, to Russ's finger probing deep inside her. She had come before ten in the morning and had loved it.

She'd wanted wild. Here it was.

In the form of a short plaid skirt, black tights, chunky high-heeled Mary Janes, and a tight black tank top, covered by another one in white that stopped approximately three inches above her waist. Aside from the fact that it seemed beyond ridiculous to flash her midriff when it was twelve degrees outside, she felt half-naked. "Are you sure the hair isn't too over the top?"

Catherine had stuck her hair into two little pigtails on either side of her cheeks. "I think I look like I'm trying to attract a pedophile."

Cat laughed. "No, because you have the chains on the skirt and the black leather bracelet. That prevents you from looking like you're posing for porn. Trust me."

Since she had no idea what the appropriate clothing etiquette for clubbing was, she was going to have to trust Catherine. Which she did. She just wasn't sure she trusted herself not to make an ass out of herself.

"I brought a bottle of wine with me." Cat picked at her hair in the mirror, stretching one spike farther out. "Let's go have a glass before we go."

Laurel turned her back on their images and reached for her scarf. "Good idea."

Cat touched her arm and shook her head, eyebrows raised. "Leave the fleece scarf, Laurel."

"Really?" Darn it, she was going to freeze with her neck exposed like that. The flu was going around, too.

"Really."

Cat was so vehement that Laurel tossed it on the bed and headed for the door, the wine, and the wild life, only wobbling a little on the chunky shoes.

Trevor held his cigarette low so the amber glow wouldn't be visible when Laurel flicked the kitchen light on and walked into the room.

So this was what was more important than meeting him. Getting whored up and hanging out with a Goth friend. He couldn't hear what they were saying from his position outside the bay window, but they were breaking out a bottle of wine and laughing.

He didn't like being brushed off. He didn't like it when a woman rejected his overtures.

Normally he didn't take these things personally. The rare occasions when a woman had responded to him with a lukewarm reception, he had just moved on to the next one, who would look at him with adoration and longing. He should just forget about Laurel Wilkins.

It was the smart thing to do.

If he did, he wouldn't be standing outside in fucking five-degree weather getting more and more pissed off with each passing minute.

But there was something about Laurel. There was her money. There was her house. Then there was the way she looked, like a Barbie, all curvy and perky and innocent. Everyone knew Barbie was a slut even though she had that angelic smile. Trevor thought Laurel was the same.

The outfit she was wearing tonight cemented the opinion.

He'd come over here, disturbed that her recent e-mails had a different something than before. A different tone, a confidence, an amusement, maybe, that hadn't been there prior to his standing her up at the coffee shop. He wanted to know what had changed. If he didn't know better he'd think she suspected something was off about him.

But seeing her swinging her ass in that short little skirt, he thought maybe there was a different answer. Laurel was getting fucked. And he didn't like that. Not when he had plans to seduce her into giving him all she had.

Life hadn't been fair to Trevor. He'd grown up piss-poor, the unwanted kid of a junkie and one of her many boyfriends. So Trevor had figured out that if he wanted to get anywhere, stop sleeping in a trailer or in the nearest shelter, he'd have to do for himself. At twelve he'd left his mother sleeping off a high in jail after assaulting her latest boyfriend, and he'd struck out on his own.

He'd done well. He could con anyone, make them believe anything about him. Make them believe he was respectable, with a good background, and a family who gave a damn about him.

But it wasn't enough.

His cell phone vibrated in his pocket and he pulled it out, knowing no one could see him. There was nothing but trees and the lake back here, and Laurel was warm and cozy in her kitchen fifteen feet away, unable to hear him.

"Hello?"

"Hi, it's me."

It was Jill, checking up on him, as he'd known she would. It pleased him that she worried. "Hey, sweetheart. What are you up to?"

"Nothing, just watching TV. You've only been living here a week and it's like the apartment's empty without you." She gave a laugh, like she was teasing, but he knew she meant every word.

Laurel sipped her wine in front of him, fiddling with the waistband of her skirt, a ribbon of pale flesh peeking out at him.

"I miss you, too. Traveling for work is a bitch." He took a hit off his cigarette, shifting for a better view, easing the pressure on his knee from hunching down the way he was.

"I think it stinks when they've been so lousy to you lately."

"They pay the bills, Jill, so I can't complain."

"You'll be home tomorrow?"

"As soon as my plane lands. Let's hope it doesn't snow here in Chicago." He had booked himself a hotel in downtown Cleveland for the night, wanting some space and a room with an adjustable thermostat, and because it amused him to have Jill dangle after him.

She gasped. "I never thought of that. God, you could be stuck there for days if we get a blizzard."

"It probably won't happen. But would you miss me?" Trevor ground out his cigarette as Laurel emptied her wineglass. "Would you get horny without me?"

Jill's breath hitched. "Pete!"

"Well? I need to hear you say it." He let himself sound needy, coaxing.

"Yes, I'll miss you. Yes, I'd get horny without you." There was a pause. "I'm already horny."

"Oh, really?" He could picture Jill, wearing those damn flannel pants that were big enough to be pitched as a tent. Her plain face, free of makeup, her hair in a disheveled ponytail. "I am, too. And I'm picturing you spread out beneath me, my finger inside you, my mouth on your nipple."

"Oh, Pete." She gave a shuddery sigh.

"Touch yourself, Jill, so I won't feel embarrassed that I'm the only one doing it."

"You're touching yourself?" She sounded scandalized, excited.

Trevor propped the phone on his ear, patted down the pocket of his leather jacket for his pack of smokes. It was too cold to be without one, and he wasn't quite ready to leave yet. "I can't help it . . . just thinking about you gets me hot."

"I can hear you breathing hard."

"I'm not going to come, I promise, I'm just going to touch a little. Touch yourself, Jill, please."

"Okay."

As he lit his cigarette, he could hear the rustle of fabric, sense her growing excitement, her breathing faster and harder.

He talked her through it, with coaxing words and put-on moans, and a minute later when Jill was whimpering as she came, Trevor was watching Laurel Wilkins.

Just watching.

Chapter 15

"What's with that naked broad with no arms stuck up there like that. You ever wonder what that's supposed to mean?" Anders asked him as they drove past the Stokes building and turned the corner.

Russ glanced at the sculpture floating on the façade of the building. It was a woman—Lady Justice, he imagined—staring out with a prim, yet somehow licentious, look. "I think it's Justice, you know. But I don't know why the hell she's half-naked."

Anders snorted. "Because justice can be bought and sold like a cheap whore?"

Russ laughed and pulled into a parking lot on West 6th Street, then shook his head at the sign posted. "Damn, I can't believe it costs ten bucks to park."

He paid the fee against his better judgment and climbed out of his truck, frowning when a bitter wind smacked him in the face.

Anders followed suit and slammed the door shut with a shake of his head. "You know, Pam's going to kill me if she finds out about this."

Rubbing his face as they walked across the park-

ing lot and down a precarious slope of icy sidewalk, Jerry sighed.

"So don't tell her," Russ said, preoccupied with
scoping out the area. Bad lighting. He didn't like
that.

"You clearly have no idea how to do this whole
girlfriend thing." Jerry hunched his shoulders over
and shook his head. "Anything you fail to mention
is going to get found out. Women are freaking psy-
chic. Better to fess up ahead of time. That way she'll
only withhold sex for two days instead of three or
four."

Since Jerry actually sounded serious, Russ stopped
walking. "Look, if this is going to cause a problem
between you and Pam, you don't have to come. I
can go by myself."

Sometimes Russ wondered if Jerry and Pam's
relationship was all that healthy. They always seemed
to be angry with each other, but he figured what
the hell did he know about it. To date, his longest
stint with a woman had been six months, and that
had been because she had traveled three times a
week as a flight attendant.

But Jerry shrugged at his suggestion. "Technically, we're broken up right now. I said something
stupid, it turned into a big fight, and well, who gives
a crap, you know? Pam's always mad at me. Seems
like according to her, I can't do anything right,
and I'm getting sick of it."

"Hey, sorry, man, I didn't know you broke up."

Jerry stuck his hands in his pockets. "No big
deal. There was a time when I thought Pam might be
it, but she's not. So just ignore my whining. Besides,
I can't let you make an ass out of yourself all alone."

"I'm not going to make an ass out of myself."
Russ blew on his hands, eyeing with suspicion some

guy hanging around the club entrance, pants just about around his knees. Hadn't the look died out yet? God, he couldn't stand that.

"When the woman that you're sleeping with tells you she's hitting the clubs with her girlfriend, and you just happen to show up at the same place, you're asking for trouble, man, I'm telling you."

Russ started walking again. "I'm just checking the place out, that's all. Laurel isn't exactly nightlife savvy. I'm just going to make sure she's alright, then I'll leave."

Jerry snorted. "You're going to piss her off. How did you get her to tell you where she was going without getting suspicious anyway?"

That gave Russ pause. Maybe he had been a little devious there, but it had been for a good cause. Keeping Laurel safe. "I asked her this morning, right after she woke up." And right after he'd given her an orgasm while she was still half-asleep.

"Aah, the old trick of catching her while she's too fuzzy to think about why you're asking. Fuel on the fire, man. You're screwed. Hope the sex was good, because you're not getting any more."

"Laurel's not like that. She's not going to get mad at me." He opened the door to the club and violently loud music with screaming lyrics hit him in the face. "Laurel probably wants to be rescued. She's probably cowering in the corner in those teacher clothes she wears. She'll be glad to see me."

They scanned the room, seeing nothing but pulsing bodies and strobing lights ahead.

Jerry jerked his thumb to the left. "Uh, Evans, I think you may be off on that just a little." He clapped Russ on the back. "Sorry, man."

Russ turned and followed Jerry's gaze. What he

saw made a red haze of shock and fury blur his vision.

Which didn't get rid of the sight of Laurel dancing in the middle of a group of punked-out guys, wearing the most outrageous clothes he'd ever seen in his life, a fishbowl-sized drink in her hand.

"I don't think she wants to be rescued."

Russ barely heard the words as he started across the room, wishing like hell he was wearing his weapon.

Laurel had figured out quickly the dance floor was the place to be. Words weren't necessary when you were gyrating. Not that she was gyrating. On a good day she didn't know how to gyrate.

Tonight, after a glass of wine and four or five sips of the drink Catherine had brought her, anything more than wiggling was out of the question.

But even though no one could understand a word she was saying in the noisy club, all of Catherine's friends were very nice. Laurel had the advantage in that she could lip-read everything they were saying to her, but her speech was probably getting lost under the noise. The music was so loud even Laurel could feel the beat.

Still, despite the communication problems, they were all smiling at her and offering to buy her drinks. She had three guys right now dancing next to her, taking turns doing a bizarre sort of shimmy-shake thing in front of her. They were all a little odd-looking, not her type with all the piercings and tattoos, but she didn't want to judge anyone on appearance, and she would have felt rude walking away from them.

So she smiled back and tried not to feel alarmed when one clamped a colorful arm around her waist, perilously close to her butt. Fortunately, her drink gave her an excuse not to wrap her arms back around him. She wielded it like a shield between them, even though she'd stopped drinking it after the guy with the shaved head had taken a healthy sip out of it.

It was flu season and she wasn't taking any chances.

"You are so hot," the guy said, his hand sinking lower, a finger tracing the waistband of her skirt.

What the heck was she supposed to say to that? *I have good genes? It's the alcohol talking? You're hot, too?* Laurel tried to smile. "Thank you."

A little nervous now, Laurel tried to put more space between her and Goatee Guy. She hadn't come clubbing to pick up men, but just to have fun. The only man she was interested in wouldn't be caught dead in this place, she was sure.

Looking around for Catherine to help her out, she studied the thorns decorating this guy's neck. Ouch—tattoo or not, they looked awfully grim and painful. She thought his name was Shane, but she could have totally misread that.

Her curiosity got the better of her, and since she was trapped in his arms, she figured she might as well ask the thought that went through her head every time she looked at all those tattoos. "Aren't you worried that you'll get a disease from the needle at a tattoo parlor? How do you know someone, the shop, is reputable?"

He must have caught enough of what she said, because he answered. "You watch them open the bag with a clean needle in it."

"Oh. So this is like art, then, to you?" She pointed

to a very intricate design of a woman having sex with Satan on his forearm.

He laughed and nodded, letting go of her long enough to flex his arm for her. When he did, Satan thrust his erection into the woman.

Oh, my. Laurel blinked. "Well, that's very clever."

Shane, or whomever he was, smiled again and pulled her even closer. "You're really pretty cute, you know that? Different."

Somehow that didn't feel flattering to Laurel. Not that she necessarily wanted to fit in here, but she didn't want to be an oddity, either.

Whatever answer she might have given never emerged, because the guy dropped her without warning and moved to the left. With a meaty forearm, he gave her a hefty shove behind him, sloshing her drink over the side of her glass and onto her white tank top, where it landed right smack on her nipple.

"Hey!" What was his problem? Sheesh. Peering around his shoulder, Laurel nearly dropped the darn drink. "Russ!"

Ohmygod, what was Russ doing there? Looking like he could rip Goatee Guy from limb to limb and feed him to Ferris.

Keeping a careful eye on Russ, the guy half-turned. "You know this guy?"

She nodded. He was her . . . something. Her sort of date partner, her affair participator, her orgasm generator, her . . . lover. Love. Laurel sighed. She was starting to really think that she was falling in love with Russ.

Cute, adorable, sexy, good, good, Russ.

And she was starting to think she was drunk.

Whatever transpired between Russ and Shane resulted in Shane shooting her a look of reluctance before walking away. Russ stared at her, looking her up and down, his nostrils doing a strange flare in and out, his shoulders all tense beneath his jacket.

"Hi," she said. "What a coincidence that you're here."

Then it occurred to her that it wasn't a coincidence at all since he'd known she was coming here, since she had told him in a cozy postcoital moment when he had asked her where she and Catherine were going. Then it occurred to her that he'd just walked up to her on the dance floor, interrupted, and sent some poor guy packing without even bothering to say hello to her first before he'd gone caveman.

And now he was taking her drink out of her hand. She tussled with him, hanging onto it.

"Give it to me, Laurel."

"No! I paid nine dollars for this." She planned to sip it for the next week or so. Or she had, before Baldie had drunk from it. But she wasn't going to tell Russ that.

"That schmuck you were dancing with dropped something in it. I saw him." Russ yanked harder and used his fingers to peel hers back from the stem of the glass.

Laurel could not believe he was doing this on the dance floor of this really cool club where she was trying very hard to blend in and not be a total geek for once in her life. "He did not! Now let go. I can't believe you showed up here. You don't even trust me to go out without getting myself into trouble."

He snorted. "With good reason, apparently. I find you drunk, wrapped up in another guy's arms, about to sip from a drink he drugged. Another hour you'd have been on your way to his apartment passed out, and tomorrow you'd have woken up naked after being gang-banged."

Her mouth dropped open. She felt an embarrassed, angry flush rip through her face. "You're overreacting. And I don't like you checking up on me like a two-year-old playing in the sandbox for the first time."

"Tough." Russ let her keep the drink, but took her hand and started to lead her off the dance floor.

Laurel dug her heels in. "Stop it, Russ. If I want to dance and get drunk, I most certainly can." She wasn't even sure why she was protesting so vehemently. She didn't really want to stay, and she hadn't been having all that great of a time.

Shane had been a little scary and Catherine was nowhere to be found. But she just loathed that Russ thought she was so dumb, so naive, so clueless that she needed a babysitter. It wasn't considerate, it was high-handed.

Russ didn't seem to have a problem with high-handed. He picked her up at the waist and flung her over his shoulder, her breasts colliding painfully with his collarbone. She squawked in protest as his hand closed over her butt to hold her in place as he strolled towards the door of the club. Half of the drink splattered over his shoulder, which she thought he deserved.

If it weren't for the clunky Mary Janes, she would have kicked him, but she didn't want to hurt him, despite his incredibly high jerk quotient. Nor did she want to make a bigger scene than they already were, given the dozen or so people gawking at them.

So she rested her elbows on his shoulders and tried to look dignified, like she was an Egyptian queen being carted around by her buff and very stupid manservant.

Shane gave her a little wave before the front door opened and the bright light of the streetlight and the cold air simultaneously hit her.

Jerry watched Russ sling Laurel onto his shoulder and physically haul her towards the front door. That was never a good thing.

"Oh my God!" Laurel's friend smacked his arm. "Did you just see that? That was totally repulsive, barbaric, inhumane. Aren't you going to go stop him?"

Jerry rolled his eyes. Maybe Russ had made a stupid move, but it didn't warrant that kind of reaction. The woman's indignation got on his nerves, along with the eighteen different shades of blond and black in her hair and the chain that stretched between her ear and nose like a freaking laundry line.

Man-hater. He knew her type. "I'll give them a few minutes to work things out before I head out after them."

He figured he had enough time to drink a beer at least. He flagged over one of the chicks wearing an apron and ordered a Bud.

"Work what out? The fact that he's an asshole?"

Alright, nobody called Evans an asshole but him. "He's looking out for her. She was obviously in over her head here."

The woman next to him gasped. "Laurel is a grown woman. She can handle herself. It's not his job to swoop in and save the day. That's so out-dated and archaic."

He groaned, thinking he should have skipped the Bud and gotten the hell out of here. "Oh, Christ, you're one of those feminist Nazis, aren't you?"

"And you're one of those small-minded men who's threatened by a woman's equality." Her jewelry rattled as she quivered in outrage.

Jerry gratefully accepted his beer from the waitress, not even caring that it cost six bucks. He needed it badly. Lately it seemed like every damn word out of his mouth was wrong. At least when it came to women.

He was thinking of giving women up for Lent. Except it was only the end of January. Maybe he'd start early this year.

"I embrace equality, alright? I think a couple should be partners and all that happy crap, but you can't tell me that there aren't just differences between men and women. And I'm not talking body parts."

"That's because we've culturally brainwashed our children to see only those differences."

Jerry looked towards the door with longing and downed half his beer. "Whatever, sister."

A black spike from her hair poked him in the eye as she got in his face. "Don't do that. Don't dismiss me."

Crazy broad. Jerry backed up. "I'm not dismissing you. I'm trying to avoid an argument neither of us can win. We're not going to change each other's minds, and we're not going to like each other." At least he was never going to like her. "Maybe I should go see if Russ needs backup out there."

He stood up, took one last sip, and patted his wallet to make sure it was intact.

"I'll come with you."

Jerry sighed. Great. Now he was stuck with Goth Girl for who knows how long. Evans owed him big-time for this. Freaking big-time.

Chapter 16

Russ walked down the street, Laurel still on his shoulder, and tried to clear his thoughts.

The cold air felt good after the stuffy, smoke-filled club, and he was so relieved he'd gotten Laurel out of there, his knees were trembling. When he had seen that scum drop that pill in her drink, he'd been filled with a fear he'd never known and a rage so intense that it had taken everything in him not to drop the guy like a rock on the dance floor.

Laurel might not be his for the long haul, but for now, while they were sleeping together, he was responsible for her, and the thought of the harm she might have come to had him sick to his stomach.

She punched his back, obviously not coming from the same place as him on this one. "Put me down! Russ! Where are you taking me?"

He didn't bother to answer, since she couldn't see his mouth from her current position. When he got to his car, he undid the locks and carefully set Laurel down on her feet.

She wobbled a little, still clutching that damn drink to her chest. Russ took it and unceremoniously dumped what was left on the pavement. She snatched the empty glass back.

"You had no right . . ." she started, poking him in the chest with a fingernail she'd painted a deep, bruised purple, so different from the pinks she usually favored.

"I had every right." He cut her off, impatient. "You promised, Laurel. I said no guys but me while we were seeing each other. No other guys."

Now why had he blurted that out? Jesus, was he actually jealous? He hadn't really thought that Laurel was interested in those attention-hungry nut jobs. But he hadn't wanted her to be. He hadn't wanted to even contemplate any other man's hands touching Laurel, and that guy had been doing just that. His hand had been on Laurel's waist, sliding across her bare skin.

"I wasn't . . ." Laurel seemed to lose some of her anger. "Okay, maybe it looked like I was. But I wasn't. They were just being nice to me."

Hah. "They were being nice because they wanted up this very short skirt you're wearing." Russ still couldn't believe the outfit he was seeing her in. It was so unlike her, so gratuitous, so goddamn sexy. He wanted to peel it all off her, one naughty piece at a time.

Laurel blushed. "Maybe. But that didn't give you the right to haul me out of there like that. I would have handled it."

Russ couldn't prevent a snort. "Oh, please, bunny. Just give me a goddamn break."

Her eyes flared again, and he realized he'd just

renewed her anger towards him. She opened her mouth, but he was distracted by the shiver she gave and the way her teeth chattered. She wasn't wearing a coat, and her stomach was exposed.

"Get in the car," he told her, opening the door and giving her a little push in the right direction.

"Arrghh!" she said, but she got in the car and slid past the steering wheel to the passenger side. "I'm only getting in this car because I'm cold. Otherwise, I'd tell you to stuff it."

Russ followed her. "Got it."

"I'm very angry with you," she said, setting the glass down on the dashboard and rubbing her arms.

He took off his jacket, handed it to her, then started the car to warm it up. "I know. And I'm very angry with you for putting yourself at risk."

"So we're both angry." She took the jacket and pulled it over the front of her like a blanket.

"Yep. Looks that way." He wasn't budging on this one. He wasn't wrong, damn it. Laurel didn't have the street smarts for clubbing with that crowd. That was the bottom line. Maybe it wasn't any of his business if she wanted to flirt with other guys. They had no promises to each other, and flirting and dancing wasn't the same as going home with some guy.

He had told Laurel it was just fun between them, that he wasn't looking for a relationship. And he had meant that. But he couldn't erase the feeling that he wanted to keep her locked in her room so no man but him could ever look at her.

He wasn't having his most rational moment here, he'd have to admit.

"So what do we do if we're both angry?" She glared at him, her hair in pigtails, brushing the collar of his jacket.

He knew what he wanted to do. "We say we're sorry and kiss and make up?"

This very good plan was greeted with a snort. "It's not that simple, Russ. There are trust issues at stake here."

"I trust you, Laurel. I don't trust anyone else when it comes to you." Like it or lump it, that was the way he felt.

The expression on her face softened, and her hands fell to her lap, his jacket sliding down. He thought maybe he had scored a point there by being honest. "Russ . . ." Her eyes pleaded with him, for what he didn't understand.

So he touched her pigtail, flipped it back and forth. Traced her lip, breathed in her scent. The car was getting warmer, the windows fogging up a little. Russ didn't want to take Laurel home angry, so he kissed her forehead, a coaxing, please-baby, kind of kiss.

She sighed. "That guy told me I was hot."

Every muscle in his body tensed up again. Damn, did she have to tell him these things?

He put his hand on her breast in that tight tank top, in a move that was nothing short of rude and possessive. But he couldn't help himself.

Laurel bowed into his touch and his gut clenched. She was so incredible.

"You *are* hot. You are very, very freaking hot. Why do you think I'm so jealous?"

"You were jealous?"

It wasn't every day he was going to admit that, so

he hoped she appreciated it. "Yes. I didn't want anyone else touching you."

"You don't have any reason to be jealous." Her hand closed over his.

"No?" He moved their hands together, massaged her breast, brushed her nipple.

The car suddenly felt as warm as the tropics.

"No."

"You're mine?"

Her breath hitched. "I'm yours."

Oh, damn. Russ pinched her nipple, and even as she cried out in pleasure, he was shoving that shirt out of the way, peeling down her bra. It amused him that she was wearing one—most women wearing a skin-tight tank top to a bar wouldn't have bothered with the bra—but that was Laurel.

Not as wild as she wanted to be. But he thought she was perfect. She was kind and sweet and well-mannered, yet when he peeled her clothes off, she was an enthusiastic and uninhibited lover.

Russ dropped his seat back so he could maneuver better. Laurel was clawing at him, digging in his hair and leaning towards him, the jacket bunching between her skirt and his rapidly growing erection.

He kissed her hard, wanting to show her how he felt, how he couldn't stand the thought of anyone being inside her but him. He didn't have the words or the romance or the ability to promise her anything more than now, but for now he wanted her, and he wanted it to be good.

But when her hand started tugging his shirt up, it occurred to him they were in a car. Parked next to a windowless building and an SUV, with a busted lamplight keeping them in the shadows, but it was still a parking lot.

"Laurel." He broke away, breathing hard, forcing his finger off her rosy nipple. "We shouldn't do this. You're drunk."

She gave him an indignant look, which was tough to pull off with the pigtails and the top shoved up to her shoulders, but she managed it. "I am not. I had one glass of wine and three sips of that drink. I had three glasses of wine at Christmas and I wasn't drunk."

"We should still head back to your place, though . . . shouldn't we?" There, he'd done his duty. The rest was up to her.

He was good to go in the car, but he wanted to make sure she had no problems with it.

"I don't want to wait that long," she said, and lifted her ass off the seat and shimmied her black tights down her legs.

Russ made an incoherent grunt as he watched her. He undid his zipper, pulled his cock out. Ready.

Laurel's eyes widened. "It's a lot easier for you to get ready than for me, isn't it?"

Since she was still bent over fooling with the buckles on her shoes, he had to agree. He also didn't feel like waiting. Condom quickly in place, he reached for her, hauled her clear over the gearshift, and settled her on his lap.

With the tights around her ankles, she was spread just fine. Enough for him to feel the creamy wetness of her inner thighs, enough to reach down between them and stroke her swollen folds. She must have pulled her panties off with those tights, the little vixen.

"Mmm, very nice. You been walking around that club all night wet, Laurel?"

She held onto his shoulders, her breasts teasingly close to his mouth. She gave a naughty little smile. "Nooo. Just since you picked me up and dragged me out of there."

Russ twitched, thrust his hips up a little, but she wiggled away down his thighs. "I thought you didn't like my hauling your ass away from your new friend with the tattoos."

"I didn't like it. But it was still very sexy." She ran her finger across his lip, then leaned forward and sucked it.

Everything in him wanted to shift an inch, push inside her hot opening, but Russ wanted Laurel to do it. To take that final step to join them in a way he knew would be explosive.

"Same as that outfit of yours," he told her when she pulled back. "I don't like it, but it's very sexy. Pigtails and all."

"What about the skirt?"

He glanced down. It was short enough that it barely covered her pubic hair now that the tights were gone, and with her warm behind sitting on his thighs, her delicious center pressing against the base of his cock, it was very arousing. He could feel everything, but it was all hidden behind that little swatch of plaid. "Actually, I like this skirt. You should wear it in private just for me. Often."

She gave a little laugh, a breathy laugh that ended in a gasp when he stroked his thumb across her clitoris.

Laurel wasn't drunk, she was sure of that, but she was a little tipsy. Enough to remove any doubts she might have had about having sex in a car. But even as she rocked against Russ, her nipples brushing the cotton of his shirt, she did think to ask, "If we get caught doing this, could you get in trouble?"

He was a cop, after all, engaging in public indecency.

Russ tugged her tank top down so her breasts were covered. "What are we doing? You're just sitting in my lap. Nothing wrong with that."

Good point.

Laurel shifted, joined them together, clamping her eyes closed as his hard penis filled her, stretched her. Sucking in air, clutching his shoulders, she forced her eyes open and her head back up. "I'm still just sitting in your lap. No big deal, right?"

Russ's lips weren't moving because his teeth were gritted, but she was pretty sure he said, "Right."

She moved a little, trying to figure out how to manage this. She lifted an inch or so, dropped back down. Her panty hose was restricting her movement, and the gearshift was in her way. Not to mention that she didn't have a lot of experience with lap rides in cars.

But it felt so good, just resting there, having him deep inside her, that she wasn't all that worried about it.

Only Russ didn't seem inclined to just sit there. He thrust up. Hard. The way he knew she liked it, and suddenly she was scrambling to keep up with him, take all of him, more, everything.

He kissed her, with lots of demanding tongue, his whiskers scraping her jaw and his teeth knocking hers.

She spread her legs farther, burrowed against him, smelled the sweet scent of Russ's sweat as he made love to her fully dressed. Laurel slapped her palm on the window for balance, bit her lip as she felt herself spiraling out of control, higher and higher, each thrust stroking her further into ecstasy until she was panting, desperate.

"Russ, please . . ." she didn't know what she was begging for, not when he was giving it all to her already, but she ached, she burned, she squirmed on him, until suddenly without warning her body let her fall.

There was a delightful, still pause as she hovered on the edge, then with a surge, she tipped over into exploding pleasure. Russ's hand tightened on her hips as she bucked back, and rode it on and on. And just when she thought it was over, Russ joined her, the expression on his face renewing her own aftershocks.

When she collapsed on his chest, Russ kissed her forehead. Then he pulled back, touched her arm. "You should sit on my lap more often."

Laurel pushed back sweat-dampened bangs and laughed. "I think we can work that out."

Jerry checked under the sheet.

Yep, he was still naked.

A glance next to him showed him he still wasn't alone, so he wasn't dreaming either, which had pretty much been his last hope.

Shit. He rubbed his eyes and tried not to move. Of all the dumb-ass things to do, this was about on the top of the list.

He'd slept with Goth Girl.

Not only had this pretty much screwed over any chance of Pam taking him back, he didn't even like the broad next to him, clutching a sheet over her half-naked breast. It was a nice breast, he'd admit that, but it was Goth Girl. Christ.

This was all Russ's fault. When he'd left the damn club, he'd found Russ gone. Disappeared. He'd been left with no ride. And when what's-her-name had offered to let him walk the block to her apartment and call a cab, for some perverse reason he had said yes.

A heated argument, a bottle of tequila, and here he was.

He didn't even remember her name, which pained his conscience. He wasn't a twenty-year-old horndog anymore, he didn't pull crap like this.

Not usually, anyway. He had the naked proof that he did, in fact, pull crap like this.

His head was pounding, and he swallowed, wondering when his tongue had doubled in size. She was still sleeping away there next to him, though she was moving a little. The sheet gave way, revealing both her breasts and a tattoo of a shamrock right on the perky part of one.

A memory of licking that clover popped into his head, and Jerry felt the unmistakable beginnings of a boner. *Stop it,* he commanded himself and his dick. It had been a mistake, one he would not be repeating.

Except it all came flooding back to him, in one carnal surge, that with this woman, sex had been incredible. Creative. Lengthy. Adventurous.

Oh, shit, no, no, no. He had to be wrong. The alcohol was fogging his memory.

The best sex in his life could not have been with this woman.

Her eyes opened slowly, focused, then popped

wide. She fumbled around on a black nightstand, shoved her glasses on her face. Then she screamed, yanking the sheet back over her breasts.

"What are you doing here?"

That was the million-dollar question.

"The same thing you are. Waking up after too much booze and a night of hot sex." No sense in walking around this thing delicately. Not when a glance around the room showed no sign of his clothes.

She clapped her hands over her ears. "No! Don't say that!"

Jerry started to enjoy himself a little more. At least he wasn't the only one mortified here. It was kind of fun to watch her groaning and losing that bitchy self-assurance she'd had in such abundance the night before. Her hair had gotten droopy, and with her makeup smeared off during the night, she almost looked normal. Pretty, even in a hard-ass, bitchy kind of way.

"If you don't want to talk about it, we don't have to." He threw the sheet back and gave her a full frontal. "Just help me find my clothes, and I'll call a cab or take the bus home."

She shrieked again. "Ohmygod! Cover up." She held her head in her hands and groaned. "I never do stuff like this—never. I don't sleep with strange men. I have safe sex while sober when I'm in a committed relationship, and I never, ever sleep with Neanderthal sexist pigs."

"That might explain why you're so uptight."

She whacked him with her pillow, which caused the sheet to fall and flash him her chest again. "Get out of my bed before I call the cops."

Jerry laughed, seriously enjoying himself now. "I

hate to break this to you, sister, but I'm a cop. Detective Jerry Anders. And you can call my buddies if you want, but I'm not exactly breaking the law here." He stood up, wincing a little as his tired muscles protested.

Crap, what had she done to him? He seemed to remember a whole standing-up thing while she held onto her dresser over there. "Don't worry. I'll leave as soon as I can find my pants." And he could shove his hard-on into them.

She seemed to pull herself together, wrapping the sheet around tightly before standing up. "Maybe they're in the other room. Just be gone when I get back." Wiggling and jumping a little, she went into the attached bathroom and slammed the door.

Jerry snorted. "Freak." But he didn't really mean it. As he searched for his clothes on the floor, he found four opened condom wrappers, a plastic cup, and a lime. A bad combination altogether.

His jeans were under the bed, and he tugged them on without his briefs, which were still missing. On the nightstand he discovered money, a lipstick, a driver's license, and a little empty handbag, like it had been dumped in a search for something. Probably the four condoms.

A quick glance at the driver's license at least gave him her name. Catherine Renney. Age twenty-eight.

Jerry tugged on his shoes without socks, then his sweatshirt, and decided it was time to get the hell out of there.

"I'm leaving," he called to the closed bathroom door with a painting of a headless blob hung on it. He tilted his head. Was that supposed to be a dog?

"Thanks for a lovely evening, Catherine. Maybe we can do this again sometime."

"Screw you," she said, muffled but unmistakable.

Jerry laughed. God, what a bitch. He kind of liked that about her.

Chapter 17

"So are you guys going to be all H and H all night, or can we go get something to eat?" Sean propped himself onto the door frame and eyed them in what Russ thought was part amusement, part disgust.

Russ let go of Laurel, who was trying to wiggle away from him, and leaned on the kitchen counter. "What the hell does H and H mean?"

"Hot and Heavy." Sean gave the sign for hot, then looked to Laurel. "How do I say heavy?"

She showed him, her cheeks pink with what Russ thought was both embarrassment and pleasure. In the three weeks since he and Laurel had been seeing each other, she and Sean had hit it off really well. He pestered her constantly to learn sign language, and not only did she seem to enjoy teaching him, she was having a positive effect on his homework habits. Sean's math teacher had actually sent Russ a note saying how pleased she was with Sean's improvement and questioning what had changed.

While Russ was glad to see Sean buckling down at school, he had to admit that he was annoyed that it was Laurel causing the change, not him.

Without her, he had no doubt Sean would still be pulling D's and F's, and it made him feel lousy.

But he was willing to get over it for the time being.

"Did you finish your homework?" Laurel asked Sean. "Let me see it. Then if you're done, we can go get something to eat." Only then did she think to look at him. "Okay, Russ?"

"Sure." Russ couldn't think of any reason to say no. But he felt a niggling of discomfort.

For three weeks, he had seen Laurel almost every day in some form or another. And that was because he wanted to. He enjoyed her company. He was very possibly falling in love with her. But he wasn't used to this boyfriend/girlfriend thing, and sometimes it felt too foreign, almost suffocating.

Most of the time it was great, and he felt great. They ate meals together, they hung out with Sean or just the two of them. They went to the movies, bowling, to listen to some live jazz music. There were plenty of steamy nights of teeth-grinding sex, though he hadn't spent the night since they'd romped in Candyland. But that was because of Sean, no other reason.

Everything was perfect. Yet something wasn't, and he wasn't sure what was off.

They had never intended to still be seeing each other after three weeks. They had never intended to be shopping together, eating meals together, redecorating his kitchen together. Yet they were, and neither of them was talking about it.

Russ didn't say anything because he didn't know what the hell to say. He didn't know where he wanted their relationship to go, wasn't sure if it could go anywhere.

Sean went to grab his homework, and Russ started

tidying up the wood samples he and Laurel had been looking at. Somehow or another, he couldn't quite pinpoint how it had happened, he had decided to remodel his kitchen, and Laurel was helping him pick out cabinets, a countertop, and vinyl flooring. Or more like she was picking it all out, and he was yeaying or naying each choice.

But the thing was, she could pick out all the Sandstone faux ceramic tile vinyl she wanted—he was still just Russ Evans, Cleveland cop, living in a modest house with modest aspirations. He didn't want much out of life. He just wanted a roof over his head, his brother to grow up into a responsible happy individual, and a shot at putting away some criminals.

He didn't think Laurel fit into that, or Laurel could be happy with that.

"What's the matter?" she asked, tucking her hair behind her ear.

Russ watched her, thought she was just unbelievably pretty. Thought he didn't deserve her. Thought he was stupid for questioning any time at all that he got to spend with her. He should just appreciate how wonderful things were right now and quit worrying like an old woman.

"Nothing. Absolutely nothing."

"Here." Catherine shoved a bag into Laurel's hands in the back room, where they had lockers for their purses and a table to eat lunch.

Cat darted a nervous glance over at John, a new hire, who was reading a magazine and smoking a cigarette, and pulled on her bangs.

"What's this?" Laurel shifted the plastic grocery

bag and frowned at Catherine, who was avoiding looking at her.

Catherine compulsively zipped and unzipped her black hooded sweatshirt and pushed her tongue ring up and out between her lips. "Just give it to Russ. He'll know what to do with it."

"What is it?" Laurel asked, bewildered. "Are there drugs in here or something, Cat?" She was joking, but still shook the bag, getting a little worried. Catherine was usually so calm and in control, but she looked downright rattled.

"It's not drugs! I don't even know where people get drugs from, Laurel. I'm a total virgin about stuff like that."

"Okay. So what is it?" She undid the tie, curiosity getting the best of her.

"Don't!" Cat clapped her hand on Laurel's wrist. John looked up at them curiously.

But Laurel shook off Cat's hand, not in the mood to be discreet. She'd seen a flash of something and wanted to confirm what it was. It was. "This is a pair of underwear! And socks."

She stared at Catherine in outrage. Why did Cat want to give Russ underwear? *Male* underwear.

"Shhh! Not so loud. God." Cat bit her nails and pulled her towards the doorway, away from John. "I'm sorry, Laurel, this is awful."

"Did you sleep with my . . . Russ?" Whatever he was. Laurel actually felt the floor tilt, her head spin, stomach heave.

"No! God, no, no, no, of course not. He would never, I would never . . ." Catherine grabbed her arms and shook them. "No, it's worse than that. I slept with Jerry."

"Jerry? Jerry Anders, Russ's partner?" Laurel repeated dumbly, sure she'd read that wrong. Cat and Jerry? That would be like stilettos and comfort. The two just didn't go together.

"Yes, Jerry. It was the night we went clubbing and Russ left Jerry without a ride. I offered for him to use my phone, and the next thing I know we've knocked back a bottle of tequila and I'm waking up naked. Next to *him.*" Catherine shuddered.

Laurel clapped her hand over her mouth, simultaneously horrified and wanting to laugh hysterically. "Oh my God."

"And when we woke up, I was so embarrassed, I just kind of threw him out. Then two days later I'm vacuuming and I find his underwear behind my wastebasket and his socks under the bed. I didn't know what to do with them. It seemed rude to throw them away, but I can't keep them. They're driving me crazy, mocking me, a visual reminder of my stupidity." Cat pushed up her glasses. "I mean, it's *underwear.* Yuck."

Laurel retied the bag. She didn't really want to be seeing Jerry's briefs, either. "So he hasn't called you or anything?"

"No, thank God for small favors. I'm sure he realized, just like I did, that it was a terrible mistake. One that I never want another living soul to know about."

"Jerry's really a very nice guy, Cat. I'm sure you can trust him to keep quiet." Not that Laurel really knew Jerry all that well. But Russ trusted Jerry with his life, and Laurel trusted Russ.

And she was incredibly relieved that Catherine wasn't returning underwear to Russ. Her heart had about stopped when she'd thought Russ had slept with another woman.

They didn't talk about the future, and Laurel took it one day at a time, but something she had always been sure of was that Russ wasn't seeing any other women. For a second, she'd doubted that, and it had felt pretty damn crummy.

"There's the doorbell. I have to go back out there."

Catherine turned and left the back room, only to reenter two seconds later. Laurel hadn't even had time to do more than open her locker when Cat tapped her shoulder, face leeched of color. "He's out there, Laurel! Right now. Russ and that other person are out in the store."

Since Catherine didn't look in a rush to assist them, Laurel figured it was up to her. She also didn't even have to ask who that other person was, and wasn't surprised to see Jerry bent over a Laffy Taffy display, shifting through it. Russ had a handful of Pixy Stix and was studying a candy ring.

She slowed down, a shiver of desire rolling through her. The memory of him licking that powder off her nipple had her breath hitching and her belly tightening. Then he looked at her, their eyes locked, and he grinned a slow, sensual smile that had her swallowing hard.

Russ twirled the candy ring idly, suggestively, making Laurel's cheeks burn. She didn't know what he could do with that, but clearly he had some ideas. He cocked his head and nodded to the candy, as if asking permission.

Laurel signed yes. Then turned her back on him, heart thumping, before she totally gave herself away with tight nipples and damp panties.

Which she already had, but Russ and all of Sweet Stuff didn't need to know that.

Laurel went up to Jerry and touched his arm. "Hi, Jerry."

"Hey, Laurel." He glanced at her in surprise. "Russ wanted to know if you can go to lunch, but I have to tell you if you say yes, you're stuck with me, too. I'm hungry."

"Sure, I'd like that." She pushed the plastic bag at him, unbelievably embarrassed to be doing this chore. "Catherine wanted me to give this to you."

"Really?" Jerry dropped the taffy in his hand and took the bag. "What is it?"

"I believe it's something you . . . left at her place." Laurel stumbled over the words and took a step back, hoping he wouldn't look inside.

He did. Jerry laughed, then shot her a grin. "Thanks. Is she here? Catherine? I'd like to talk to her."

"Well . . ." *Yes, but she's hiding from you,* didn't sound very appealing.

"She's hiding, huh?" Jerry looked amused.

"Well . . ."

"Guess she doesn't want to accept that a guy she can't stand could give her four orgasms."

Laurel's eyes widened. "Four?" she asked before she could stop herself. No wonder Catherine was a basket case. There was nothing like mind-blowing sex to, well, blow your mind.

"Yes. Four." No small amount of male pride flashed across Jerry's face.

His eyes shifted to her left, and Laurel felt and saw Catherine come up next to her. She must have spoken to Jerry, because he lost that sense of smugness and frowned. "Whatever, Goth Girl."

Cat whacked him on the arm and Laurel retreated to let them hash things out, hoping no blood would be spilled, and wondering who exactly would be left standing at the end.

She'd place her money on Catherine.

Russ was walking towards her. He said, "What do you want to do tonight?"

With a smile, she gave the sign for sex and laughed when Russ's eyes went huge.

"Laurel!" He looked around like she'd broadcast her suggestion over national television. Then he grabbed her hands and held them, like she couldn't be trusted not to talk dirty.

She laughed even harder, giving him a quick kiss. "You asked."

"I meant, maybe you want to see a movie or something."

She had known that, but it was much more fun to shock him.

And while he did look shocked, he also looked aroused, his brown eyes turning into that rich chocolate color that assured her he wanted her very badly.

"We could do the movie, too. I'll even let you pick which we do first."

His eyebrows shot up. "How nice of you."

"I'm a very nice girl." Who was feeling very naughty. Laurel wished like heck she weren't at work so she could show him.

Russ looked ready to ignore that fact and kiss her anyway, but then he pulled back and glanced over towards Cat and Jerry. "Maybe we should intervene before she pulls his gun on him."

Laurel turned in time to see Cat beating Jerry with the plastic bag of clothes. "Oh! Isn't that assaulting a police officer?" She liked Catherine and really didn't want to see her in jail.

Russ didn't look too worried, if the grin he was sporting was any indication. "I think this falls more under the heading of domestic violence. But what did he do to her that has her so pissed?"

"He gave her four orgasms."

"Well, that would make anybody mad."

Chapter 18

Russ pulled into Laurel's driveway, spare tooth-brush in his coat pocket. Sean had been in-vited to a hockey game and then to spend the night with one of his buddies from Lakewood, and Russ was free to stay overnight with Laurel as long as he was home by nine A.M.

He was looking forward to teasing Laurel, tak-ing her to the movies first, then pretending like they'd run out of time and he needed to go home. He wanted to see her disappointment, see how much she wanted him, before he confessed that he was free to touch her all night.

Russ stepped out of the car and into Laurel's driveway, heading towards the garage. Since it had snowed again that morning, he'd ring the kitchen doorbell so he wouldn't track slushy, dirty snow through the front rooms. She'd left the garage door up for him, and a glance inside showed it was nice and tidy, no evidence of a man in residence. No scattered tools or lawn mower parts.

When he'd asked Laurel once who took care of the maintenance on the house, she'd looked at him oddly and told him that they hired someone for anything that needed to be done. It was an old, big house, and he imagined that meant there was someone coming around fairly frequently. He'd already noticed they had the driveway plowed by a snow removal service.

It bothered him that Laurel came from such a different background. Because sometimes in the back of his mind he pictured making things permanent, and then he walked up this driveway, smelled the lake, saw the brickwork, and knew he was kidding himself. He couldn't ask her to leave this, come live in his matchbox house with his grubby kid brother.

He had a good job and a decent paycheck, a roof over his head that he owned, and a decent bit of money socked away. It was a good life, enough for him, but how could it ever be enough for Laurel?

Russ paused at the edge of the driveway, stared out into the backyard. There was a patio back there, a silent brick retreat, covered with snow and hulks that must be covered lawn furniture. He felt comfortable here in her yard, watching the dark, half-frozen water, just like he felt comfortable in her cozy little third floor room. The rest of the house didn't sit well with him. Laurel had given him a full tour a few weeks before and he'd spent the whole time with his hands in his pockets so he wouldn't knock a vase to the floor.

His breath floated in front of him in an ephemeral cloud, like cigarette smoke, and for a second, as the thought rolled through his head, he swore he could actually smell burning tobacco, the sweet odor wafting across the crisp night air. Russ turned with a frown, stepped onto the patio, looked toward the house.

He could see Laurel's kitchen window, the big one

that the table sat in front of. Idle curiosity turned into suspicion. His instincts, honed from nine years on the force, told him something was wrong here. He just didn't know what it was.

Laurel came into view, wearing those stretchy black pants he loved because they cupped her perky backside so nicely. She held a paperback book and a glass of milk, which she sipped from as she sat down.

Russ moved closer to the window, knowing she couldn't see him because of the interior light. It would be easy to just watch her like this, drinking in the sight of her innocent moves around her kitchen, while she trusted that she was alone with her thoughts and actions.

But Russ didn't need to watch her, because he had access to Laurel. They were dating, whether he wanted to call it that or not. She knew him, cared about him, trusted him. Let him inside her body.

But what if she didn't?

Russ scanned the yard, then looked down at the ground under the window. And confirmed what he'd already suspected.

Cigarette butts lay on the ground, an arrogant calling card, a total confidence that he would never be caught. Wet footprints and eleven butts. Eleven.

Russ went hot with rage. That motherfucker had been watching Laurel on and off long enough to smoke his way through eleven cigarettes.

Movement to the right caught his eye. He didn't hesitate, just started running toward the cluster of trees. Even though it was night, between the moon and the reflective snow he caught a glimpse of a man cutting through the trees to the intersecting street.

Dean. Russ knew that blond head and weak shoulders from the description some of his victims had supplied the department.

But he'd have known it was Dean anyway. He could feel it.

Russ ran harder, the cold air pushing into his lungs and making it hard to breathe, but he wanted this guy. He wanted him on the ground, under his fist, for having the goddamn nerve to watch Laurel, *his* Laurel.

It was hard to run through the snow—it tugged at his shoes and had him slipping—but he was in better shape than Dean and was gaining on him. But then he heard the beep of Dean's car lock and even as Russ burst through the trees and ran for the street, Dean was already pulling away in a blue Honda Civic.

"Shit!" Russ skidded to a stop and bent over to catch his breath. He could pretty much guarantee that car didn't belong to Dean, though he'd run the license plate number just to be sure.

He entertained the idea of getting his car and following Dean, but it would be too late to catch up to him. Plus he didn't like the idea of leaving Laurel home alone, unaware of what was going on.

As he jogged back through the woods, he pulled out his cell phone and called Anders.

"Hello?"

"Hey. I'm at Laurel's and I found Dean hanging out in her backyard. He's been stalking her, Jerry." Russ heard the tremors of anger in his voice and rubbed his forehead. He wanted to kill Dean. Slowly and methodically, and he needed to get a grip here.

"No shit? Well, that's a different MO for our boy."

"Yeah, and it pisses me off." Russ kicked a tree

branch out of the way as he made his way back into Laurel's backyard.

"No doubt."

"Listen, I got his plates. I want him picked up for trespassing." It was the only thing they had to hold over him, but it was something, an outlet for Russ's frustration.

"We can't do that, Evans. He'll get like a fifty dollar fine and they'll let him right out. And then he'll know we're on to him."

He really hated it when Jerry was being the rational one.

"We got nothing, buddy. We're going to have to let this one ride. We've got other cases to work on."

"He made it personal now, Jerry." Russ had wanted him before because Dean was a scum and because he'd taken women's trust and shattered it. But now he wanted him because he couldn't stand the idea of him watching Laurel with cold, calculating, soulless eyes.

"He doesn't know that. He doesn't know Laurel's your girlfriend. And when we started this whole thing, she wasn't."

Russ hovered in front of Laurel's garage, scanning left and right, making sure everything was normal. "I don't know what he knows and that scares me."

"Don't worry about it, man. He's just a con artist. A coward. He's never hurt any of these women."

"Well, he sure in the hell won't be hurting Laurel, because I'm not letting her out of my sight until he's behind bars. She's moving in with me."

Anders snorted. "Look, I gotta go, but you can tell me tomorrow how Laurel reacts to that suggestion."

When Russ pressed the OFF button on his phone, he wondered what the hell Anders was talking about. Laurel was a reasonable woman. She would see that he had her safety in mind, and if that meant living a week or two without creature comforts like a three-head shower, well, that was life.

And life was better than death, in his opinion.

Laurel gaped at Russ. Maybe she should ask him to write that down, because he could not be serious.

"Pack yourself a bag. You're moving in with me."

There. He'd said it again. Laurel clutched her glass of milk and worked her mouth, trying to force words out. So far nothing was emerging.

Russ was already heading for the stairs.

Laurel grabbed his arm before he could escape. "Why? And isn't that the sort of thing you usually *ask* a woman?"

He ran his hand through his hair. Russ looked worried, deep grooves in his forehead, his mouth grim and determined. She got the distinct feeling that this wasn't a romantic moment in her life.

"Dean has been sitting outside your kitchen window watching you."

No, that definitely wasn't romantic. "What? Tonight?" she asked in confusion, gaze darting to the big bay window. Nothing but darkness and shadows and her own image reflected back at her in the glass.

"Yes, tonight. And God only knows how many other times, the sick bastard."

Russ's jaw twitched and Laurel saw how carefully he was holding on to his rage. She slowly set the glass down, her heart leaping into her throat.

"How do you know?" The idea that anyone had been peering at her, seeing her as she moved around her own home, nauseated her. That it was Trevor Dean was actually something of a relief. She wasn't scared of a con artist whose methods revolved entirely around seduction.

She was safe from that, being immune to seduction from any man but Russ. But those nameless, faceless men who climbed in windows, tied women up, raped them—now that scared her.

"I saw him! I went around back because I smelled smoke and I found cigarette butts under your window, and there he was, running off through the woods like the miserable coward that he is."

"This is so strange. I've been trying to maintain the e-mails with him, you know, just in case we could set up another meeting, and he's been brushing me off."

"Because he doesn't need friendly e-mails—he's been sitting under your window!"

None of it made sense to Laurel, but she figured she didn't know anything about how the criminal mind worked. Maybe he had liked her coaxing e-mails, asking him if something was wrong when she didn't hear from him for days at a time. "Can you arrest him now?"

"Just for trespassing, which would have him out in a couple of hours." Russ connected his fist with the wall. "Damn, this makes me nuts! I'm teaching you self-defense tomorrow. But come on, let's go pack a bag for you and get Ferris. You got a crate for him?"

While it was amazing that Russ was willing to take her cat into his home, she hedged a little. It didn't seem like a particularly brilliant idea to just dash off to Russ's house for an indefinite period of time. There was the first and most difficult hurdle of length of stay. It could be months—or never—before the police had the evidence to convict Dean. Russ couldn't possibly expect her to live with him just shy of forever.

Which led her to the next problem. She wanted to live with Russ. She wanted to wake up next to him every day. She wanted to cook him breakfast, force Sean to eat something besides Twinkies and Doritos, and rip that brown carpet up with relish. She wanted Russ permanently, because she was in love with him.

But he wasn't asking her for any of that. He was asking her to stay with him for her own protection, because he clearly thought her incapable of having even a modicum of common sense.

"What about Sean? It's not appropriate for me to be living with you with him there."

Russ waved his hand. "We'll just explain to him why. Come on, he's almost fourteen. It's not like he hasn't figured out we're sleeping together."

"Him knowing it, and us flaunting it, are two different things."

He frowned, like she was being unreasonable. "You want me to sleep on the couch?"

Laurel spoke carefully, trying to articulate feelings she wasn't even entirely sure of. But she did know she didn't want to wiggle her way into Russ's home under the guise of protection, denting her self-assurance and independence, and sending their relationship into an awkward false future.

"No. I want to stay in my house, and you to stay in yours, and continue dating the way we have been."

"Is this because my house is a piece of crap? I know I'm not rich, and I don't have fancy furniture and everything, but that shouldn't matter when you're in danger."

Laurel was astonished. "Your house is not a piece of crap, and I don't need fancy furniture to be comfortable! I am not a pampered princess, Russ Evans, and I resent you suggesting that I am."

"You're used to nice things, just admit it."

That wasn't fair, and it hurt that he thought her so shallow. "Everyone likes nice things. But I work in a candy store—I am not, and never have been, a snob. And if you think so little of me, I can't even imagine why you want me to live with you."

"Oh, Jesus Christ." He rolled his eyes. "Don't do that. I don't think you're a snob. Hell, you're dating me, aren't you? I just think a girl like you can do better than what I have to offer, but I'm worried about you. I want you to be safe and out of danger, and that's why I want you to move in with me."

Not because he loved her. Not because he couldn't stand being away from her. Because he wanted to protect her. It should make her feel pleased, that he cared, that he was considerate, such a dedicated public servant.

Instead it just pissed her off and made her want to pinch him. "What danger? So some guy watches me outside the window . . . I'll have floodlights put in and I'll make sure the alarm is on all the time. I'll put blinds on the kitchen window. Dean wants my money, and he's not going to get it. He's not going to run me out of my house, either."

"Don't be insane. You can't protect yourself!" Russ shot his hand out, tossed it around indignantly. "This house is huge! And it's not like Ferris could protect you from anything other than overeating. Use your head here, Laurel. The guy could be in the house and you wouldn't even know because you can't hear him!"

Laurel was so stunned she didn't have any retort but the tears that rose into her eyes before she could prevent them. Russ had never treated her deafness like a disability, and to have him bring it up now, like it was, just to force her to see his opinion, sliced pain through her entire body and had her turning away, clutching her mouth.

Russ saw Laurel suck in her breath and recoil backward from him like he'd hit her, tears popping out and silently rolling down her cheeks.

Damn it. His gut twisted, and panic, regret, fear rose up in his throat. He reached for her. "Laurel. I didn't mean that the way it sounded . . . I just meant, practically speaking, it's harder to protect yourself when you can't hear."

"I know what you meant."

He waited for her to yell, scream, rant, and rave at him that he was an insensitive bore, that he didn't know jack shit about what she wanted, but she didn't. Laurel just sort of crumpled in, shoulders hunched over, arms wrapped protectively around her middle, hair falling but not covering sad, sad eyes.

Russ hadn't felt this terrible since he'd stood at his parents' graves while the minister had spoken meaningless words of comfort.

"Laurel, baby, I just want you safe." He took her hand, limp and unresponsive, and beat back the panic. This was no big deal. He hadn't meant anything other than the obvious truth. She couldn't hear. He didn't mean that was a problem for him, no matter how it had sounded. "Please tell me you understand that."

"I understand." She locked eyes with him, cheeks pale, lips trembling. "What you don't understand,

Russ, is that you can't use my deafness to control me."

"What are you talking about?" He brushed her hair back, clutched her hand a little tighter. He didn't want to control her, Jesus. That was Dean's specialty, controlling women. He just didn't want to lose her, to Dean or to his own stupidity. "How am I trying to control you?"

"You assume you know what's best for me. People have been doing that my whole life, and I've let them, because the truth is, I've never really understood what I wanted or where I belong."

Laurel traced his jaw, ran her delicate fingers over his scratchy chin. "You know who you are, where you were meant to be. But me, I've spent my whole life trying to decide if I align myself with the speaking deaf and, by default, the hearing world, or if my deafness defines everything about me and I immerse myself in ASL and deaf culture. Most of the time I've chosen to sit on the fence, scrambling between both, always an outsider, never fitting in."

"You're right, I don't understand that. How can I?" Russ stroked her back, understanding one thing only. He loved this woman. Her generous soul and sweet smile, and everything that made her who she was.

"My parents never agreed on how to educate me, you know, and I wound up getting a little of everything. I was a constant source of contention and worry between them. So I just tried to do whatever I thought would please them, so that no one would see me as a problem. I don't see being deaf as a problem, and I didn't want them, or now you, to feel that way."

Russ gripped her harder. "No, Laurel, I've never

felt that way." What he felt was deep respect for her and a love so strong, so unexpected, that he felt propelled into desperation. "When I look at you, it's not a problem I see, it's a beautiful, amazing, intelligent woman who ties my guts up in knots. And all I know is that if you belong anywhere, it's right here, right now, with me."

Laurel's tears had dried in splotchy little streaks on her smooth skin, and he rubbed them away with his lips. She shivered. "Historically, there was a huge percentage of deaf people on Martha's Vineyard—a hereditary deafness—and the people there were completely integrated into society because everyone on the island, deaf and hearing, spoke sign language." Laurel gave a heartfelt sigh. "To me, that sounds like heaven on earth."

Her longing made him ache. He'd never seen this side of her, the one that struggled to communicate. He always saw Laurel as confident, happy, modest. "If I'm doing something wrong, tell me, and I'll fix it, Laurel. I've never been very good at relationships. I can't give you heaven on earth, but I can damn well try."

She studied him, cupped his cheek. "You're a good man, you really are. And what I want you to do is let me make my own choices, whether they're mistakes or not."

"Okay." Just don't leave, just don't walk away, not when he was feeling like she was the best thing to ever happen to him.

"This house . . ." Laurel let go, moved away from him, swiping at her cheeks. "It may belong to me, but it's not mine. Do you understand what I mean?"

Even though Russ was starting to think she was talking in code just to try and trip him up, he did know what she meant. The house wasn't Laurel.

She didn't fit in there any more than she did in his fixer-upper. "You just haven't found your place yet, have you, bunny? Your job, your mother, your house . . . it's all just a holding pattern, isn't it?"

"That's exactly right."

Russ wanted to move to her, take her in his arms, but he was afraid to do the wrong thing, afraid to touch and have her break. He knew his place. It was in his house, at the station, out on the street. He didn't know his place here with Laurel, whether he was wanted or not.

Fortunately, she took the decision away from him. In a rush, she closed the gap between them and threw her arms around his neck.

Russ closed his eyes, closed his arms around her, squeezed her hard against him, not wanting to let go. "I'm sorry," he whispered in her ear, for all the stupid things he'd done in the past, and all the mistakes he was going to make in the future.

Laurel shivered, her hands rushing over his back, around to his waistband. She popped the snap on his jeans. "Russ, make love to me. Please."

He could do that.

Chapter 19

"I'm going to make love to you, Laurel. But not in here." Russ's cop face slipped back on, while his thumb jerked to her window.

Laurel didn't want Trevor Dean pulled back into this moment between them. She just wanted to touch and be touched, lose herself in the desire, the comfort, the feeling of right that overcame her when she was with Russ. Nothing artificial or false or greedy belonged anywhere near them when she had stripped her emotions raw in front of Russ, and he had come the closest to confessing his feelings she imagined he was ever going to get.

Without a word, she took his hand, started up the stairs. At the landing he tugged away, and she turned back to find him stripping off his shirt, jaw tense, eyes low enough to show her he had been watching her backside while she ascended in front of him. The shirt fell to the floor as he took her head, hands digging through her hair, and kissed her.

Laurel loved the way Russ kissed, with all of his focus on her mouth, his tongue questing and lips possessive, like he wanted to absorb all of her.

There was desire in that kiss, passion and need, and urgency, but there was also a new level of understanding, intimacy, in the embrace.

Neither of them could claim they weren't having a relationship now, not after the things they'd said and the way they touched.

When she pulled back, Laurel sent her sweater sailing down the stairs with Russ's shirt. He didn't smile or laugh, but just leaned forward, pressed a kiss on her abdomen, trailed his tongue up to the underside of her breast. It took everything she had to keep walking up that second flight of stairs, to turn her back to him when she knew he was watching her.

But they needed to get to the bed and the condoms so she didn't wind up with rug burns—and pregnant.

Another minute, and that might be a very real possibility.

Russ's hands cupped her backside, walking with her, sending her off balance and her body burning. He had big hands, blunt hands, that were clumsy with buttons and hopeless with chopsticks, but when they were touching her, they were perfect, skilled, possessive.

When they stopped in front of her room, Russ stepped out of his shoes, tore down his jeans. Waited. Laurel did the same with hers, wiggling and holding onto the wall, the inside of her chest doing a strange imitation of a helium balloon. It felt inflated and frightened and too full not to burst.

She ripped her socks off, leaving them in little inside-out bundles on her jeans, and reached for his hand again. Leading him to the bed, she walked carefully across the cold floor, aware that this was the first time she had taken the lead, the first time she had initiated sex. He was allowing her to lead him, and he sat on the edge of her bed when she waved him down.

Laurel wanted this, wanted him, wanted to have this one night where he saw and felt everything that she was feeling. To know that she was in love with him.

She went down on her knees in front of the bed. Russ's eyes closed, his mouth drooped.

Peeling his briefs off, Laurel studied his erection, the thick smooth shaft with the cluster of dark hair behind. He had muscular thighs, with an interesting little mole in the dimple between his hip and thigh, and she dusted a kiss on the spot, brushing her cheek across his penis.

Russ's hands were on the bed, and she was glad he didn't take her head, thrust her forward. She wanted to do this all on her own. One slow stroke at a time.

Gripping the base of him, she closed her mouth over the hot flesh, licking the little bead of clear fluid hovering at the tip. He tasted so good, and if intimacy had a flavor, this would be it.

In the dark room, lacking in any light but the hint of the moonlight struggling through the cracks of her shutters, Laurel loved Russ with her mouth and her hands, going down over and over again, until his penis was slick and her breathing was desperate. Until her nipples brushed the duvet on the bed painfully, and her eyes rolled shut. Until he was under her armpits, hauling her up the length of his body to join her moist mouth with his eager one.

Russ handed her a condom, lying on his back, allowing her to run the show. Even though she had trouble opening it, and took a break to undo her bra and shove down her panties, she never hesitated. The shadows fell across his face, obscuring his eyes, but she could feel them on her, and she lifted her hips a little to roll the condom on, to squeeze him and feel him pulse with pleasure.

Then Laurel took him and joined them together.

Breasts flat against his chest, hands on either side of his head, she moved, rocking herself onto him, while he lay still, letting her take him. Russ's hand splayed across her ass, teasing little strokes up and down between her cheeks, his mouth hovering against hers. Not kissing, just holding, just breathing together, just being.

He started to lift his hips, to grind them closer together, to press her clitoris more tightly against his hot flesh, and Laurel let an orgasm roll over her like a warm ocean wave, a bold, tender shattering of her body over his, her heart and soul in her gasping little moans.

Russ held her to him, still, then pushed deep, jerking her a little as he came, nipping at her lip, hot breath rushing past her ear.

Laurel lay on his chest, slick with sweat, closed her eyes, and rested her cheek on his shoulder. She could hear his heart pounding violently in his chest, feel his fingers idly brushing across her back.

Then he was forming letters again, one at a time on her back, while Laurel clung to him, full of heart and body, still joined to him intimately. Wanting his words, needing them, moved profoundly by them.

I love you.

One letter after the other, until they were all there, telling her everything she needed to know here in the dark.

Russ could feel Laurel tensing on him, her breath quivering, fingers twitching along his side. Her weight was a pleasant blanket, keeping him warm, and he'd had to tell her how he felt. He had to let her know that no matter what happened outside of this room, he loved her. With his whole heart, in all the ways he was capable of.

For as long as she would let him.

Her head lifted off of his chest. In the dark he couldn't see much beyond the pale gleam of her chin, the soft spot of color that was her bottom lip.

But when she said, "I love you, too," in that silent, soundless way she had of speaking sometimes, he heard it with total clarity, and never had anything sounded so beautiful.

It wasn't the light filtering through the shutters that woke Russ up. Or Ferris climbing onto his chest.

It was a woman's voice, speaking in a shrill urgent tone that he knew didn't belong to Laurel, even when he couldn't explain in his sleep-fogged brain why he'd be hearing any other woman's voice.

He forced his eyes open.

And saw a middle-aged woman standing in the open doorway holding his jeans and making a strangling, choking noise like a bad actress after she's taken a fake bullet.

This must be Mrs. Wilkins, Laurel's mother.

With incredibly bad timing.

Russ turned, checked on Laurel. She was sleeping blissfully unaware, her hair scraggly, and a pillow dent on her left cheek. That wasn't the only cheek showing, unfortunately. Laurel's bare butt had popped out of the side of the sheet, and while it was damn adorable, it probably wasn't thrilling her mother the way it did him.

"Mrs. Wilkins?" he asked, when it looked obvious the poor woman couldn't think of a word to say.

"Yes." Laurel's mother fluttered her hand to her throat, displaying a big old rock on her ring finger and some perfectly done fingernails. "And you would be?"

She didn't sound angry, but more like she might faint. Yet she clung to politeness valiantly, and Russ appreciated the awkwardness of both their positions. Especially his, since he was naked. "I'm Russ Evans, ma'am, a friend of Laurel's."

Slight understatement, since Laurel was mooning her mother. He was tempted to twitch the sheet over her, but was afraid to draw more attention on the off chance her mother hadn't actually noticed yet.

"These must be yours, then." Mrs. Wilkins held up the jeans and cleared her throat. "I'll just let you get back to things . . . I had no idea Laurel had a guest. I guess I should have called and let her know I was coming home early."

She folded his pants and set them on the easy chair with the floral print, on top of a stack of books. Then she left the room without a backward glance, closing the door softly.

"Jesus." Russ rubbed his eyes. He hadn't been caught by anyone's mother since high school. He debated whether or not to wake Laurel, and decided to let her alone for now.

He wanted to talk to her mother about the security of the house and the importance of not letting anyone in, even for maintenance, unless they were familiar with him.

Five minutes later, Russ called to Ferris, who

leaped off the couch eagerly, and started down the stairs. He'd put Ferris through his moves later, though given the way the cat was meowing and swatting at Russ's leg, he didn't like being put off. Russ and Ferris had developed a little routine, a sort of obstacle course where they raced down the long hallways, and Ferris leaped between furniture trying to catch the string that Russ would leave trailing out of his back pocket.

It wasn't Pilates, but at least he had the cat moving. And in the process, they were starting to grudgingly respect each other. He hadn't planned to play around this morning, in case Laurel woke up before he'd had a chance to talk to her mother, but he figured what the heck.

"Alright, come here, boy." He slapped his leg and whistled, letting Ferris know he was ready. Then he slowly let the string out of his pocket, dodging left and right so when Ferris reached he missed it every time.

Russ laughed. "Gotta be quicker than that." Then he ran down the hall, Ferris on his heels, leaping for the string.

He skidded to a stop, watching Ferris scramble to catch himself on the hardwood floor, his back claws making an offensive scraping sound. Russ winced. Probably not a good thing. He let Ferris have a swat and a chew on the string, then went down the stairs in a jog, Ferris doing a little back and forth leap on the banisters that would have been graceful if it weren't for his old man gut dangling over the rails.

They hit the ground floor running and turned the corner, nearly plowing into Laurel's mother.

"Good God, what are you doing?" she asked.

Russ drew up short. "We're just playing around."

He let his hand go slack and Ferris took advantage of the opportunity to pounce on the string.

"It sounded like a herd of elephants racing down the stairs." Mrs. Wilkins let out a small laugh, fiddling with her diamond earring.

"Sorry." Yeah, he was one classy guy alright. Herd of elephants or Russ Evans. One and the same.

"That's okay. I'm just not used to so much *activity* in the house." She looked down curiously. "And I've never seen Ferris move that fast in my life. What did you do to him? Promise him a lifetime supply of tuna?"

Russ pulled the string up so Ferris would leap a foot in the air and laughed. "Nah. We've just decided our relationship had to go in a different direction than his with Laurel. I won't take any cat whining from him, and he's found out he likes to play."

"Has he lost weight?" Mrs. Wilkins asked in amazement, leaning over to study the cat more closely.

"Could be. We've been running a lot."

"Well." She laughed again, a nervous, but amused sound. "Come on in the kitchen. Would you like some coffee?"

Russ remembered his Starbucks experience. "Is it black, or is there creamy stuff on top?" He followed her into the kitchen.

"Black. It's the only way to start the day."

Alright. Score a point for Mrs. Wilkins. "I'd love one."

Laurel's mother was wearing trim black pants and a soft gray sweater. She was an attractive woman, still blonde, with chin-length hair, and Russ imagined Laurel would look fairly similar in thirty years.

"Look," he said as she pulled two cinnamon brown mugs down from a cabinet. "I'm sorry about the way you found us. It wasn't meant to be disrespectful, we just didn't know you were coming home."

She gave a choked laugh. "Well, that's obvious. What did you say your name was again? I was a little too caught off guard to catch it."

"Russ. Detective Russ Evans, of the Cleveland Police."

Lips pursed, she poured the coffee. He couldn't tell what she was thinking, and he'd had a large amount of experience observing people on the job.

She handed him a mug with a sudden smile. "Nice to meet you, Russ. I'm Beverly Wilkins. You can call me Bev, given that I've seen you naked."

Russ laughed, but it was anguished. Damn, was he blushing? And he hadn't been totally naked. That sheet had been over him. Hadn't it? At least she was taking this whole thing pretty well. It wasn't every day you walked in on your daughter like that.

"Don't be embarrassed, though Lord knows I am. But Laurel is an adult. If anything, I'm more surprised than upset. I've always wanted Laurel to get out and date a little, but she never seemed interested. I guess I was wrong."

Russ sucked down half the cup of coffee, hoping for inspiration on what the hell to say. He leaned against the counter.

Bev did likewise, on the other side of the room. "How did you meet Laurel, if you don't mind my asking? Clearly you've been dating a while since you're such good friends with Ferris."

Carefully, so he wouldn't alarm her, he gave the abridged version of the Dean case and where Laurel fit in.

It didn't work. Bev drained of all color and clutched the coffee mug until her fingers turned white. "Oh, dear. Laurel's very trusting, you know."

"Don't worry, we've got it all under control." Not really, but he was trying. And he wouldn't let anyone hurt Laurel, that he could promise. "I won't let him touch her, you have my word."

He didn't tell her about Dean hanging around under the window. He figured that was Laurel's right, so he wouldn't scare her mother any more than he already had.

Bev cocked her head. "How serious are you about my daughter?"

The question made him uncomfortable, but he supposed if circumstances were reversed, he'd be asking the same thing. "Very."

Bev fought the urge to turn a cartwheel across her kitchen. Not that she really knew enough about this man to judge if he was right for Laurel or not, but just the fact that her daughter was dating had her thrilled.

That she had picked a police officer was even better. Bev couldn't see Laurel with some starched-up businessman. She needed a down-to-earth guy. A manly man. This one certainly was that, and then some. Bev set her coffee down and tried to banish the vision of his muscular chest from her head, aware it was a little inappropriate to ogle her daughter's boyfriend. Up until now, she'd never had the chance.

And the man was a dish, no doubt about that. Laurel was clearly her mother's daughter—she had darn good taste.

"We've been seeing each other for almost a month. I, uh, don't usually spend the night."

The little cutie was actually blushing. Bev hid her grin behind her coffee.

"I've got a thirteen-year-old brother that I have custody of. I need to be home for him."

Cute, law-abiding, *and* responsible. Better and better.

She didn't like the idea of Laurel fooling around on the Internet and chatting with strange men, but nothing heinous had happened. She hadn't actually met the con artist, or fallen victim to his con, and along the way, she'd met Officer Orgasm here.

"Well, my sister is fully recovered from her hip replacement, so I'm home permanently. I guess we'll just have to all be adults and use a little discretion."

He just nodded. "Listen, will you talk to Laurel about being safe at home and online? I know she's a grown woman, but I just want her reminded not to open the door to strangers, or give out personal information online. To use the alarm system on the house and to use basic common sense."

Bev wondered if there was something he wasn't telling her, but she just nodded. "Oh, I can tell her, but she doesn't listen. She thinks I'm cynical. But Laurel isn't stupid. She won't be walking alone at midnight down a dark alley. But in my mind, she trusts people in reverse. I don't trust someone until they've earned it. Laurel trusts until they give her a reason not to."

Over the years her daughter had given her an entire head full of gray hairs that she now had dyed every four weeks. Bev knew in her heart that Laurel was a better person than she was, and when she looked at her daughter, she was filled with pride at the generous, intelligent woman she had become. But it had worried the color right out of the hair on Bev's head.

Russ stared into his mug. "That's part of what makes Laurel so special."

"I know. But sometimes I think that Laurel is the way she is because she only sees what people say, she doesn't hear it. She's never once had to listen to the cruelty of ugly, hateful words."

"Cruelty can be seen and felt just as easily as it can be heard. Laurel is the way she is because you raised her well and because she's just intrinsically a good person. One of the best I've ever met. And I've met a lot of people."

Bev watched his face, lean and chiseled, tight with emotion, and she knew, as clear as her Waterford crystal vase. He was in love with her daughter.

I'll be damned, she thought. She needed to go away more often.

"Russ, is that coffee I smell? You should have woken me up." Laurel plodded into the kitchen with sleepy eyes, wearing her robe and not much else.

And screamed.

Chapter 20

"Oh my God! Mom!" Laurel gaped in horror at her mother, who was sipping her coffee calmly like it was any other day of the week and she hadn't popped up out of the blue.

And like she wasn't drinking coffee with the man Laurel was sleeping with, who looked very casual and comfortable holding up that counter, his shirt rumpled and his hair mussed. Laurel wondered who had found who first, and squeezed her robe shut at the neck as a raging blush soared up her neck and cheeks.

They had left a trail of clothes from the first floor to the third the night before. Oh, help. There was no way her mother hadn't seen that.

"Good morning, Laurel. Sorry to startle you. Aunt Susan is doing fabulous with her recovery, so I came home early."

Her mother crossed the kitchen and bussed her on the cheek. Laurel kissed her back automatically. "How wonderful. I'm glad Aunt Susan is feeling so much better."

But a goddamn phone call would have been nice.

"Have you met Russ?" Of course she had. They were chatting each other up over coffee.

"Yes. I like what I see so far." She smiled. "And I've seen quite a bit."

What did that mean? Laurel felt a little sick.

Russ moved to her side. "Are you okay, honey?"

No. Duh. She was dying of mortification, and his tossing out endearments in front of her mother was not helping. Neither was that kiss he plopped on the top of her head.

"I'm fine. I just need something to drink." And some clothes.

He poured her some coffee into his used mug and handed it to her. Laurel took a tiny sip. Russ squeezed her hand. "I've got to go. I need to get home before Sean does."

"Of course." She nodded, grateful for his broad shoulders shielding her from her mother's curious eyes.

"Pick you up at eight?"

She hesitated, then wasn't sure why. The naked cat was already out of the bag. Her mother obviously knew they were dating. "Sure."

"Don't talk to anyone you don't know. Don't go anywhere alone."

"And don't take candy from strangers. Got it." She rolled her eyes at him.

"I'm serious." Russ shook her hand a little. "This is serious."

"I know." But if he weren't so cute, he'd just be annoying.

Then he further ruined her ability to be irritated with him by looking very earnest and saying, "I love you."

Her heart flipped in her chest like a beached fish. "I love you, too."

Then he was gone, and she was left staring at her mother.

Her mother had gotten herself a melon slice and was sitting at the table eating and flipping through *Better Homes and Gardens.* "Well," she said, looking up so Laurel could see her, "you've been busy while I was gone."

Laurel sank into the chair across from her and twisted her hair into a bun. "Are you mad at me?"

"Mad at you?" Her mother looked genuinely astonished. "For what?"

"For . . ." Sleeping with Russ, that's what for.

"Laurel Anne. You are an adult. I think it's fantastic that you're dating someone."

Laurel was confused. "I thought you didn't like me dating. You were always discouraging me when I showed an interest in a guy."

"I didn't like you bringing home the freeloading losers you did in high school. They were stray dogs, Laurel, that you wanted to fix and improve. But they were just losers, plain and simple. I have no problem with you dating men who are gainfully employed and treat you well. In fact, I embrace that."

Oh, now she found that out. After six years of celibacy. Not that it would have changed anything. Laurel still hadn't possessed the courage to seek out men on her own. Not until now, when boredom and loneliness had finally compelled her to chat with Russ, who wasn't really Russ.

"Oh."

"I'm sorry if you thought I didn't want you to date. I just wanted you to choose well. But really, I want you happy, baby, and if Russ Evans makes you happy, then I'm happy." Her mother put down her fork. "You know, Laurel, I made a lot of mistakes raising you."

"No, you didn't!" Laurel was shocked and plunked her mug down on the table, sloshing coffee over the sides.

"Yes, I did. See, I was terrified that I would fail you when we found out you had lost the majority of your hearing. And being frightened and confused, it was easy for me to just listen to what the medical professionals were telling us to do. They told me that in order for you to be successful, we had to teach you to speak. That was the prevailing opinion at the time, and I thought they were experts so they knew what was best."

Laurel nodded. She understood that.

"They told us ASL would interfere with your learning English, and since I wasn't thrilled about being unable to communicate with my own child if you didn't learn to speak, I went along with it all. But I never stopped doubting and worrying and second-guessing, and had you start learning ASL at ten, plus maintain your speech lessons and keep you mainstreamed in school. I think we just confused the issue altogether. And all of that tension, fear on my part, worked its way into you. I made you cautious and shy when you didn't need to be."

The regret on her mother's face made her heart ache. "Mom, you did a wonderful job raising me with love and a solid set of values. If I've been cautious, that's my problem, not yours. And I'm happy, even if I've been feeling a little restless. I want something more for my life, but I'm not sure what that is." She squeezed her mom's hand. "I just know I'm going to get it, whatever it might be."

Her mother clasped her other hand over Lau-

rel's. "I know you will, too. I am so proud of you
and your father would have been as well."

Russ was picking her up in five minutes, but Laurel hadn't checked her e-mail in three days. When
she clicked her mailbox, she had seventeen e-mails,
mostly spam.

She ignored the offer to increase her manhood,
to funnel millions of dollars in misappropriated
funds from the Nigerian government, and to work
from home. Deleting them all, she paused a second at the one that boasted, *Want to be hung like a
horse?*

Laurel winced. Did any man really think a woman
wanted a horse-hung lover? No, thanks.

She had a chatty e-mail from Michelle talking
about her baby and one from Catherine.

Laurel clicked on the one from Cat and nearly
fell off her chair.

I slept with Jerry again. And I was sober.

That's all it said, though Laurel guessed that
pretty much covered it. Good God.

She could not understand what they saw in each
other. They were complete and total opposites and
seemed to have a grating effect on each other. But
clearly they had a mutually agreed upon lust.

She was still trying to recover, eager to tell Russ
and get a better lowdown on Jerry so she knew
what her friend was dealing with, when she saw an
e-mail at the bottom of her box. It was a failed delivery notice.

A quick click showed it was her last message to

Dean. It had bounced back, stating the account did not exist.

Laurel chewed her fingernail. That account had existed until three days ago. She'd been e-mailing Dean there for almost three months. Maybe it was a glitch with the server.

She resent the message, checked her hair in the mirror over her dresser, and put on some lip gloss. By the time she glanced back at her screen, her message had already bounced back.

So Dean had really closed that account. Interesting.

A week ago Russ might have shrugged, knowing the case was slipping away anyway, but Laurel knew he'd be very interested to hear this now. Since he had caught Dean under her kitchen window watching her.

She shivered. That really was an awful thought, despite what she had told Russ. The night before, with him snuggled up beside her, she had felt completely safe, but now, with just her and her mother, she had to admit it was a little disturbing.

But if Dean was canceling accounts, maybe he was skipping town, moving to another area to pick a new victim.

Or maybe the person Russ had seen in the backyard wasn't even Dean. That was probably the worst thought of all. At least with Dean, she knew what and who he was. A petty con artist, not a violent rapist.

Shoving the fear away resolutely, she bent over her desk to type a reply to Cat, intending to use lots of exclamation points, when her connection went out.

Darn it. She hated when it did that without warning. She tried to reconnect and watched for several minutes as the modem dialed but never established a connection. Frustrated, she ran her antivirus software to see if a virus was gumming up the works, then vowed to chew the phone company out on Monday. They were notorious for dropping connections, but if she wanted high-speed Internet access, she was stuck using them.

She'd ask Catherine to call them for her, since Cat was better at demanding her rights than Laurel's mom was, and because she actually understood the way the computer worked.

But then her light flashed on her desk, letting her know Russ had arrived, and she shoved her annoyance aside, to deal with when the weekend was over.

Right now she had a cute cop she wanted to kiss.

"Five."

"Five?" Laurel looked at Catherine in disbelief. "Five? In one day?" Two or three, okay, she was fine with that—in fact, aimed for that herself—but five? She would be a babbling, boneless mass if Russ ripped five orgasms from her in one night.

Catherine didn't look entirely thrilled about the whole thing, either.

Sucking a Dum Dum vigorously, Cat nodded and leaned back against the counter, then popped the sucker out. "It's insane, isn't it? That I would find my sexual soul mate with a total cretin? What have I done wrong? Clearly I have done something, because this is some butt-kicking bad karma."

Laurel thought hormones were the more likely culprit than karma, but she just glanced around the store to make sure there were no witnesses to this conversation. Since it was two o'clock in the afternoon, they weren't busy.

"How did this happen anyway? Last week you were beating him with a bag full of his underwear."

"That night he just showed up at my apartment. He rang the bell, I made the mistake of letting him in, and then suddenly I'm coming on the couch." Catherine shook her head, which was now dyed completely black. "I don't understand this. It's like I don't even know myself. I'm a total hypocrite!"

The sucker waved back and forth violently. Laurel actually was starting to find the whole thing funny, despite Cat's dramatics. "How is sleeping with Jerry hypocrisy?"

"Men like him are small-minded and sexist. I can't stand his tacky jokes, yet I can't seem to keep my hands off of him."

John came around the corner and Catherine waved to him with the shiny ball at the end of the Dum Dum stick. "If I were normal, and not a disgusting, horny hypocrite, I would be attracted to John. Which I'm not."

John looked amused. "Not even a little?"

"No." Cat shrugged. "Sorry."

"That's okay. I'm not attracted to you, either." His lips pursed in a whistle as he bent over the counter looking for something.

"But I'm not attracted to Jerry, either," Cat said. "At least not to who he is. It's just when he touches me. So maybe any guy would have the same effect on me right now. Maybe I'm sexually peaking or something."

Laurel wasn't sure she was buying that.

Cat nudged John with the toe of her black canvas Chuckie's. "So John, will you touch me sexually and we'll see what happens?"

Laurel laughed, shocked at Cat. Poor John stood

straight up and moved three feet away, hands held out.

"Whoa. I don't think so, Cat. We have to work together."

Catherine sighed. "You're probably right. And I probably wouldn't have liked it anyway."

The look on John's face was comical. He looked torn between horrified and mortally offended. "Hey. I could make you like it."

Cat rolled her eyes. "Oh, now I've hurt your ego. Men are so predictable."

"Maybe Jerry is a nicer guy than you've given him credit for," Laurel suggested. "Maybe that's why you're attracted to him."

"I'm a nice guy," John said.

Laurel laughed and Cat looked amused. "We know."

"And since you're so nice, can you do me a favor?" Laurel wanted to ask while they weren't busy in the store, with no immediate tasks looming over them. "Can one of you call the phone company for me and see if they can figure out why my Internet is out again?"

"I'm so nice, I'll do even better than that," John said, fiddling with the roll of cello wrap he had retrieved. "I'll come over and fix it for you, so you won't have to pay a hundred bucks for a service call."

"You know how to fix it? But I'm not even sure what's wrong with it."

John shrugged. "The wind or the ice probably disconnected the cable to your box outside. It's happened to me like three times, and your house faces the lake, right?"

"Yeah." Laurel hoped it was something as simple as a disconnected cable. But it seemed like the thing was always going out. "Well, if you don't mind." She'd feel really bad if John wasted an hour or two fooling with her computer and couldn't fix the thing. But maybe she could buy a pizza for him or something.

"No, I don't mind." He grinned. "It sounds easier than sexually satisfying Catherine."

Cat whacked him in the chest. "You'll never know."

Chapter 21

Trevor glanced around Laurel's bedroom with interest. The expensive, understated taste, the neat arrangement of furniture, yet the minor clutter, all confirmed for him what he'd suspected of Laurel. Sweet as sugar.

Which worked to his advantage.

It was time to move on this.

He opened up her desk drawer, poked around. Found a paperback book and her hearing aid. A hair clip and little thing of hand lotion.

The room and the house were silent, and his ears were attuned to any movement from below as he pulled her computer keyboard towards him. She was already logged into her e-mail, so it was easy enough to glance through it. He found a purchase confirmation from an online bookstore, her credit card number in the receipt.

"Thank you, beautiful." Trevor wrote the number down in his Palm Pilot.

There was nothing else of interest in her mail, nothing to give him the identity of the guy who'd chased him, the guy who he was sure was Laurel's new boyfriend. So he returned to searching her desk. An expandable folder was in the deepest drawer, and when he opened it up, Trevor knew immediately this was what he was looking for. It had all her bills, all her identification, and a copy of the deed to the house.

Five minutes later, he had everything he needed recorded. Her social security number, her bank account numbers, driver's license number pulled off of a tax record. He smiled in satisfaction. "You're such a good girl with all your records so neat and tidy, Laurel. Sorry I have to do this to you."

He had wanted Laurel in an entirely different way, but he was going to have to settle for her money. In the end, it was the practical thing to do.

If he wanted a quick lay, there was always Jill for now, and when he got to the Caribbean on Laurel's dollar, he'd coax a local girl into his bed.

But then again, it had never been about a quick lay. He was fascinated by Laurel, wanted her for no discernable, logical reason, took unnecessary risks and it had to stop.

Money would last longer than his bizarre interest in a deaf girl.

He didn't have the time or the patience to wait for her budding little romance to fizzle. Trevor was cold to the goddamn bone and wanted out, while the getting was good.

Footsteps were on the stairs, and he quickly replaced the folder and shut the drawer. He closed her e-mail and clicked to establish a connection.

"John?" Laurel came into the room, two glasses in her hand. "You thirsty? I brought you a Coke."

"Thanks." Trevor stood up and patted his pocket to confirm he'd tucked his Palm Pilot away.

"Is it hopeless?" Laurel handed him one of the glasses and glanced over at her computer. "Hey, it's connected! What did you do?"

Plugged back in the cord he'd ripped out when he'd strolled through her yard the night before. "It was like I thought—your box on the back of the house was open and the cord was loose. Probably the wind. I fixed it, and was making sure everything was working before I got your hopes up."

And to give himself time to search her computer and desk.

"That's great!" Laurel leaned over the keyboard and clicked on a few things, like she was confirming it really did work.

Trevor watched the curve of her ass dispassionately. It really was a shame he didn't have the time to charm Laurel into his bed.

She smiled up at him. "Thank you so much, this was so sweet of you. You saved me a huge hassle."

"No problem." Trevor took a sip of the drink and set it down. "Well, I should head on out." He had work to do. Money to steal and a bus ticket to buy. It truly was regrettable that he'd have to take the Greyhound, but with airline travel so rigid these days, he didn't want to risk it.

"Well, thanks again. I'll see you tomorrow?"

"No, I have tomorrow off. I don't have to go into the store until Thursday."

"That's my day off, so I'll see you on Saturday."

"Great." Trevor gave her the nice, choirboy smile she was expecting.

"Let me walk you downstairs, John. Gosh, this was so nice of you to do this." Laurel gave him another smile and headed for the door.

"I don't mind in the least."

* * *

Laurel pushed the intercom button at Sean's junior high and bit her nails. She didn't understand why Sean's school had called Sweet Stuff to tell *her* Sean was in trouble, and she didn't understand why such a good kid was fighting in the first place. There wasn't a whole lot she knew about teenage rebellion, never having done anything more radical than wearing white after Labor Day when she was in junior high, and she had avoided conflict with other students like Atkins's followers avoided carbs.

But Sean was struggling to cope with his parents' death, and he and Russ hadn't settled into a routine with each other yet. Laurel also strongly felt that Russ needed to stop focusing on the results and start focusing on why Sean was acting out. And getting into a fistfight at school was definitely acting out.

She held her hand on the door and kept pulling it every few seconds to see if it had been buzzed open. When it was, she stepped inside a dark and institutional hallway and headed towards the office.

When she was ushered by the secretary into a waiting area outside the principal's office, she saw Sean immediately, slumped in a chair looking unconcerned. He also had drying blood on his lip and a shiner under his left eye.

"Sean!"

He looked her way and signed hello. Then he looked past her to the secretary. "You can't talk to Laurel's back, Mrs. Rockman. She's deaf."

Laurel turned in time to see the secretary go red with embarrassment. "Oh, I'm sorry, Mrs. Evans,

I didn't realize . . . I just said I'll let Mr. Henry know you're here."

After "Mrs. Evans," Laurel couldn't read a darned word. She looked at Sean in amazement.

He shrugged with a grin. *Sorry,* he signed.

You'd better be sorry, she signed back, not sure if he would understand but unable to stop herself from saying something.

She also couldn't stop herself from reaching over, touching the swollen skin under his eye. "Does it hurt?"

"No." But he winced.

She sank into the chair next to him. "What happened?"

His Adam's apple moved up and down and his fist hit the arm of the chair, but he stayed silent. She raised an eyebrow at him.

Sean sat up straighter. "These jerks, they were picking on this kid, Darren, who's got Down syndrome. They were being nasty, Laurel, and I told them to stop. So the one guy tells me to fuck off and shoves Darren, so I shoved him." Sean gave another shrug. "I got one down on the ground and cracked another one's nose before they pinned me against the wall. Three on one ain't fair."

Laurel swallowed hard. *Oh, boy.* How did she handle this one? Everything in her screamed that Sean had done the right thing—especially since she knew what it was like to be picked on for being different—but fighting was wrong. Sean was supposed to be working on getting his grades up, making friends, fitting in at his new school, and fighting wasn't going to help achieve any of those goals.

Conflict resolution shouldn't be handled with a

fist. But how could she argue that standing up for someone who was defenseless was a bad thing?

She hedged. "So, why did they call me instead of your brother? And why do they think my last name is Evans?"

Sean had the decency to go pink in the cheeks. "I knew Russ would freak out. I figured I'd rather he freak out at home. So I told them you and Russ are married. I knew you'd come."

His bloody lip shot up in a grin, obviously pleased that he had been right. Then his eyes darted to the left. "Oh, we can go in now."

He stood up while Laurel tried not to be extremely pleased that he had turned to her when he was in trouble. She put her hand on Sean's back and urged him forward, even though he was a good three inches taller than her. Maybe for the first time she really understood the tenuous position Russ was in with his brother. There weren't enough years between them to have established a paternal relationship before their parents' death, yet Sean was too young to make all his own decisions.

Guidance was definitely needed, and rules had to be established, but Sean didn't respect Russ's authority.

If Russ felt unqualified to handle Sean, Laurel figured she was akin to a toddler driving an SUV.

The principal was in his forties, trim and tidy, wearing a floral tie. He smiled and held his hand out. "Thank you for coming so quickly, Mrs. Evans. I'm Mr. Henry, the principal."

While Mrs. Evans had a heck of a nice ring to it, as she shook the principal's hand Laurel was about to come clean. Only she made the mistake of glancing at Sean.

No. Please?

She was starting to regret he'd been such a quick sign language student. *Okay, fine.* She also regretted that she was such a complete and total pushover.

The principal was watching them closely. She forced a smile. "I apologize, Mr. Henry, for Sean's interruption. Now I understand that Sean was defending a special needs student when he was attacked by three boys."

Mr. Henry's eyes went wide. He took a long look at Sean, who was slouching in the chair, drumming his fingers on his knee. "That's not what Sean told me."

Laurel felt a tremor of concern, but held her ground. If Sean had told her that's what had happened, she believed him. "What did he tell you?"

"Nothing, as a matter of fact. He refused to talk about it."

That renewed her confidence. Sean was like Russ in that respect. He didn't like attention drawn to his good deeds. "Well, he told me that three boys were picking on a student with Down syndrome. What was his name, Sean?"

Sean finger spelled *Darren* to her, still refusing to look at the principal.

"His name is Darren, and when these boys shoved him, Sean intervened. Now I realize that fighting under any circumstances is not appropriate for school, and I'm sure Sean's brother would agree that Sean should be punished. But considering that he did not instigate the attack, and that he was defending another student, I think that should be taken into consideration."

Mr. Henry leaned back in his chair, tapping a pen idly on the desktop. "I think maybe I need to bring Darren into my office and ask him what he remembers happening. I'd like to believe Sean, and I'm well aware the other three involved are not exactly eighth-grade angels, but Sean here isn't a stranger to trouble, either. Are you, Sean?"

Sean just shrugged.

"Cutting classes, profanity, failing grades . . . it makes it hard for me to give you the benefit of the doubt."

Sean met the principal's gaze defiantly. "Then don't. I don't give a shit."

"Sean!" Laurel touched his arm, horrified.

But Sean just gave another shrug. "Thanks for trying, Laurel, but he'll never believe you. He made up his mind what happened before I even walked in the door."

While Laurel thought that was probably true, in all fairness she could see the principal's point of view. Sean wasn't a model student by any stretch of the imagination. He'd been making progress, that was true, but he'd had a whole year of bad grades and bad attitude to make up for.

"Look, I said I'll talk to Darren. I already gave the other three two days' suspension, and I was planning to do the same for Sean. If Darren's story jibes with Sean's, we'll reduce it to an in-school suspension."

"Can I go home now?" Sean asked.

"As soon as your brother gets here," Mr. Henry said.

At that, Sean sat straight up. "Why did you call him?"

Laurel wasn't all that thrilled about that announcement either, given that she was sitting here pretending to be his wife.

"Because his name and your grandmother's are the only names on the emergency authorization forms. He's the only one close by who can pick you up from school." Mr. Henry turned to Laurel. "I'm sorry, but I can't allow you to take Sean since Mr. Evans didn't give permission for you to do so."

"That's okay, I understand."

Mr. Henry and Sean both glanced behind her, Mr. Henry pasting on a smile, Sean going even more sullen, a trace of fear on his face. Laurel took a deep breath, turned, and saw Russ entering the office. His shoulders were tense and he held his car keys in his hand.

But he drew up short when he saw her. "Laurel, what are you doing here?"

That seemed to be the question of the hour.

Russ's attention shifted to Mr. Henry, and Laurel turned and caught the tail end of what he was saying. ". . . thought we couldn't reach you, so he asked us to call your wife instead."

Russ's eyes narrowed. He glanced carefully between Sean and her. Then he took the seat to her right, and Laurel didn't even bother to try and read his lips. She wasn't sure she wanted to see what he was saying.

Instead, she patted Sean on the arm and smiled reassuringly. He gave a little tilt of his mouth in return. Then he finger spelled *jerk* into his hand and flipped his thumb to Mr. Henry.

Stop, she reprimanded him. But he obviously didn't respect her authority any more than he did Russ's because he just grinned.

Laurel turned back to Mr. Henry.

"As soon as I speak to the other student, I'll contact you and let you know our decision."

The principal stood up and so did Russ. They shook hands and then Russ tapped her on the arm. "Let's go."

Mr. Henry said, "Oh, while you're here did you want to add your wife to the authorization forms?"

Russ shook his head. "No."

The response was so short Mr. Henry blinked.

Laurel hadn't expected Russ to say anything other than no, since she wasn't his wife and never would be, but for some reason it still hurt to hear that flat pronouncement. After quick good-byes, Russ had them out of the office and striding towards the parking lot.

Sean walked slowly, pulling on his coat, dragging his feet to the front door like he knew he was in for it. Laurel felt almost the same way. Russ looked really, really angry.

"Get in the car," he told Sean when they reached the parking lot.

"Why?"

"Because I goddamn said so!"

Sean caught the keys Russ lobbed at him and stomped off.

"Russ, calm down," Laurel started, thinking he was going to eradicate all the progress they'd made with Sean in the past few weeks.

"I don't want to calm down! And I want you to stop coddling him."

Laurel was so stunned she couldn't think of a thing to say.

"I know exactly why Sean called you. He knew you'd believe whatever bullshit story he was going to tell you and he'd walk away without any punishment. He knew he could play you."

Fury poured through her—not hot, but bitter and ice-cold, like the wind that swirled the snow on the blacktop around their feet. "I'm not an idiot, Russ. I know when someone is telling the truth and when someone is lying. Sean needs more from you than your anger and punishments. He needs your understanding."

"Understanding about what?" Russ threw his hands up in the air. "Me to understand that he's a selfish punk intent on destroying his life?"

"No!" God, Russ was so fixated on the behavior, he couldn't see what was causing it. "He wants you to understand that he hates this school, that he has no friends, and he wants to go back to Lakewood."

"I understand that, but I can't do anything about it. He's just going to have to get used to it. He needs to try." Russ rubbed his forehead.

Laurel took his hand, felt the tension in him, tried not to feel hurt when he didn't clasp her back.

"Maybe he can go back to his old school. If you claimed my address as your residence, he could go back to Emerson." She knew that until Russ understood that when Sean had lost his parents, he'd also lost his home and his friends, the brothers would be at a stubborn impasse.

"That's fine for now—just a pain in the ass since I'd have to drive him every day. But it's a temporary solution. What happens if we're not seeing each other anymore, Laurel? He's got four and a half years of school still, so he might as well get used to where he is."

That Russ could say that so casually, as if it were a foregone conclusion that their relationship had no future, and that it wouldn't affect him as anything more than an inconvenience, ripped Laurel into little pieces and scattered them across the parking lot.

She must have made a sound of distress, because he suddenly looked contrite. "I'm sorry, that didn't come out right."

"No, I think it came out exactly the way you intended it to." She pulled her hand back from his and flipped hair out of her stinging eyes. "I get the message—butt out of Sean's life. I'm just a novelty, aren't I?"

To his credit, he looked like she'd slapped him. "You know that's not true. I love you."

"But not enough to think it could last? Not enough to trust that I could care about Sean?"

"I'm just being realistic . . ." Russ's voice trailed off. He rubbed his jaw, looking frustrated and stubborn and oh-so-cute.

Laurel knew she needed to leave before she really said something pathetic and grasping and small. "Just do me a favor, Russ. Sit down and talk to your brother and actually listen to what he's telling you. You might be surprised at what he has to say."

She turned and walked away, fumbling for her keys, tears in her eyes, hoping he wouldn't run after her, wanting him to.

He didn't.

Chapter 22

"**D**amn it!" Russ told the parking lot and Laurel's retreating back. That had not gone at all the way he had intended.

He had never meant to take his frustration with Sean out on Laurel. He knew she was only trying to help, but it made him feel so goddamn inadequate that he couldn't handle one thirteen-year-old kid.

And when he'd realized that Sean had turned to Laurel first, it had hurt. Sean and Laurel had their little friendship, their homework sessions, their lessons in sign language, and damn it, Russ felt left out. All he got from Sean was lip and a bad attitude.

When she had suggested he use her address to register Sean at his old school, Russ had been appalled. Claiming that he could ever afford to live on Edgewater was laughable, but also it had made him see what it would feel like to be married to Laurel.

Like a kept man. Relying on his wife's money. Laurel could snap her fingers and give Sean everything he wanted, and Russ couldn't. He couldn't give him the friends or the school he wanted, he couldn't give him his parents back, and he couldn't even give him the love and affection that had flared up so easily between Sean and Laurel.

Whenever Russ tried to show Sean he cared about him, Sean rebuffed him.

Russ yanked open his car door and found that Sean had already started the car. He was about to peel out of the parking spot when Sean shot him an accusing look.

"You just made Laurel cry."

"I did not." At least he didn't think he had. She'd been upset, but she hadn't been *crying*.

"Look, you can yell at me, you can punish me, you can do whatever. But don't take it out on Laurel. I called her. It's my fault."

"My relationship with Laurel is none of your business." Russ backed out, wondering if he could just hit rewind and start the day over. Work sucked—they were working a half-dozen cases and getting nowhere on any of them—and now he'd managed to hurt Laurel's feelings while trying unsuccessfully to control his little brother.

Sean didn't say anything the rest of the five-minute drive home. Nor did he even look at Russ as he headed for the kitchen and the refrigerator.

Russ found Sean's silence irritating in the extreme. Shouldn't he at least pretend that he was sorry?

"So, what really happened at school?"

"Mr. Henry told you what happened."

"He didn't sound convinced you were telling the truth."

"Then why does it matter? If I tell you what happened, are you going to believe me?" Sean stood up, a single-serve cup of chocolate pudding in his hand. "It's not like you listen to me, or talk to me, or anything."

What the hell was that supposed to mean? "I do so."

"No, you don't! You won't let me talk about Laurel, you won't listen to me when I'm telling you I hate school, and worst of all, you act like Mom and Dad never existed!"

Whoa. Time out. "That's not true."

"It is true. When was the last time we talked about them? It's like every time I do, you're all, 'We've got to move ahead, not get stuck in the past.' Well, screw you! I miss Mom." Sean's voice cracked at the end, and he dropped his chin into his chest.

Russ moved to him without even thinking. "I'm sorry, Sean, I'm sorry." He wrapped his arms around his brother and pulled him to his chest. "I know you miss her . . . God, I do, too. I know this sucks for you—getting stuck with me—but I just wanted to pretend that everything was okay. That we were okay."

Sean's sobs were silent as he tried to control them, and Russ prayed he could take away some of that pain, any of it. "I'm not very good at communicating."

"No shit," Sean said, pulling back and wiping at his eyes.

Russ figured he deserved that, but it still hurt. "Cut me some slack. I don't know what I'm doing here . . . I'm just trying to feel my way through. I didn't even realize I wasn't talking about Mom and Dad. I guess that was my way of coping with losing them."

"Well, I hate it." With a sniffle, Sean pulled the

foil top off of his pudding cup and licked it. "I hate that you sold our house without even talking to me about it. Why'd you do that, Russ?"

Because he hadn't wanted to deal with it. The house or the emotions it created. "At the time, I thought it made sense. I couldn't take care of it . . . it was too big, a financial drain, and I thought maybe you needed a fresh start."

"You should have asked me. I'm not a little kid, and half that house was mine."

For the first time, Russ saw the situation from Sean's perspective. Not only had he lost his parents, he'd lost everything in his life that he'd had since birth. His home, his neighborhood, his school. While Russ had been unable to deal with his grief, he'd taken away the one thing that might have helped Sean deal with his—stability.

"Maybe you're right."

"Well, that's a first. You thinking I could be right."

"I'm going to make mistakes, Sean."

To which Sean gave a shaky laugh. "No kidding."

"But we're in this together, alright, and I can't help you or fix my mistakes if I don't know what's wrong." Russ waited, hoping like hell Sean would trust him, hoping they could build a better relationship from here on out.

"Mr. Henry . . . what he said was true. I was just sticking up for a kid some assholes were picking on."

Russ knew he had to trust Sean on this one, so he just nodded. "Okay."

"And while you're working on that whole communicating thing, maybe you should go and apologize to Laurel for being a jerk. I'll even go stay next door in Diaper World so you can do it." Sean reached into the drawer for a spoon and dug into the pudding with relish. Apparently a rough day didn't dent his appetite. "Maybe pick up some flowers or something on the way."

"Thanks for the tip," Russ said wryly.

Sean grinned. "Here's another one—you should marry her."

"Oh, really, Cupid. And why is that?"

"Because she's smart, she's sweet, she's really pretty. And she's the only one who's going to be willing to put up with you."

Russ laughed. Damn, he thought maybe Sean had the right of it. "You know, when I was seventeen and Mom told me she was pregnant, I was embarrassed. I mean, come on, having to tell people my mom was knocked up? But then she told me that for fifteen years she and Dad had been trying to have another baby since they loved me so much."

"Hard to believe." Sean licked his spoon clean and grinned.

Russ leaned against the refrigerator, kept his tone light. "So after that, I was happy for her, because she was so happy. Then when you were born, they let me into the room to see Mom, and she was crying. And I thought, 'Damn, no wonder. That's the ugliest kid I ever saw.'"

Sean let out a snort.

"I mean, you were all sort of bluish-red, and you had this white stuff smeared all over you like the glaze on a doughnut."

"Nasty."

"Your eyes were all watery, and your head had this funny point on it. But Mom was crying, because she was happy. Because she'd gotten exactly what she'd wanted—another son." Russ looked at his baby brother, half grown up, and smiled. "And after a while, you stopped being so ugly."

Sean slugged him on the arm. "Too bad I can't say the same for you."

And Russ knew they were okay. That they would get through this. He pushed off the refrigerator and headed for the living room.

"Where you going?"

"I'm heading up to the attic to pick through some boxes. I feel like looking at Mom's photo albums. Want to come with me?"

"Yeah."

Jerry rolled onto his back and struggled to breathe. He was starting to think he was too old for this. Catherine was killing him.

And already her fingers were starting to tickle along his leg towards his dick, which didn't even have the energy to jump a little. He grabbed her hand before she was disappointed.

"Not yet. Give me five minutes." Damn, she was insatiable. He loved that about her. With Pam, it had all been about politics. She used sex to control him and always wanted it all on her own terms.

Catherine just wanted him. Period. They saw each other, and thirty seconds later the clothes were coming off. He didn't understand it, but he sure in the hell wasn't going to argue with it.

Cat nibbled his shoulder. "Three. That's all I'm giving you."

"Alright." He gave a mock sigh and whacked her on the backside. Cat had a great body, despite all the weird shit she'd done to it. That was another thing he didn't understand—the tattoos and the piercings—but he had to admit, tracing the patterns of her five tattoos with his tongue got him hard every time.

And really, when she was standing there naked, pale and long-limbed, the tattoos covered very little of her creamy body. In recent days, she had taken out that chain hanging across her face—a good thing—but she'd gone and dyed her hair all black, which he knew for a fact wasn't her natural color.

He fingered the dark blond hair covering her mound, lazily stroking back and forth. "Shouldn't you dye this too? You know, so you match?"

Cat bit his shoulder. "Jerry, this works so much better when you don't talk."

"What? I'm serious. It was a legitimate question." It looked pretty damn strange, in his opinion.

"Shhh." Cat held her finger in front of her mouth. "Just shhh."

Jerry got mildly irritated. "What, I'm not allowed to talk? I'm just a dick to you?" A dick that was starting to swell back up, mindless bastard.

But Cat's breasts were tumbling across his chest, and her leg was slung over his, giving him a hint of the wet heat between her thighs. Lamplight cast her bedroom in a warm glow, and she had some kind of sexy, bluesy music playing on her stereo.

He was helpless against that kind of onslaught.

"So what if you are? Men have been using women for sex for thousands of years."

Oh, damn, he'd set her off on one of her feminist tirades. "So what do you want, Cat? Me to be your sex slave?"

He wasn't sure that was so far off the mark anyway. Not that he was really complaining, but a guy has feelings.

"No. Well, maybe sometime just for fun." She

squinted at him, like she always did when she took her glasses off. "But I just want you to treat me like an equal. Talk to me like you would a guy."

Damn, hadn't she been listening? "I do."

"You do?" She moved back, taking her breast with her, looking astonished.

Jerry reached out and brushed her nipple, wanting it back. "Hell, yeah. You know, I was raised to treat women differently from guys, sort of cautious-like. To watch everything you say and do and hope like hell it doesn't bite you in the ass. To expect women to sort of be perpetually pissed at you."

He had her attention, and she was scooting closer to him again, fitting her nipple into his hand. "But with you, I just tell it to you like it is. I say whatever I'm thinking. And I don't hold back my lust either, which I normally do. Always figured raw sex would scare a woman."

"Doesn't scare me," she said with relish, her hand taking a stroll over his head, and not the one he was using to talk.

"I noticed."

"So, you're being honest with me? You're giving me total equality?"

He'd never thought of it that way, but it was true. "Yeah, I am. Like I can tell you that I think you're pretty messed-up looking, and I know you won't get all bent out of shape. I never would have felt comfortable saying that to any other woman."

Jerry was kind of joking, but not really. Catherine looked kind of whacked-out most of the time with all that crap stuck all over her face. He didn't understand why she needed to take a perfectly decent-looking face and vandalize it with jewelry.

Cat squeezed his dick a little tighter than should be strictly necessary to turn him on.

"Hey, watch it, babe, easy."

Catherine laughed and loosened her hold, though for a second she'd been tempted to maim Jerry. *Messed-up looking. Geez.* But then she had realized that if she were going to ask him to tell it to her like it was, always being honest, then she had to be able to listen without getting pissed.

And whatever he thought about her body art, it didn't seem to interfere with his attraction to her. "You don't like my piercings?"

"Not the ones on your face. It's distracting. I don't mind the eyebrow or the nose, but the lip ones throw me off. I think you're pretty under all that, but it's kind of hard to tell."

Catherine still wasn't entirely sure what she saw in him, but God, he made her laugh. No moody artiste here, which was her usual type. She never had to second-guess Jerry.

She also wasn't about to take out her lip ring just because he didn't like it, but she wanted to tease him a little. There wasn't really any great motivation behind her tattoos and piercings—more like once she'd started, she'd just kept going. It had been fun at first, a way to stand out in a crowd, and the attention she got was amusing, but lately she'd been starting to think she was a little old for it. It had looked cool at twenty-four, but dang, she was sliding towards thirty.

But she'd had them so long she wasn't sure what she looked like without them. Her head might feel lighter.

"Let's do this . . . for every ring I take off my face, I'll put one someplace else."

"Can you just take them out? Won't you have holes all over the place?" Jerry flicked his finger across her three lip rings.

"The holes will just close right up, like I never had them."

"And do you have any place left to put new ones? I mean, babe, you've got them all over the place."

"Not everywhere." Cat licked his ear and whispered a suggestion for possible placement.

Jerry groaned. "Damn. Is that possible?"

"Oh, yeah." She was getting hot just thinking about it, picturing his tongue doing little leaps through a gold hoop in that particular spot.

"You know, Catherine, I'm starting to really like you."

Jerry flipped her on her back and she gave a breathy moan. "You're not so bad yourself."

Chapter 23

Jill should have known. Maybe she always had.
Men like Pete Trevor didn't fall for girls like her.
Average girls who may have had an interesting feature or two, but whose overall effect was nothing special. Girls who didn't have the advantage of beauty or money or great intelligence to pave their way in the world.

Girls who were normal, and generous, and worthy, but who never caught the attention of the pretty people.

Pete was one of those, and Jill had never quite believed that she had him.

She hadn't.

She wasn't sure what had made her start following him. Maybe it was the way he popped in and out, or the way he was so secretive about his computer, or the fact that he didn't seem to have any furniture or towels or anything when he moved in with her. Pete always had reasons for all of those things, and they always made sense, but somewhere along the way Jill started to think that if something was too good to be true, maybe it was.

It wasn't reality that Pete Trevor would love her.

So she'd started following him.

Jill pulled into the parking lot and ground her Chevy Cavalier to a stop. She glanced at the suitcase on the passenger seat and fought tears.

When she'd first discovered that Pete wasn't a computer consultant like he'd told her, but was working at a candy store, she'd been confused, but had thought immediately he must have lost his job. He must have been embarrassed to tell her where he was working to make ends meet.

But then she'd managed to sneak into his e-mail one night after he was asleep and she'd found some pleading e-mails from a woman named Laurel, asking to see him. They had suggested a relationship, one that he was clearly ending, since the woman was asking if she'd offended him, if something was wrong, when could they see each other.

Jill might have believed it was a previous girlfriend except that he'd kept the e-mails, and something about the tone, the nervous pleading a half-step below begging, reminded her so closely of herself that she was ashamed and mortified. And had been compelled to follow him again, and this time had discovered that he spent a lot of nights going in the back entrance of a big house on Edgewater. A house that Jill had searched public records for and discovered belonged to a woman named Laurel.

The insecure side of her wanted to wait for him to come home from work and confront him with everything she knew, but the strong side of her, the one she'd almost forgotten she had, realized that would be a disaster. If she let Pete come home, and they talked, an hour later he would have her arguments turned in circles and she would believe anything he told her.

No, it was better this way. She wanted her dignity back. Jill picked up the suitcase, opened the car door, and hauled it across the steering wheel.

Trevor was enjoying himself immensely. Laurel had bought him lunch as a thank-you for fixing her computer, and they were eating sub sandwiches in the back room and chatting, all while he tried not to laugh out loud. He'd stolen almost three hundred grand from her, and she was buying him lunch.

It was downright hysterical.

After his shift at the candy store, thankfully his last one, he was catching the bus to Chicago, and from there he was going south. If he never had to see another snowflake or a goddamn gummy worm it would be too soon.

He'd left everything at Jill's except his computer, but he didn't give a crap about his clothes. Let Jill keep them. He'd buy new ones with the five hundred bucks he'd nipped from Jill's credit card that morning.

"So how's your new boyfriend?" he asked Laurel, still curious, though it was irrelevant at this point.

Laurel, the little hypocrite, blushed. "Well, actually, we kind of had a falling out yesterday. I was hoping he'd stop by last night, but he didn't."

Poor thing. Trevor had a momentary urge to stick around and comfort Laurel, but he knew it was time to leave. It was only a matter of days or, at the most, weeks before she discovered he'd opened an equity line of credit using her house and withdrawn the entire amount.

"Maybe he just needs time to cool off. What's

his name again?" Trevor took a sip of his raspberry iced tea and glanced out into the store. They'd propped the door open since Catherine was in the store alone handling the Saturday crowd.

He had thought he heard a familiar voice for a second, but he must have been imagining it.

"Russ. Russ Evans, for all it seems to matter at this point."

Trevor swung his head back to stare at Laurel. Russ Evans. The name he'd been using? The cop from the CPD? How the hell was that possible?

Cat leaned her head into the door while he was still gaping, processing the information that Laurel was dating the cop whose name he'd stolen. "John, can you come out here? We have this woman here who's freaking out, insisting that her boyfriend works here. I told her there's only you, but she's throwing a hissy."

Trevor stood up, but before he could say anything, Jill was in the doorway behind Catherine.

"There you are! I knew you were here!"

Shit. He was caught. Swallowing a curse, Trevor took in Jill's appearance. She had hair spilling out of a ponytail, blotchy skin and eyes, and she'd missed a button when doing up her shirt.

But even as he was trying to figure out how'd she found him and what she was doing, he was maneuvering his way out of the possible disaster. He shot Jill a look of concern. "Jill, sweetheart, what's the matter? Why are you so upset?"

The ungrateful bitch actually hurled his suitcase at him, clipping Laurel in the arm before he caught it in midair. "Jill, now come on, you just hit Laurel. Calm down."

He set the suitcase down on the chair he'd been sitting in and tried not to get pissed off. Here he'd picked Jill out, showered her with attention and affection, giving her great sex and never once complaining about her stinginess, and now she was going to fuck everything up.

"Laurel?" Jill turned to Laurel, who was rubbing her arm and inching towards the door. Jill looked furious. "You're Laurel?"

Trevor narrowed his eyes. How the hell would she recognize the name Laurel? And while he normally enjoyed jealousy from women, this was bad timing.

"Slut!" Jill spat at Laurel. Then she started weeping and slapped at him when he tried to take her arm. "Don't touch me, you lying asshole."

He didn't have a problem with that, but he was impatient for her to leave, knowing the longer she was there, the greater the possibility of exposure. But he kept his tone placating, the bewildered boyfriend. "Can we just talk about this at home, please? I'm working, and you're making a scene. I need this job, Jill, I need the money."

"You're not coming back to my apartment. I'm kicking you out, and I want my key back."

"Honey, you don't want to do this. Whatever this is about, we can work it out." He'd never seen Jill so ticked, and she didn't even know he'd withdrawn cash on her credit card yet.

Laurel was leaving the room, kicking the doorstop out of the way so the door would close behind her. Trevor was glad, in case Jill blurted something he didn't want Laurel to see.

But Jill had noticed what she was doing and charged for the door. "Don't bother leaving, Laurel. I'll go, and then you can have him all to yourself!"

"John?" Laurel looked at him, her eyes wide.

Damn it. Trevor just shrugged, like he didn't know what was going on.

Jill rounded on him. "John? Why is she calling you John? Your name is Pete Trevor, or was that a lie, too?"

Given the blank confusion on her face, Laurel either didn't understand what Jill had said or didn't see the significance of it. She just stood in the doorway with her hand on the knob, like she wasn't sure what she should do.

There was no point in arguing with Jill. There was nothing to gain from her at this point. He reached into his pocket, removed her key from his key ring, and handed it to her. Yet he couldn't resist staying in character. "Call my cell phone if you change your mind, Jill."

It wouldn't be working by tomorrow, but that was unimportant. "I thought you cared about me enough to at least have a rational conversation, but I guess I was wrong. Now please leave before I get fired."

He stroked her hand as he passed the key to her, and for a split second, she wavered, long enough to be gratifying. Then she yanked away from him and ran out the door and towards the front of the store.

Thank God. Crazy bitch.

Trevor ran his hands through his hair and gave an embarrassed laugh. "Sorry about that, Laurel."

Laurel nodded to John, completely mortified that she'd been in any way involved in that conversation.

"Come back and finish your sandwich. I have no idea what Jill was so upset about. She's normally a very sweet girl." He shifted the suitcase off his chair and sat down. "Guess I'm in the doghouse for some reason or another."

John looked embarrassed, his movements just a little bit stiff.

Laurel wasn't having the best of days. She felt like someone had rammed cotton up her nose and drilled into her brain with a screwdriver. She hadn't slept much the night before, waiting and watching for the doorbell to ring. Wanting Russ to come over so they could talk. Being devastated when he hadn't.

She shouldn't have walked away from him like that. He had been in the middle of a crisis with his brother, and she had added to his burden by arguing with him. She should have just backed off and waited until he'd had time to calm down before she brought up her suggestion of using her address as Sean's residence.

But she hadn't, and she hadn't heard from Russ. She wanted to stay in bed and cry, and instead had been forcing herself to chitchat with John. Who had one very angry girlfriend.

Laurel picked a piece of lettuce off her sandwich and ate it. "I didn't know you have a girlfriend."

"Apparently I don't anymore."

She didn't know John all that well, but she had still worked with him a couple of times a week for almost a month. It seemed like in all that time it would have popped up once or twice, considering he seemed to have been living with his girlfriend.

Not that it was any of her business. Not that it mattered. But she watched John make short work of his veggie sub and felt something like unease poking at her. "Why did your girlfriend act like she knew who I was? Like you were cheating with me or something?"

John shrugged. "She's very jealous. Jill's a very sweet girl, but for some reason she's really insecure. She's followed me before, so maybe she saw me at your house."

Laurel felt horrible. "God, John, you should have told me! I wouldn't have had you come over if I had thought it would cause trouble."

John leaned back in his chair. "Don't worry about it. Jill will come around. And come on, I should be able to help out a friend without her freaking out."

That was true. But Laurel still just felt like pond scum. "I guess neither of us are having the best of luck with our relationships right now."

"So you care about him? This Russ?"

Laurel just nodded.

But John paused while lighting up his cigarette and studied her. "You love him, don't you? You do, I can see it."

Heat rose in her cheeks, and Laurel's discomfort grew. The question seemed personal, probing, for a coworker, and something about the way John was looking at her bothered her. Like he knew something. Like he wasn't quite so casual or cheerful or nice as she'd always thought him to be.

She didn't say anything, just watched the smoke curl around John's handsome face, his blond hair cut short above his azure blue eyes. Mysterious eyes that seemed to shift and change and close even as she was watching them.

Jill's words popped back into her head. Laurel hadn't been able to understand all of what she had been saying, since her words were slurred and upset, but she had said something about his name. *John, why is she calling you John?*

Laurel had been so embarrassed at the time,

she hadn't given any thought to it. But then what had Jill said? *Your name is Pete . . .*

Pete something, Laurel had thought at the time. Now she knew. Pete Trevor. Trevor Dean.

Oh, God.

Her arm jerked across her sandwich paper before she could stop it, and she knew he knew.

His expression changed, became amused. "You think you've figured something out, don't you, Laurel?"

"You're Trevor Dean," she said in amazement, then clapped her mouth shut. She shouldn't say anything to him. She should get the hell out of there and call Russ.

But she gave herself away by looking towards the closed door. Dean's eyes followed hers.

He shifted his chair so she would have to go around him to get to the door, and she was trapped.

Chapter 24

Russ was grateful that Catherine answered the phone at Sweet Stuff. He could ask her about Laurel without looking like an ass.

"Hey, Cat, it's Russ. Is Laurel working today?" He'd already been to her house and hovered for thirty minutes until the old man next door had come over and asked him what the hell he was doing. He'd been forced to admit he was waiting for Laurel to come home.

After inspecting him like he was a potential stalker, and studying his badge with his bifocals, the guy had suggested that Laurel was probably at work. She worked most Saturdays.

Russ had known that, of course, and if he hadn't been in a total panic it might have occurred to him all on his own to look for her there. But he was in a total panic, having the horrible feeling that Laurel had broken up with him or something the day before.

He had spent so many years shying away from relationships and delivering I'm-not-ready-for-this speeches that he wasn't sure he'd realized that

Laurel had given him the boot in the school parking lot. He still wasn't sure.

Sean, on the other hand, with all the wisdom of a thirteen-year-old who's never had a girlfriend, was positive he'd been dumped. Which had Russ driving around town like an idiot looking for Laurel to assure himself they were fine. Yesterday was a speed bump, that's all. He hadn't been knocked out of the course.

"Yeah, she's here. She's in the back eating lunch with John."

"Who the hell is John?" One day later and she was already cozying up to John in the back room?

"Calm down, tiger. He's just a guy we work with. He's been here about a month, and he has a girlfriend who's a lunatic, by the way. We just had a huge scene here."

Jealousy somewhat abated, Russ turned left, heading towards the candy store. He'd planned to ask Cat what time Laurel got off for the day, but he got the idea that maybe he wanted to see her right now. It could be hours until she got off work. "What kind of scene?"

"His girlfriend threw his suitcase at him, kicked him out of the house, seemed to think he was cheating on her with Laurel. It was crazy."

Jealousy came back, more vicious and painful than before. It stabbed behind the eyes and churned his gut. "Have you forgotten who you're talking to? That maybe it wouldn't thrill me to hear that someone suspects Laurel and another guy of having a relationship?"

Cat snorted. "Oh, come on. This is Laurel. She wouldn't cheat. But I guess the chick got the idea because John was over Laurel's the other day fixing her computer."

Russ braked at a red light and frowned. "Her computer?" Some instinct had him feeling for his holster, which wasn't even strapped on since it was his day off. "What does John look like? How old is he?"

"About thirty, blond, blue eyes, very clean-cut, cute, nice guy. But it was weird . . . I didn't even know he had a girlfriend, then there was this hysterical girl calling him Pete or something like that. It was just weird."

Russ glanced at the intersection. He was five minutes away. He gripped the steering wheel and drummed his fingers, propping the phone with his shoulder. "What did the girl look like?"

He waited for Cat's answer, feeling sick, angry, violent.

"She was kind of plain, actually, just kind of pale, brown hair, a little heavy, wearing sweatpants or something. Why? Is something wrong, Russ?"

"Call Jerry and tell him to bring his gun and his cuffs. I'll be there in five minutes." The light turned green and he floored it. "Four."

"His gun? Shit, Russ! What's going on? What do you want me to do?"

"Lock the front door so customers won't come in. And just try and act normal."

"Oh my God . . ."

Russ hung up on her so he could use both hands to drive. Like that would somehow get him there faster.

"Let's talk a little, Laurel. I'm curious about a few things, and I've got a few hours before I leave town." Dean took a hit on his cigarette.

"You're leaving?" Laurel was equal parts terrified and relieved. She knew she should be trying to figure out a way to entrap him, to extract information from him so the police could track him down, but her mind was like mud. All she could think was that this man lied all the time, to everyone, about everything. And he was damn good at it.

But he didn't look violent. Russ had told her he'd never hurt anyone. Then again, she didn't really think anyone had discovered who he was until now. That couldn't thrill him.

He just laughed. He actually laughed. "Don't look so happy to see me go. I kind of thought you'd gotten to like me, Laurel. But before I head out this back door, just tell me this. How did you know Trevor Dean was Russ Evans online? Or didn't you?"

Laurel swallowed, gripped the leg of her khaki pants. She wasn't sure what she should tell him, but she had to say something. It seemed like telling him the truth was the smartest thing to do. "I didn't at first. But the night we made plans to meet in the coffee shop, the police were waiting for you."

His eyebrow rose. "Really? Well, it's a good thing I decided to stand you up, then."

"Why did you stand me up?" That had never seemed logical to her.

Dean flicked his ashes onto his sandwich wrapper and crossed his legs. "Well, I shouldn't go revealing all my secrets, but I like you, Laurel. So let's just say I never wanted you to meet Russ Evans. That name was just a way to get to know you a little, find out some details, see if you were anyone I might be interested in. I decided you were, so I got the job here to, ah, pursue that interest in you."

Laurel felt nauseous. He'd been working with her, watching her this whole time. He'd picked her out as an easy mark, and even when Russ had told her all about Trevor Dean, she'd never for one second suspected John or really thought that any con artist would be targeting her.

He waved his cigarette at her, his face a mock reprimand. "Laurel Wilkins, you've caused me a heap of problems. You've caused me to break rules, skirt too close to the edge. I'm kind of pissed about that."

Laurel struggled to stay composed, but he must have read her fear.

"Oh, don't worry. I'm not going to hurt you. That's not my style. But you're going to let me walk out this back door and you're not going to call the cops or your little boyfriend." He put out the cigarette in his iced tea and crumpled his wrapper up. Standing, he threw it in the trash, all neat and tidy, like it was an ordinary day.

"If you do decide to call the cops, it won't matter. I'll be long gone. And then I'll punish you by taking everything that's yours, Laurel. Cash, trust fund, your house, your credit cards, until you'll have nothing and it will take ten years of perfect credit for you to get a loan for even fifty bucks."

Her mind was frozen, her hands clammy. He meant it. She could see that, now that he wasn't pretending anymore. His eyes were cruel, selfish, empty. Laurel didn't care about the money, but that house was her mother's last connection to her father. She loved that house with her heart and soul.

"I won't call the cops, John. Trevor. Whatever your name is."

"I didn't think so." Dean picked up his suitcase, wiggled it. "I'd written these clothes off. How thoughtful of Jill to bring them to me."

Laurel just stared at him in horror. "You're repulsive."

"Now, don't exaggerate. I'm not a murderer or a rapist or a child molester. I'm a thief—what of it? And if you think about it, without me, you'd have never met your stud that has your eyes going all soft and pathetic when his name is brought up." Dean pulled his keys out of his pocket, got his coat off the hanger by the refrigerator. "So, really, you owe me a little something, which I've already taken the liberty to collect. Think of it as a matchmaker's fee."

Laurel jerked in surprise, knocking her knees against the table. She hadn't even noticed that she was edging her chair back, away from him.

"Do me a favor and ask Cat to send my last paycheck to Jill. Maybe she can buy herself a sense of style."

Something about the way he said that, so crude and dismissive, so derogatory to the woman he'd been living with, ripped through the fear and infuriated Laurel. "You asshole!"

His eyebrows rose. "My, my, Laurel, I didn't expect that from you."

She stood up, deciding she didn't need to listen to any more of this. He could just leave out the back and she could go straight to the bank and put a freeze on her assets. It wouldn't get him arrested and she'd probably already lost money, but she didn't give a damn. She wanted away from him and his cold, calculating venom.

Only the door opened and Laurel saw the side of Russ's face as he stuck his head in.

Dean sighed. "Damn it. You really are a pain in the ass, Laurel."

She was walking past him, intent on getting

away. In a move so fast she couldn't anticipate or react, he grabbed her and closed his arm around her neck in a tight headlock, pushing her face towards the floor. She let out a startled scream, her hair falling across her face, blinding her, her throat constricted, air obstructed, panic setting her fingernails clawing at his skin.

She could see feet moving, Russ's boots and Cat's maybe, felt the sharp bite of a knife pressed against her side, pricking through her sweater, forcing her to go still.

"Just let him go, Russ," she said.

There were no words, no answers, only the movement and the fear and the sudden intense certainty that Dean would gut her like a trout if she let him. She couldn't just stand there, bent over, trapped in silence, and let herself be victimized. It made her angry that Dean had followed her, watched her, stolen from her. And as if that weren't enough, now he had the nerve to make her feel helpless, to frighten her, like a common playground bully.

Before she could think and talk herself out of it, Laurel remembered the things Russ had showed her. She dragged in a painful rush of air, the crook of Dean's arm still wrapped tightly around her neck. Then she stomped on his foot at the same time she reached back and grabbed the front of his neatly pressed khaki pants. She squeezed with every ounce of energy in her, felt his startled jerk, felt the knife nick into her, before his hand went slack.

With one last twist and yank on his testicles, she let go and stumbled forward, trying to get out of the way. The blow to her midsection sent her reeling, tripping and going blind with tears as the pain tore through her. Cat caught her, dragged her with both hands to the doorway. Afraid for Russ, remembering that knife, Laurel turned to scream, to yell, to beat at Dean, or something to protect Russ. But what she saw had her covering her mouth with her hand.

Dean was already down on the floor and Russ was hitting him. With a violence and fury that made Laurel's already shaky stomach heave. He brought his fist down on Dean, while Jerry stood next to them and watched.

Laurel couldn't watch. Appalled at the whole situation, she turned away while her stomach churned and her side ached.

Russ felt Jerry tap him on the shoulder, and he eased up on Dean. "What?"

"Time's up, unless you want to get kicked off the force." Jerry stuck his foot on Dean's gut and reached for his cuffs.

Russ didn't want to stop pounding the bastard, but he knew Jerry was right. He'd already gone too far and pummeled him beyond the point where he could claim resisting arrest or self-defense. But when that motherfucker had grabbed Laurel, he'd lost it.

He'd never known fear like that, so deep, so paralyzing. He'd stood there breathing too hard, unable to react. Until Laurel had gone for the balls, just like he'd taught her, and he'd been spurned into action. He was also reaching for Dean when the bastard had landed a punch on Laurel's kidney. And he'd had the goddamn nerve to call her a deaf and dumb bitch while he had delivered the blow.

Russ had lost it. Completely and totally lost it. It wasn't just because it was Laurel. It was the idea of any man touching any woman, but that slur, to his woman, the woman he loved, had sent him into a rage he hadn't known he was capable of.

But Jerry was right, he needed to back off. Russ shook out his wrist, pulled in a breath, and glanced down with satisfaction as Dean spit a tooth onto his chest that had been knocked clean out.

Then he left the scum to Jerry and turned to Laurel, who had her eyes closed. He touched her arm, gently. "Laurel? Are you okay, honey?"

She shook her head, but opened her eyes. She was shaking, he realized, when she looked up at him. "I couldn't look."

"Shhh, that's okay." He wrapped his arms around her, drew her to his chest. He dusted kisses on her head, holding her so tight she couldn't move. The fear started to recede, leaving him with a trembling that started in his toes and rode up his whole body until his hands vibrated on her back.

"Jesus Christ. Don't scare me like that." He knew she couldn't see him talking, but he didn't care. He stroked her back, her hair, closed his eyes for a split second.

When he opened them, Jerry was hauling Dean to his feet, having read him his rights.

"You don't have anything on me," Dean said.

"Just shut up," Russ told him. "Nobody asked you for your goddamn opinion. Need help, Anders?"

"Nope." Jerry gave Dean a nudge forward to get him moving.

Dean paused in the doorway, and Russ turned Laurel away from him, so she wouldn't see any last parting shots he might be inclined to deliver. "See you around, Cat. And for the record, I could have made you like it."

Cat curled her lip. "You need to get over yourself."

Dean's eyes trailed over her. "Freak."

"Hey." Jerry jerked the cuffs. "Nobody calls the woman I'm going to marry a freak but me."

Russ had to have heard that wrong. He gaped at Jerry. "Marry her? What the hell are you talking about?"

Cat folded her arms across her chest and raised an eyebrow at Jerry.

He just shrugged. "This is a dramatic moment. I thought it needed a nice finishing line."

Russ was thinking along the lines of calling Anders an idiot when Catherine started laughing. Laurel looked up and tried to ease back out of his arms. Russ wouldn't let her.

"There is something so completely *wrong* about you." But Cat moved towards Jerry. "Are you serious?"

Anders grinned. "Kind of, yeah. Whatta'ya think?"

She twisted one of the rings in her lip. "I'm thinking, maybe, yeah, in a while."

"Can you do this later?" Dean asked, sounding bored. "I'm bleeding here."

Russ was tempted to crack him again, but Jerry just snorted. "Alright, let's go. I'll call you later, Cat."

His training urged him to follow Jerry, make sure he got Dean in the car without incident, but he was reluctant to leave Laurel. She was very quiet, very still, her face a waxy pale mask, her hands frigid. Russ rubbed her back, kissed her head again, struggled whether to leave her with Cat or follow Jerry.

"Well, how do you like that? I think I just got proposed to over an arrest . . . he'll call me later, he says." Cat shook her head. "Tell me why I like him, Russ. Why I actually think I might be in love with him."

"He's a good guy." One of the best. Russ was about to expand on that, when in caressing Laurel's side, he felt a cold wet spot on her sweater.

Without hesitation he tore the material and saw her smooth skin pierced by a knife wound, blood sluggishly working its way down into the waistband of her pants. "Holy shit! Call 911, Cat." Russ grabbed the bottom of his T-shirt, pressed it against Laurel's skin. "Why didn't you say something, bunny?"

Her fingers clutched at the front of him, and she swayed just slightly. Her eyes were glassy, breathing shallow. "I don't think it's that bad. Everything just stings and burns, Russ . . . all over my middle."

And everything inside Russ stung and burned, and he gripped Laurel's side, hating feeling helpless, knowing that he'd do anything to take away her pain and hurt. Knowing that if something happened to her, he couldn't handle it.

Chapter 25

Russ cursed every pothole as he drove Laurel home from the hospital. There was no avoiding the damn things in February in Cleveland. The salt to keep the roads ice-free chewed giant holes all over the asphalt and repair crews wouldn't come through until April. He drove slowly, but he didn't want to get home at midnight, not when every wince Laurel gave made his gut churn and his chest tight.

The ER doctor had assured him that Laurel's cut was superficial and needed only minimal stitches. The blow Dean had delivered to her back had bruised her muscles and her kidney, but she'd recover. She was just going to feel pummeled for a few days, sore and stiff.

Laurel's mother had met him at the hospital and had been a big help, staying much more calm than Russ could have ever imagined. Much more calm than he was through the whole damn waiting process. He'd tried to claim that he needed to stay with Laurel as an interpreter, but she had shooed him away with an angry look, like he'd said something wrong.

But she had agreed to let him drive her home. Not that he would have taken no for an answer. He wasn't going to let Laurel even go to the freaking bathroom without him until he was sure she was recovered.

He pulled into his driveway, relieved to be there finally.

Laurel leaned against the window, facing him. "Why are we at your house?"

"No stairs. Your mom agreed. She's bringing some things by for you later."

Laurel wanted to argue that she should have been consulted, but she was too damn tired. And mortified. Here she'd just been nicked with a knife and taken one lousy punch to the side, and everyone was treating her like she'd survived a war. Or like she was five. It was embarrassing and made her a little angry.

Russ loved her, she knew that. But he didn't treat her like an equal. It had infuriated her when he'd tried to manipulate the hospital staff to bend rules so he could stay with her, using her deafness as an excuse. She couldn't let him do that.

But she was too tired to debate it right now. Too tired to worry about anything that was logical or important to her future when she just wanted to close her eyes and slide into the medication they'd given her.

Still she managed to say, "You don't need to take care of me, you know. I'm fine. I just want to go to bed."

Russ stared at her, jaw clenched. "I don't care how fine you think you are, let me do this, Laurel, please. I need to see you're all right."

There were things she wanted to say to Russ, about Dean, about them, about how she felt like she needed to find her independence, but she didn't have the words. She was too tired, and she didn't want to say it wrong, have him think she didn't want his love. She understood where he was coming from, the need to do something when you felt helpless. If Russ were hurt, she'd want to take care of him, whether the injury was serious or not.

"Come on, let's go in the house."

Russ was hovering over her, his arms tight around her, body too close as he walked her up the path to the front door. She stumbled from his legs interlocking with hers. Part of her wanted to just turn, sink into his arms, let him handle anything and everything, while the other half wanted to stand up straight, on her own.

She didn't know which she wanted more, or if she could fuse the two.

When she tripped again, Russ pretty much lifted her off the ground and carried her the remaining two feet. He took her right down the hall, straight to his bedroom, before she even had a chance to kick off her wet shoes or her jacket.

"Sit down," he said, giving her shoulders a gentle push so she was forced to sit on his bed.

It was a very masculine bedroom, with rumpled navy sheets on the unmade bed, the window free of anything but dusty gray miniblinds. She'd never spent the night here. They'd never made love here. The bed was softer than her hard mattress, with a dip in the middle, and wedged against the wall with the window, covering the bottom third of it. The room was crowded with the queen-sized bed, his dresser, and a chair that served as a laundry station.

His lampshade was tilted crazily, like he'd bumped it on his way by, and there was nothing on the walls, but it was clean.

Russ slipped her jacket off of her arms. "Lie down, honey."

Laurel wanted to protest that she could undress herself, but she didn't have the strength. When she leaned back, the bed rushed up to meet her quicker than she'd expected, pushing a shot of air out of her lungs, her head spinning a little.

"Why did you really bring me here, Russ?" Her house was big enough. One of its downstairs rooms would have sufficed as a temporary bedroom.

He was staring at her, running his hands along her arms, her thighs. "I wanted to see you here, in my house."

"I've been in your house lots of times." Laurel licked her dry lips and tried to ignore the way all of her muscles throbbed, and the persistent sting in her side.

"Not like this." He spread his hands wide. "Not in my bedroom, not in my bed, not surrounded by these walls, like you're a part of it. I wanted to see it, since I had such a hard time picturing it."

He still didn't believe it, didn't trust it. Russ bent down and slipped Laurel's ankle boots off her feet. He was a simple guy, with simple wants and needs, and he wanted Laurel. He wanted to believe she could fit here, in his world.

"Where's Sean?"

"He actually chose to go spend the day with our grandparents on the east side. It was kind of cool to have him ask for that."

"Russ, we need to talk . . . about yesterday. About things."

"Not now." He didn't want to talk, he just wanted to feel. He wanted to wrap his arms around her, close his eyes, and hold on for as long as she would let him. Reassure himself that she was okay, that because of her quick reflexes and nimble fist she had escaped with just a minor injury, no thanks to him.

He reached over her, undid the button on her pants, moved the zipper down.

"What are you doing?"

"Helping you change your clothes." He had no intention of doing anything other than innocent nursemaid duty.

For about two seconds.

Then his honorable intentions evaporated as he pulled her pants down over her hips and her little satin-covered mound lifted towards him just a little. His thumb went out of control and stroked across her, feeling the heat, the soft give beneath his touch.

He lifted his hand away, closed it into a fist. Turning, he pulled a crew shirt out of his drawer, long-sleeved, soft, and big even on him. It would work for pj's for Laurel. "Let's take your sweater off. It's covered in blood."

Laurel sat back up and started to raise the sweater. Russ grabbed her hands to stop her. "Just lift your arms. I'll get it so we don't tug on the bandage." She had a gauze pad taped over her stitches, about two inches square, and he didn't want to disturb it.

Russ fingered the hard rust stain on her sweater after he pulled it off and felt that anger, that fear, all over again. He gripped it harder, swallowed a painful lump. Then swore out loud when he looked back up and saw Laurel had unhooked her bra and was wiggling it down her arms.

"Good idea," he told her. His love for her was so strong, so powerful, that he hurt everywhere just looking at her, seeing what Dean had done to her, seeing how fragile and vulnerable she could be, her skin so pale and that bandage so stark. "You'll be more comfortable without your bra."

Laurel smiled, a soft, sleepy smile as she lay back down. Russ braced his feet apart, propped his arms on either side of her so he wasn't touching her, and kissed her. He kissed her with everything he had, with all his heart and fear, with deep pushy thrusts of his tongue. She wasn't so much kissing him back as she was permitting him to take, and Russ pulled away, aching with something he didn't understand.

Jerry had told him someday some woman was going to knock him flat on his ass, and he'd been right. Russ was down on the ground, out for the count. And wanted to stay there.

He trailed his lips down her neck, taking in her scent. He didn't mean to touch her, knew she was worn out, but he couldn't help himself. She was so beautiful, so generous with her heart; and even as he stood up, pulled his lips off her cool flesh, he grazed a fingertip across her breast.

"I'm really sleepy, Russ."

With both hands, he brushed all over her flesh, wanting to touch, to claim, to assure himself that she was alive, his. "That's okay. Just go to sleep, Laurel. I'm just tucking you in."

Russ wanted her to relax, to fall into sleep steeped in comfort, not in pain and confusion. But he also wanted to taste her, to touch her, to brand her in his bedroom as his, no one else's. He traced her eyebrows, her temples, down her cheeks and over her lips, dusting a kiss on the tip of her nose.

"You're silly," she said, on a funny little sigh, head falling to the side.

He'd been called a lot of things, but silly wasn't

one he could remember in recent years. Probably the last time that adjective had been used for him was his first-grade report card. And he wasn't feeling particularly silly now.

Russ peeled back the sheets on the bed, urging Laurel to lift her body with his hand on her back, then her behind. Her panties were smooth beneath his hand, her flesh warm. He watched her breathing, steady and quiet, her eyes firmly closed, and he decided to skip putting the bulky shirt over her.

He skimmed off her underwear, lingering over the angry, mottled, purple bruise staining her right side. He kissed everywhere around it, running his lips along her smoothness, breathing in her natural scent, hovering beneath the antiseptic and bandage smell that clung with determination.

"Feels good . . ." she murmured.

He spread the lightweight sheet over top of her, up to her armpits. Stripped his own shirt off and shoved the laundry off the chair opposite the bed. He sat down, settled back, stiff muscles protesting, and watched Laurel.

She was already asleep, hair falling across her flushed cheek, a peaceful and still sleep.

But he still watched her, and would as long as she let him.

Chapter 26

Laurel woke up feeling sore, but clearheaded and minus the pain of the day before.

She knew she wasn't in her own bed the minute her eyes opened. The room was darker than hers, the ceiling low, the furniture crowded around her like people on a full public bus. And Russ's eyes were on her.

In front of the bed, he was slouched forward in an old nicked wooden chair, his arms propped up on his legs. And he was staring at her, eyes dark and serious, hair standing on end, shadows under his eyes like he hadn't slept at all. His body and posture were tense, tired, but protective and caring. Despite the argument they'd had over Sean, he had been there. Still was. Solid and steady.

Wearing just a pair of jeans.

Which was more than she was. She was totally naked, and she shifted her thighs together restlessly. She remembered Russ helping her onto the bed, remembered his hands and mouth rushing over her shoulders, her face, as she'd dozed off.

"Good morning," she said. Stifling a yawn, she

tried to gauge what time it was and gave it up. It was either still early out, the skies were February gray, or Russ had armored miniblinds. The room was pitched in shadows. Yet despite the gloom, and the aches and pain in her unhappy body, she was looking forward to starting the day.

It seemed clear to her now what she needed to do. What she should have done years ago. What she could have with a little courage and some hard work. What she needed to tell this man in front of her who had already given her so much.

"It's morning. I don't know if it's good." Russ rubbed his forehead. "Jesus, I should have never let him hurt you, Laurel. I should have taken him in weeks ago. I shouldn't have just barged into that storage room like that."

It had never occurred to her to blame Russ, and she certainly didn't want him to. Laurel tried to sit up, wincing at the stiffness in her side. The sheet slipped, and instinctively she grabbed it and held it to her as she leaned back against the headboard. It wasn't like she had a reason to feel modest in front of Russ. But she didn't like being naked, without even her panties on, when the mood between them wasn't sexual. It made her feel self-conscious, exposed.

"Russ . . . please don't blame yourself. You couldn't have prevented this. We didn't know Dean was John. I'm fine, you arrested him, and that's all that matters."

Something had been bothering her since the night before, though, had rolled around in her pain-weakened mind and disturbed her. She needed to know now. "But what did Dean say when he pushed me? I got the feeling he said something about me, I don't know why. Tell me what he said."

Russ stared, thumb drumming on his knee, then shook his head. "No."

Still shaking off sleep, she was startled by his stark response. "What do you mean no?"

Laurel stared back at him, until he looked away and she sighed. This was the root of the problem between her and Russ—he thought she couldn't handle it, that she needed protection and cosseting. And for the first time in her life, she really wanted to reach out and grab her independence, prove to herself that she could do whatever she wanted. She wanted, needed Russ to support that. "You don't have the right to not tell me something if I ask."

But Russ had a stubborn set to his jaw. "No. I'm not repeating that filth."

Laurel took a deep breath, tried to meet his eyes, which were darting to the left. She gripped the sheet and said what she knew would hurt them both, but that needed to be clear. She loved Russ, wanted to move forward and be with him desperately, but they had to establish the parameters of their relationship before they went any further. "Russ. You have to tell me, trust that I can handle it, or we have a serious problem. One I'm not sure we can fix."

"Laurel . . ." Dark brown eyes locked with hers for a long, frustrated minute. He swore. "You don't want to hear this."

"Yes, I do."

Russ sighed. "He called you a deaf and dumb bitch."

"Oh!" Laurel gave a painful laugh, startled that seeing Dean's slur coming off Russ's lips hurt. The force of those words, the cruelty and the meanness proved to her that she had been completely wrong about one thing. Sometimes there was a legitimate reason to protect those you love.

"I guess you were right, after all. I would have preferred not knowing that." Damn the tears that leapt into her eyes, eager and bright, determined to humiliate her in front of Russ. Here she'd made a big deal about being able to handle it, and one juvenile uninspired insult had her choking up.

Russ stood up, came towards her, his fist raised in front of his chest. "I'm sorry . . ."

"For what? You're not the one who said it." Laurel blinked hard to hold back the tears that hovered.

"For making mistakes, for not understanding what you want." He reached for her, took her chin, ran his thumb over her lip. "I'm sorry that my caring is overbearing. I don't mean it to be that way, I just want you safe and happy. I want to take care of you because I love you. And I want you to take care of me. Forever."

Laurel kissed his finger, her lip trembling over the pad of his thumb. Her thoughts were scattered, confused, unsure. He looked so sad, so tired. Russ Evans, tough, foul-mouthed cop, was sharing his heart with her, entrusting her with his feelings.

"When I saw Dean hit you yesterday, I thought that I might lose you before I even had you, and the thought has been killing me ever since. I want to be with you, Laurel, I want this pain in my gut to go away. I've never admired or respected a woman the way I do you . . . and I need to know that at the end of the day I've got you to climb into bed with." Russ cupped her cheek with his hand. "Marry me, Laurel."

Whoa. Somehow she hadn't actually expected that. Had never allowed herself to believe that Russ wanted marriage. Her vision blurred and she realized she was crying, hard and fast, the way she had wanted to several times the night before and hadn't given in to. Russ wanted to marry her and she was going to burst, a shattering of all the love and emotion she felt, of all the hope and determination she finally had to really live her life.

The tears clearly panicked him. He started swiping at her cheeks, eyes wide, but she couldn't force the words out to reassure him. Couldn't begin to explain that she had never expected to feel so happy, so overwhelmed, such a part of something wonderful.

"I'm sorry—shit, what's the matter?"

She shook her head, still clutching the sheet. "Can this work, Russ, can it really work? I want to go back to college . . ."

"Laurel." Russ took both of her hands, squeezed them hard. "Here's the thing, honey. We have to trust each other. I have to trust that it doesn't matter to you that you have more money than I'll ever see in my lifetime. And you have to trust that I see you as an intelligent woman, capable of doing anything you see fit to do."

Fingers entwined in his, Laurel swallowed hard. She had spent her whole life hiding in the shadows, afraid to make a mistake, missing out on so much. Living life meant taking risks, and she wanted to live her life with Russ.

"I trust you, Russ. Completely. I want this. I want you."

Thank God. Russ gave a sigh of relief, his gut twisted up in knots. "This is what I want, too."

"Are you absolutely sure?" Laurel sniffled.

As sure as the goddamn sunset every day. "Of course I'm sure. You're the one who doesn't sound sure."

They looked at each other and without warning Laurel walloped him on the shoulder and bicep.

Astonished, he just gaped at her.

Laurel gave him a lopsided smile. "You said if we ever question each other like that again I should smack you."

He laughed, focusing on the fact that she was grinning at him, wrapping herself into his arms, caressing his lower back.

"I never really thought I would ever get married," she said in a soft voice.

"What a coincidence. Me either. And frankly, this is it for me." He couldn't take the strain of doing this a second time. "So is that a yes or what?"

She nodded, sniffled. Her eyes filled with a fresh batch of tears. She was beautiful, especially with splotchy skin, and he was one lucky guy.

"Now this really is the part where we kiss, because damn, I need to hold you." Russ didn't wait for her response. He took her mouth with his, a long, drawn-out devotional kiss.

He had Laurel, and she tasted wonderful.

"I want you as my wife. I want to build a family with you and Sean. I want to buy a new house, that the three of us pick out together. I even want that furball Ferris to live with us."

"That sounds perfect."

Laurel returned his kiss and Russ held her tight, close, breathing in the scent of her hair, brushing his mouth over the softness of hers, before he pulled back.

"How are you feeling today, bunny? Do you want the Tylenol with codeine the doctor gave us?"

For almost six weeks she'd been telling herself he was calling her honey, but darn it, he wasn't. He was calling her bunny, and she was so sure of it now, it distracted her from her original thoughts, which were quickly leaning towards tugging his jeans off. "Why do you keep calling me bunny?"

"Is that the sign?" Russ imitated her two fingers at the back of the head. "Maybe that should be my name sign for you."

Laurel gave a shudder. Over her dead body. "Why? What could possibly make you want to call me a rabbit?"

"That's what you reminded me of when I met you. A sweet, fuzzy bunny."

While he clearly thought it was just adorable, Laurel was mortified. "That's not very flattering, Russ!"

He looked confused. "Sure, it is. It means I was attracted to you from the first second I saw you. It means that I think you're a good person." Working the sheet down, baring her breasts and stomach, he said, "If you don't like it, I won't call you that, it's not important. But can we forget about the stupid nickname? I want to check your stitches and then seal our engagement with another kiss."

Since his fingers were wandering between her thighs, she imagined a kiss wasn't all he had in mind. Which worked for her. And now that his hand was stroking a delicious pattern along her inner thigh, she decided he could call her kangaroo for all she cared. She knew he loved her, knew he respected her, knew Russ was a loyal, honest man, who would stick by her for the long haul. Just like she wanted him to, so very much.

"I don't need the Tylenol, I feel fine today."

"I can make you feel even better if you're up for it." He looked at her, seeking permission.

Since the only ache in her body was the one his hot breath was blowing into existence, Laurel nodded. She gasped in pleasure when Russ immediately parted her thighs a little.

Russ lay down on his side and lingered over Laurel's curls, admiring the curve of her hips, the tightness of her inner thighs. Using his thumbs, he opened her to his view, sucking in hard when he saw that she was swollen, moist. She was beautiful, relaxed and bending a little towards him.

Her body lay slack, her eyes now closed, and Russ reached out with the tip of his tongue and tasted her. A little moan escaped her, pleasing him, spurring him on. Holding her apart, he licked and ate, sucking and stroking deep inside her.

She got wetter, her breathing harder, her fingers shifting on the bed restlessly. Russ stifled his own groan, fought with his urge to lift her legs up, to hold her tight. He kept his thumbs on her folds, spreading her so he could taste more thoroughly, and he bit back any insistent demands from his own body.

He didn't want to disturb her injury, but he wanted to make her feel good. He just wanted to touch her and please her and show her how grateful he was that she had come into his life.

Laurel came with a shuddering sigh, her body pulsing beneath his tongue. Russ drew it out, caressed her, until her breathing slowed.

He let go of her reluctantly. He wiped his mouth, eased back. She opened her eyes a little, looking pleased and drowsy, aroused and excited.

She reached for him, pulling until he was next to her. Laurel gave him a heart-stopping kiss, her fingers entangling in his hair.

He touched her lips. "We'll be happy, Laurel." As happy as kids with ten bucks to blow in a candy store.

"I know, Russ, because I already am."

Epilogue

Laurel smoothed the front of her gown with cool fingers and darted her eyes back and forth between the ASL interpreter and the stage, so she could see what was going on. She had worked her behind off for almost two years for this moment, and she didn't want to miss a thing.

The floor of the gymnasium was jarring concrete, causing vibrations to rumble up her legs as hundreds of graduates walked across it to collect their diplomas. She had waited and worked and dreamed she'd reach this pinnacle, and she was nervous now that it was here, afraid she would miss the cue from the interpreter to stand and take her turn.

She fidgeted in her seat, and swiveling her head in all directions, scanned the bleachers again. She hadn't been able to find Russ with so many faces in the darkened crowd, the lights focused down on the graduates. But she knew he was there, just as he always was, supporting her, loving her. As she supported and loved him, every minute of every day.

The guy next to her tapped her leg. He was also deaf, and they had been chatting during the rehearsal ceremony the day before. He was a few years younger than her, and graduating with a civil engineering degree.

We're next. He pointed and gave her a smile.

Laurel took a deep breath to calm herself down. *Thanks.*

This was it. She was a teacher, fully certified and ready to step into her very own classroom at the end of the summer. Despite the nerves, it felt really damn good.

She had done it. With honors. She rose from her seat and gave a brilliant smile to the interpreter.

"I can't find Laurel." Russ scanned the graduates again, wondering why the hell he couldn't see her. She had said she was supposed to sit in the fourth row, on the end, where the interpreter would be standing.

But there was a big pole in the way and he couldn't see a damn thing. He didn't want to miss her accepting her degree. She'd worked her ass off to get to this point, going to summer school and taking an overload of credits each semester to graduate in a mere year and a half after starting the program. He wanted to see her having her moment of triumph.

"We'll hear them call her name," his mother-in-law said, patting his leg. "Relax, for heaven's sake. You're sweating bullets."

"Oh, man, the baby grabbed the camera." Sean, who at sixteen was close to six-foot-three, bounced

Cat and Jerry's daughter on his leg. He handed Russ the digital camera, a string of drool dangling off the cord.

Russ wiped his hand and the camera off on his black pants and couldn't help but grin at his little brother, despite the slime now on his leg. Sean had a real touch with Kayla, who was seven months old. Sean still had his moments of adolescent angst, but for the most part he was doing really well. And right now he had Kayla up in the air and was blowing on her chubby stomach.

The baby squealed. Jerry shook his head. "She's going to spit up on your head, Sean. Don't say I didn't warn you."

"Nah, she wouldn't do that to me. Would you, ugly?"

Kayla gave a belly chuckle of approval.

Cat rolled her eyes, brushing back a strand of her red hair. "We're so flattered by the nicknames you guys give us. Laurel is bunny, I'm freak, and now my daughter is ugly. No chance of inflated egos with you guys around."

Russ laughed and leaned a little to the left hoping to see around the pole. "We only give nicknames if we care."

Jerry started digging around on the floor between Cat's legs. "Where's the diaper bag?" He came up with a little container of Cheerios a second later.

"She doesn't look hungry," Cat said, studying her daughter for signs of discontent.

"These aren't for the baby. I'm starving. This is taking forever." Jerry popped a handful of the cereal into his mouth.

Cat kissed Jerry's cheek, which was pouched

with cereal, and grinned. "You're a bigger baby than the baby."

Russ was about to make a crack when he saw Laurel step up onto the stage in her black graduation gown and cap. He slapped his brother's leg. "There she is."

Damn, he was so proud of her. Being married to Laurel was the most amazing experience, way more than he could ever have imagined. Every day was a gift, and they had been very, very happy in their new house with Sean. It had been wonderful watching Laurel reach for her goals, face challenges and overcome them.

She was everything to him, his wife.

"Laurel Wilkins-Evans, a Bachelor of Arts and Sciences."

You weren't supposed to make noise, so the next graduate's name didn't get blocked out, but Russ couldn't help but give out a shout, standing up to clap as Laurel accepted her diploma. Laurel's mom rose alongside him, as did Sean, Cat, and Jerry. They waved their hands silently, the deaf version of applause.

And Laurel turned and stared right at him. She caught his eye and smiled widely.

One hand clutching the degree, the other landed on her chest. *I love you.*

He grinned down from the stands. *I love you, too.*

"She was talking to me," Sean said with a smirk, nudging him in the side.

Russ watched Laurel walk off the stage with confidence. "Actually, I think she was talking to all of us, Sean."

Contemporary Romance by

Kasey Michaels